MW01538833

CHASING THE STORM

Loyalty and family mixed together are as irrepressible as the forces of nature, and just as hard to run away from.

Copyright © 2005 Dwight M. Edwards

10-Digit ISBN 1-59113-839-6
13-Digit ISBN 978-1-59113-839-6

All rights reserved. No part of this publication may be reproduced, stored in a retrieval system, or transmitted in any form or by any means, electronic, mechanical, recording or otherwise, without the prior written permission of the author.

Printed in the United States of America.

The characters and events in this book are fictitious. Any similarity to real persons, living or dead, is coincidental and not intended by the author.

Dwight M. Edwards
Dwighte@Comcast.net.
2005

CHASING THE STORM

Dwight M. Edwards

This book is lovingly dedicated to my most ardent supporter—
my wife, Janelle

Prologue

Antonio Jaillet drove through the night rain, stopping only to refuel and to grab something quick to eat, before he was on the road again. Two hours later, his eyes closed as he fell asleep at the wheel. The limousine bounced to the shoulder of the road, skidded sideways in the gravel, and scraped a fence post before shooting back on the road. That woke him up.

He wiped a sweaty palm across the front of his shirt and squeezed the steering wheel with the other. He was exhausted and needed sleep, but there wasn't time for that. He was already late and probably in trouble. Jaillet was one of several pilots employed by the Micheaux family and he was supposed to have been back to work yesterday. Now he was going to have to come up with a convincing lie to explain not only his tardiness, but also the absence of the two French Knight Guardians that had accompanied him. From the beginning, nothing had gone as planned.

Jaillet had taken one of the Micheaux's limousines and driven to Paris for the weekend. The plan was to get the woman and return by Sunday morning. What he didn't count on was that she wouldn't be at the hotel. Instead, she and a client had left the city for two days and didn't return to her Paris hotel until late Sunday afternoon. She was scheduled to leave later that night on a flight back home to San Francisco, which meant there would only be one opportunity to get to her.

It came just before midnight as she left the hotel with a garment bag slung over her shoulder. Jaillet and his men were waiting for her at the curb as she waited for her limousine to arrive. They grabbed her from behind and dragged her into the alley. That's when the plan went bad. She managed to kill the Frenchmen before Jalliet was finally able to subdue her. He left the two bullet-riddled bodies in a dumpster in the alley and sped away.

The trip had been a nightmare, but he kept reminding himself that despite the setbacks, he had pulled it off. He relaxed his grip on the steering wheel and slowed down when the car's headlights flashed against the speed sign on the outskirts of the Village of Trellone. The last thing he needed was the police stopping him.

A loud thumping noise came from the back of the car. He glanced in the rearview mirror and saw the back seat moving. Jaillet pulled off to the side of the road and waited for the other cars to pass. The seat continued to thump. He slammed the door behind him and walked to the rear of the limousine. He unlocked the trunk and unzipped the body bag. Despite being tied and gagged, the woman had somehow managed to wrestle her legs free and was using them to kick the seat. Jaillet wanted to strangle her, but his orders had been explicit. She was not to be hurt. Jaillet didn't care. He pulled a gun from his waist and smashed it against her forehead. She moaned and then was silent. Blood flowed down her sweat-covered face. He felt her pulse. She was still alive. He zipped the bag, closed the trunk, and got back in the car. In a few weeks, the Micheauxs would be home and it would be over. He'd get paid and disappear. Best of all, he didn't have to worry about anyone coming after her. He started the car and eased back on the highway.

* * *

Nine days later in London, Pierre Micheaux was in the billiard room of Westminster-Paget, waiting for his brother to show up. He and Philip had dined together at the club, but then Phillip left with one of the men to go upstairs. That was an hour ago. Pierre rested his foot on the pub rail, watching the older men playing billiards. Two waiters entered the room carrying silver platters of Rossmore Oysters and Cristal Champagne. Pierre took one of each from the tray as he walked over to the window. He looked out at the majestic view of the Thames and the Waterloo Bridge to the south. Pierre loved this city and the private club. He and his brother had arrived at the mansion two weeks ago following their trip to New York City, where they opened their newest art gallery. The brothers owned houses in Canada, France, and Switzerland, but the club felt more like home than any other place.

Westminster-Paget Mansion was a masterpiece of Victorian design that rivaled any London landmark, and membership was reserved for European bluebloods crazy enough to pay the $200,000 annual dues. In return, members enjoyed access to the best foods and wines, leather chesterfields, spas, and freedom to smoke their rum-filled stogies in peace.

Pierre heard his brother shouting obscenities as he made his way down the hall to the billiard room. Philip stormed in with a wet towel clinging to his naked body, followed by his manservant—an African waiter on the verge of tears. He stood in the middle of the room with everyone watching as Philip humiliated him with his verbal assault. The members ignored the spectacle—they were used to Philip's tirades.

A member handed Philip some pants to slip on. The waiter took the opportunity to try to apologize again for spilling Philip's drink in the pool. Pierre lightly tapped the butt of a cigarette on his gold cigarette case as he watched in amusement. His brother was an unforgiving man and nothing short of the servant's termination was going to appease him.

The club secretary was finally summoned and he promptly dismissed the waiter and apologized to Philip. Philip smiled and went over to join his brother at the bar.

The secretary watched the two brothers in the mirror hanging above the bar. He couldn't tell the two men apart. They were clones of each other: same flaxen hair, ruddy-colored skin, and angular nose. The twins' similarities didn't stop there. Both were racist French snobs, who only spoke the King's language when they had to. The secretary didn't like them, and neither did most members. But unfortunately for them, the Micheaux's great-grandfather was a founding member of the club, and their family had more money than they could count.

A Nigerian waiter entered the room with an urgent telephone message for the brothers. Pierre went to the office to take the call. Fifteen minutes later he returned with a grim look on his face as he sat down at the table.

"What's wrong?" Philip asked.

"Intruders have broken into our home in L'Ile d' Orleans and our gallery in Montreal. The private papers and ledgers from our vaults were stolen."

"Impossible. No one would dare steal from our family."

"Someone has and now they have our records. This presents a problem."

"Our men did nothing to stop this?"

"They are useless cowards." Pierre dragged a cigarette from its case. "Our sister is very upset—very."

"What did she say?"

"She will deal with the problem."

Chapter 1

On a mid-November day, a private jet from San Francisco touched down on a deserted airstrip outside Barcelona, Spain. Five African-American men exited the airplane. Three of them were brothers, dressed in identical ankle-length leather coats, fedoras and sunglasses, and carried metal rifle cases. The cooler than usual weather in southern Europe was about to heat up as the men would quickly discover.

A man named Cisco drove them to Toulouse, which was situated on the banks of the Garonne River. The rose-colored city with its labyrinthine alleyways of mansions and houseboats was the fourth largest city in France and an easy place to go unnoticed. The driver dropped them off at a seedy hotel near downtown, where they checked into their room to wait for their contact. Four hours later a girl knocked softly on the door. Xavier Toussaint cautiously opened the door.

The short, 19-year-old girl, wearing a Yankee baseball cap, shades, and backpack entered the room. "I'm here to see Dr. Sebasst."

A large man stepped from the shadows of the bathroom. His body dwarfed over hers. "I'm Sebasst," he said, tossing the towel on the nearby chair.

"My name is Tessa. We must go before they discover you have arrived. Please hurry." The men followed her into a narrow alley behind the hotel where they boarded an old school bus with tinted windows. The Spanish driver closed the doors and started the bus. The sound of gears grinding could be heard on the main street as the crippled bus limped out of the alley. Twenty minutes later it was on the highway headed south. Tessa sat next to the slim, brown-skinned man wearing glasses, who hadn't uttered a word. He seemed disinterested and absorbed in his own thoughts as he gazed out the window.

"What is your name?" she asked.

"Marcus."

"Is this your first trip to Spain?"

"Yes," he said without turning from the window.

"It is a beautiful country, especially in spring."

"Aren't you a little young for this line of work?" Marcus asked.

Tessa was surprised by the question. "I'm not sure what you mean."

He faced her. "You're too damn young to be wasting your time working for someone like Devin Leon-Francis. Take my advice and do yourself a favor. Get an education and a real job. Messing around with people like Leon-Francis will only get you hurt."

Tessa smiled. "I have no idea what you are talking about. I'm a pre-med student attending the University of Toulouse and a native of Carcassonne. Occasionally, I do some work for Jason Worrick. He wanted me to assure you that Mr. Leon-Francis is very appreciative of your efforts to secure his daughter's release, and if there is anything else you require, you need only ask."

"You can tell Leon-Francis we're not doing this for him," Marcus said as he turned back toward the window.

Doc sat across the aisle from them. "No, tell Mr. Leon-Francis we appreciate the help, and the assistance of his men Jason Worrick and Andy Preston." Marcus grumbled, but didn't say anything.

Tessa found herself staring back at the three brothers sitting in the rear of the bus. "Are they triplets?"

"Yes—the Toussaint brothers. The one on the left is Xavier—we call him X-man. The other two are Cicero and Aristotle," Doc said.

Marcus spotted a desolate castle sitting on top of a mountain ridge as the bus passed by. "Is there really a treasure buried in those mountains?"

"Some think so. In 1953, a copper scroll was found in a cave near the Dead Sea. Some say it told about an enormous treasure that had been buried by the Jewish priesthood, before the Romans destroyed the Temple in 70 AD. More than one hundred and thirty-eight tons of gold and silver were estimated to have been buried there. Legend has it that the Merovingians found it and brought it here, where it's been hidden under the protection of the families in a myriad of underground tunnels running through Lanquedoc-Roussillion. Thousands of visitors travel here each year to explore the vast network of tunnels, no doubt hoping to stumble upon the plunder. But even if it exists, the world will never see it. The Merovingians are too smart for that."

"So the Merovingians are real?" Marcus asked.

"Their existence is no secret, at least not to people who follow such things. To others, they are a fable as is their treasure. Regardless of one's opinion, the legend is the reason these mountains are one of the most mysterious and intriguing areas of the world."

"Where exactly is Micheaux Castle?" Marcus asked.

"In the Village of Trellone, near Carcassonne."

"If their castle is half as large as the one we just passed, it could get dicey."

"Micheaux Castle is much larger and more modern. I'm told they have stables, orchards—even quarters for their staff and employees," she said.

"Doc, if Worrick and Preston are right about Jaillet and Sydney being there, we're going to need an army to get her out of that place."

"More men aren't going to help. It's not that simple. This is the most geographically diverse region in France, full of towering mountains, deep gorges, and miles of underground caves. The area we're going into is even more remote, and all the maps in the world won't help us if we get in trouble. We don't know the territory well enough to get around. And to complicate matters, Micheaux Castle is on top of a 1,207-meter peak with only one way up and one way down the mountain. According to Andy Preston, the family has at least thirty security personnel and an unknown number of personal bodyguards known as the Knight Guardians who are always watching their backs. Taking them on would be suicidal," Doc said.

"So how are we going to get her out?" Marcus asked.

"The sister will bring her and Jaillet to us."

Marcus looked at Doc like he had a third eye. "You must be outside your mind. This is the best you can come up with? You're just planning to walk up to the castle door and ask them for Sydney back?"

"I never said my plan was to storm the castle walls. Jason Worrick has set some things in motion for us that will even the odds."

"I don't like this and I don't like dealing with Devin Leon-Francis' men. Why aren't his own people getting his daughter instead of us?" Marcus asked.

"Come on, Marcus, you were the first one ready to come over here to find her. I think we're the right people for the job."

Marcus turned back around. "I still don't like it."

The bus lunged hard to the left, nearly tossing them to the floor. The back tires slipped and spun as they tried to grip the rocky terrain as it made its slow journey through the mountains. They reached the abandoned farmhouse outside Carcassonne by dusk.

Tessa handed Doc a brown folder as the men stepped off the bus. "Mr. Worrick has provided everything you asked for in here, including maps and directions. The cars you requested are in the barn in the back. When you have accomplished your objective, a boat will be waiting at Perpignon to take you back to Barcelona, where your jet will be waiting. Mr. Worrick wishes you the best of luck." She smiled as the door closed and the bus made its way back to the mountains.

Doc checked his watch as he waited for the others to finish getting ready. "We don't have much time. We need to get to the cafe and get out by 9:00, which only gives us two hours to set up for our guests."

3

"You're cutting this pretty thin, Doc. What happens if the Micheauxs don't show at the cafe?" Marcus asked.

"They will. They think they're meeting with an art dealer to buy some stolen art, thanks to Worrick."

"What happens if your plan doesn't work and they don't bring Sid?" X-man asked.

"Then we've got problems. But we have a problem anyway, once the sister discovers she's been doubled-crossed."

Cicero and Aristotle brought the cars around and packed in the gear. The Toussaint brothers rode in the first car, and Doc and Marcus got in the other one.

Doc rolled down the car window. "Everybody knows what to do. You have your maps and directions in case you get lost. If everything goes okay, we'll meet up at the abbey by 10:30. If one of the cars doesn't make it back, we still go with the plan."

* * *

Carcassonne sat on the banks of the Aude, ninety kilometers from Toulouse. The café was located near Saint-Louis Bastide in the main square. A brown Saab pulled into the deserted alley behind the bakery. X-man and Cicero jumped out, and the car sped away. The two brothers scaled up the roof ladder. Cicero ran across the roof to the south side of the building, while X-man maintained watch over the alley. Cicero swung the large metal case from his shoulder and assembled his rifle. He inserted the cartridges, attached the silencer, and adjusted the optical scope.

X-man scanned the block with his binoculars. "How's it going, bro, you almost ready?" he whispered.

"Yeah, how are things shaking in the alley?"

"Everything's cool. Just don't miss or it will be hell getting off this roof in one piece."

Cicero checked the range and made a small adjustment to the scope. Three Lincoln Town cars came into view.

"Here they come," X-man said. Cicero wrapped his hands around the rifle stock and aimed. As the cars approached the intersection, a bullet tore through the hood and engine block of the lead car. The second shot took out the right front tire of the third car, causing it to swerve out of control, jump the curb, and flip over on its side. By the time the Micheaux's chauffeur realized he had lost his front and back escort cars, it was too late. Marcus cut off the lane in front of him with the Saab, and Aristotle rammed the rear of the limousine with the other car. Doc jumped out and pulled the chauffeur from the limousine. Marcus and Aristotle dragged the Micheauxs from the back seat and threw them in the trunks of the cars. Doc signaled to Cicero and he fired two more rounds, crippling the Micheaux's limousine. The bodyguards watched helplessly as the cars sped away carrying the twins.

Aristotle skidded the Renault around the block, raced through the ally, and jammed on the brakes.

"Cicero, come on, we gotta go, our ride is waiting," X-man said.

* * *

An hour later, Marcus swung the large courtyard doors open for the Toussaint's car to enter. "You're late. Everything okay?"

X-man unlocked the car trunk. "Yeah, the guy was yelling and screaming all the way, so I stopped and gagged him. Where do you want me to put him?"

"I've got a nice, quiet place picked out for them."

Later, Marcus went searching for Doc and found him working in the chapter house. "This must have been quite a place back in the day," Marcus said, admiring the intricate woodcarvings of Gabriel and St. Mark on the rectory wall. "What are you doing?"

"Going over the plan again. He tossed his pencil on the table and removed his glasses. "Something doesn't feel right about this whole thing," Doc said.

"Like what?"

"If I knew that I wouldn't be worried."

Marcus rested his hand on his friend's shoulder. "I don't like it when you get one of your feelings. We've done the best we could do. Xavier and his brothers are my best men and this place is a fortress. We'll do okay."

Cicero entered the room. "Our guests aren't happy campers. They demand to talk to you, Doc."

"That's too bad. I don't want to talk with them. Feed them a sandwich. Let them sulk for the night—maybe it'll do them some good."

* * *

5

The next morning Doc was up before dawn. He couldn't sleep. He joined X-man in the chapel tower to survey the grounds. The abbey sat in the middle of emerald green pastureland surrounded by trees and encircled by a stone wall. The only access to the entrance of the abbey was over a narrow bridge that spanned the creek flowing in front of the courtyard gate.

Doc leaned out the tower to get a better look at the road. "Worrick picked a perfect location for us. There's no way they can get in without us seeing them coming. What are you going to need?"

"Cicero and two sniper rifles. We can hold this place all day if you want," X-man said.

"Good. What about having Aristotle on the dormitory roof between the cloisters?"

"That'll work, too. How about the boss?"

"Marcus will have my back. Your job is to keep everyone off the bridge, except Sasha Micheaux and Sydney." X-man nodded.

Doc left the tower and walked across the courtyard to the dormitory where Aristotle was cooking breakfast on a portable grill. "Where's Marcus?"

"Inside," he said, pointing the spatula at the small iron door at the end of the hall.

Doc entered the storeroom. Marcus was sitting on a crate, next to the twins who sat bound back-to-back in chairs. Philip cursed Doc when he saw him.

Marcus leaned over and tapped him on the head with the barrel of his gun. "Speak English. Don't let me have to remind you of that again."

"You and your men will pay for what you have done. I promise you will die!" Philip shouted as he wiggled in vain against the tight rope binding him.

Pierre sat calmly with his hands folded on his lap. "What is it that you want from us?"

"Sydney Belleshota, and the man that kidnapped her—Antonio Jaillet," Doc said.

"What does this have to do with my brother and me?"

"Jaillet works for you and he's hiding her in your castle. When your sister turns over both of them to me, then you and your brother are free to go home."

Pierre's face turned red. "You are mad! You abduct us for something we have no knowledge of. My brother is right. You will surely not leave this place alive for what you have done to us. I will see to that."

"That remains to be seen. What *you* haven't seemed to grasp yet is that you aren't leaving here until I get what I want."

Pierre's eyes showed unflinching hatred. "I know nothing about the whore you speak of, or this man, Jaillet! You have no idea what you are doing or who we are. Release us now and you and your party will be permitted to leave in safety. We will put this matter behind us as though it had never occurred. We can even talk about some financial arrangement to compensate you."

Marcus laughed. "That's mighty white of you, thanks. And I suppose all the people you and your brother have killed to protect your little art smuggling business are supposed to put their deaths behind them too."

"You arrogant black..."

Marcus jumped to his feet. "I'm about tired of you. If I hear one more derogatory remark coming out of your mouth, I'm gonna untie you and put my foot in your mouth. You and your sissy brother over here make me *sick*. You snobbish pigs plunder cultural artifacts from all over the world, and god only knows what else that we don't know about. The little culture you *think* you have was bought at the expense of the people your family stole from and through the oppression of the poor people you've exploited. And to make matters worse, you justify all of this because you believe in some fanciful folklore that Jesus was your *daddy*? If he is, he needs to come down here and whup you twisted freaks. You think about that before you open your stupid mouths again!" The brothers sat in silence. Marcus snapped his cigar lighter closed and blew a ring of smoke in the air. "Oh, *now* you don't have anything witty to say?" They remained silent.

Doc looked at Marcus. "I wouldn't have used quite the approach you did, but sometimes directness is the most effective. I think they're starting to apprehend the gravity of their situation. But just to make sure you understand what's happening here, I'm going to explain it for you. We have in our possession information we've collected on your colorful family history, which will make for interesting reading by the authorities of several countries. For instance—the United States military would like to question you about that little airstrip you've been using of theirs in the New Mexico desert for smuggling artifacts."

"How do you know that?" Philip asked.

"We know a lot about your worthless, thieving family. How do you think we tracked Jaillet to this place," Marcus said.

"Who are you people?" Pierre asked.

7

"It doesn't matter who we are. You will never see us again, once your sister gives us our friend and Antonio Jaillet," Doc said.

"We knew nothing of these kidnappings! Antonio is our pilot—a distant cousin, nothing more," Philip said.

"That doesn't change your situation. This morning your sister received copies of the documents we took from your house and art gallery. We know about your operations and your involvement with the other Merovingian families. She has until 3:00 today to give me what I want—in exchange for you two."

"And if she refuses?" Pierre asked.

"That's bad news for you two. We will haul you back to the United States with us, and your family will be out of business for good. The only question is what to do with you. Do I turn you over to the Canadians, the United States, maybe Israel, or one of the other fourteen countries you've been robbing blind? Any suggestions?" Doc asked.

"This is outrageous. You cannot do this to us. We have done nothing to you and you cannot hold us responsible for some crazy madman's actions," Philip said.

"Hey...live with it, life ain't fair," Marcus said.

"My people will never let you leave here with us," Pierre said smugly.

"I wouldn't count on them if I were you. The only one that can save your butt is your baby sister," Marcus said.

"Sasha will have you shot for what you have done to us!" Philip said.

"For your sake, you'd better hope not," Doc said. They left the room and Aristotle locked the door behind them.

Marcus could still hear Philip swearing at them through the door. "That boy is going to give himself an aneurysm if he's not careful."

They went outside and walked around the abbey. Doc waved to Cicero in the tower. He waved back. Then he walked through the cemetery and backwoods where he waved again. This time Cicero couldn't see him.

"The woods and cemetery are our only vulnerable spots. There are half a dozen trails leading up here and we can't cover them all. If they get this far without being seen, we're in trouble," Doc said.

"Then we'll just have to make sure we stop them out front, before they have a chance to outflank us. Where's Aristotle going to be?"

Doc pointed to the jutting roof connecting the church and the cloisters. "He'll be hidden between the rafters, which will make it impossible for anyone to see him. The bad news is he won't be able to see much himself. If they get past him on the west wall, we'll never see them coming."

"Stop worrying. Sasha Micheaux wants her brothers back in one piece."

* * *

Two hours later, X-man saw a white Bentley leading a herd of cars down the winding road toward the abbey. The cars stopped in front of the bridge. Several security personnel exited the limousines, followed by a dark-haired woman wearing sunglasses. She pulled at the sleeves of her gloves and smoothed the hem of her short white dress.

X-man leveled the rifle sights on her. "This babe is *fine*."

"I'll take your word for that, brother," Cicero said, as he kept watch off the back side of the tower.

"Do you see Aristotle?" X-man asked.

Cicero leaned over the side and spotted his brother wedged between the eaves and the roof. "Yeah, he's okay. How many men are you looking at out front?"

"Sixteen and still counting."

A trio of men approached the bridge. Three bullets splintered the wood in front of their feet.

"That's close enough. No one except Madam Micheaux can pass over," X-man yelled.

Sasha's bodyguards peered into the bright sun, but could barely see the dark man in the tower giving them orders. The bodyguards pulled their guns and formed a human shield around her. She motioned to the driver in another limousine. He opened the back door of the car and pulled Antonio Jaillet out on the ground. Another guard grabbed him by his handcuffs and yanked him to his feet. Jaillet dusted the dirt off his pants and tried to straighten his rumpled suit coat.

X-man moved the scope across Jaillet's face. His long hair was tangled in clumps of mud and his beard was matted in dried blood. His eyes were dead. "Looks like the family took a little of their frustrations out on homeboy." He moved the rifle back to the guard who was now helping another person from the car. "Tell Doc they have Sid."

"They brought the packages," Cicero said over the headset.

"Okay, have them sent across. We'll meet them at the entrance," Doc said.

"Send them across," yelled X-man.

"That is not acceptable. We go where Madame goes," the guard said.

"Then you'll die." X-man fired a few rounds at his feet. The guards pushed Sasha back into her bulletproof automobile and took cover. Four men fanned out and tried to sneak across the creek. Aristotle's warning shots sent them splashing for the shore. One made it across and tried coming through the cemetery. Cicero shattered the headstone in front of him with a bullet.

"You can make this real hard or you can do it the easy way. There will be no more warning shots. Send them across," X-man said.

"We will not let madam Micheaux enter that place unescorted," the guard said.

X-man lined up the crosshairs on the man's forehead and saw the determination in his eyes. The fearless leader was resolute in his decision. "This Kamikaze isn't budging an inch and neither are his men." The stalemate was broken when Doc and Marcus stepped out into the open courtyard.

Sasha Micheaux reemerged from the car and spoke to her bodyguard. Despite his protest, he motioned to his men to step aside for them to pass through. Sydney crossed the bridge with Jaillet, followed by Sasha Micheaux. Sydney gave Doc a hug as she stepped from the bridge.

"You okay?" he asked.

"Yeah, I'm fine, but this fool isn't." She pulled on Jaillet's handcuffs and he stumbled off the steps. Marcus grabbed him by the collar and pulled him up to his feet. "Is that Xavier up in the tower?" she asked.

"Yeah, he says he's here to collect the hundred dollars you owe him." Sydney smiled and gave him another hug. "Thanks."

Sasha struggled in her high heels on the narrow steps. She lost her balance. Doc caught her in his arms. *"Merci,"* she said with a coldness that matched the look in her eyes. He lowered her to the ground, and they entered the church.

Cicero saw movement in the woods. "Hey, brother, we've got a problem over here. There's a bunch of guys in black camouflage back here."

"How many men?"

"Too many."

X-man grabbed the binoculars from his brother and took a closer look. The forest was swarming with dark clad men wearing berets.

"What are they doing?" Cicero asked.

"Waiting."

* * *

Sasha handed Doc the key to Jaillet's handcuffs. "Where are my brothers?" Doc motioned to Marcus to get them.

Marcus pushed Jaillet toward the door. "You're going to be safer with me, come on." The Frenchman limped down the cloister passageway with Marcus following behind.

"You might as well have a seat. It'll be a few minutes before they're here," Doc said. Sasha remained standing with her arms crossed, looking at the intricately designed Cherubim on the ceiling—and then at Doc. The man looked nothing like what she had expected. He was tall with keen West Indian features. The top of his head was as smooth as his face, and his eyes were bright as crystal.

"This place holds many memories for me and my family. My father and his father were christened here, and many of my family are buried on these hallowed grounds. Disgracing my family is not enough for you. You also have to commit sacrilege by trespassing on this sacred monument?"

"This is not about disgracing your family's name, madam. Your brothers seemed to manage that on their own."

"And that gave you the authority to break into our home in Quebec City, and steal what does not belong to you?" she shouted.

Doc turned his head and looked at her. "I'll do whatever is necessary to get Sydney back; including dragging you and your family down if I have to. Your brothers and Antonio Jaillet kidnapped her, so don't ask me to apologize to you for my actions."

"This is preposterous," she said, unfolding her arms. "Why would my brothers kidnap this woman?"

"Ask them. I don't know and I don't care. I'm just here to see that she gets back home safely."

"My family is not responsible for the actions of our employees. I had no knowledge of this. We are innocent."

"Kidnapping, maybe, but your brothers are not innocents." Sasha avoided his eyes. "Well?"

She tugged at the fingers of her gloves, trying to think of something to say. Finally, she sat in the chair and crossed her legs. She pulled the long gloves off and folded her hands on her lap. "Monsieur Sebasst, I will not attempt to make excuses for my brothers' actions. If they harbored Antonio, it was only to protect our family."

"I've read your family history. There isn't anything honorable worth protecting, and certainly nothing worth justifying your brothers' need to satisfy their greed."

Sasha's eyes narrowed and her lips tightened, suppressing her fury. "You would do well not to insult my family."

"I'm not here to insult you, but I won't sugarcoat the truth either. Your brothers have been stealing for years, not to mention murdering anyone that's gotten in their way. It's time they paid for what they've done."

She jumped to her feet. "You assured me in your letter that Pierre and Philip would be free to go if I cooperated with you, and I have."

"They are free to leave with you, but tell them not to make any plans. I've already notified the authorities about them. Regardless of what happens here, your brothers will be spending a long time behind bars—where they should be."

Marcus entered the room with the twins in tow. He cut the duct tape from their wrists, removed the tape from their mouths, and pushed them over to their sister.

"You will die. All of you will die for this," Phillip shouted with spit flying from his mouth. He smoothed the front of his blazer with his hand.

Sasha smiled and hugged them both. "Go outside and wait for me." She turned her attention back to Doc. "My brothers will not spend one night in prison. You are aware that my men have surrounded the grounds. I could have you and your companions eliminated."

"That's a possibility, but a lot of your people would die in the process. In the end, nothing would change. No matter what you believe, you and your family aren't God." Once again, she searched for the right words to say, but couldn't find any. His impassive expression and dark eyes made her feel small and frightened. Yet, she also felt a strange attraction to him that she couldn't understand. He controlled the moment and there wasn't anything she could do.

"Goodbye, Monsieur Sebasst. We will see each other again," she said, walking away. She crossed back over the bridge and joined her brothers. She gave them both an affectionate kiss, pulled a gun from her purse, and shot them both. Four of her men tossed the bodies in the trunk of the car and drove off.

"Damn, did you see that? She killed her own brothers. I can't believe it!" X-man said.

Cicero looked at the woods. "Her men are gone, too. One minute they're here, the next—they vanished like smoke."

* * *

Antonio Jaillet stood in the middle of the room facing a blank wall. His hands were still bound as he tried using his shoulder to scratch an itch on his face, but his long hair kept getting in the way.

"Homeboy is out to lunch. He hasn't spoken a word," Marcus said.

"He's been like that since the guards found me tied up in his cottage," Sydney said.

Jaillet coughed and blood flowed from his mouth.

"Damn, they really worked him over," Marcus said.

"This isn't good," Doc said.

Marcus removed the toothpick from his mouth. "This is going to have to wait, Doc. We need to get out of here just in case that crazy lady changes her mind."

"You're right. Get the Toussaints and pack up our things—we're going home. Sydney, give your father a call and tell him you're okay and that we'll be in Perpignon by nightfall."

Cicero and X-man brought the cars around to the front to load their bags.

Jaillet's lifeless eyes sprang to life when he saw the car doors open. "I'm not going anywhere with you. Take your hands off me!" He tried to break loose from Marcus' grip. Marcus smacked him in the mouth. Dazed, he struggled to his feet, wiping more blood from his mouth with the back of his hand. "You think you're smart." He started laughing. "You have no idea what you've done, do you?"

"Why don't you tell us," Marcus said.

A menacing smile formed on his face. "You really are stupid. Why do you think Devin Leon-Francis refused to pay the ransom for his daughter's return? It was never about money. I was paid to kidnap her."

The back of Jaillet's head exploded like a watermelon. A second shot knocked Doc off his feet. Aristotle ran to help him. Another gunshot rang out. Aristotle screamed, grabbed at his back, and dropped on his face in the courtyard.

"Aristotle and Doc are down!" Cicero shouted. X-man was in the front seat of the car. He reached in the back to get his rifle off the seat. A bullet shattered the back window, hitting him between the eyes.

"Sonofabitch!" Marcus yelled as he sprinted to the woods with bullets flying around him.

Sydney watched him disappear between the trees. Doc was stretched out on blood-matted grass, Cicero held Aristotle's lifeless body in his arms, and X-man was slumped over the front seat, dead. She choked back tears. "I'm going after the boss," she yelled to Cicero.

Marcus was stooped behind a tree reloading his guns when Sydney came running up the path behind him. "Over here," he whispered. Pointing with his gun he said, "Two shooters over there, about twenty yards in front of those trees. How are Doc and the Toussaints?"

"I don't know about Julian—Xavier and Aristotle are gone."

Marcus bolted from cover and rushed toward the men screaming profanities as fast as his guns fired.

"Marcus!" she shouted.

His rage was his only protection as he somehow managed to make it across the clearing without getting hit. One of his bullets toppled a gunman from a tree.

Sydney saw movement in the bushes. She fired and two men went down. She walked over to the dead bodies. "I know these men."

"What?" Marcus said.

"They work for my father."

Marcus snatched the dead shooter's assault rifle off the ground and smashed it against the tree. "We've been set up."

Chapter 2

Europe received its first major snowstorm in late November. By December, the continent was bracing for its fourth. Dark clouds pushed by a strong eastern wind, moved across the mountains and descended over Lake Lucerne and the paddle steamer, *D.S. Korpra.*

Iggy was in the main saloon reading the newspaper, and trying to ignore the renaissance chamber orchestra in the background. He turned to the second page and continued reading the article about Pierre and Philip Micheaux. The news of their thefts had created a firestorm of controversy and outrage throughout Europe, especially in Switzerland and France, where the brothers made their homes. They owned one of the world's largest collections of Pre-Columbian art, and were highly respected antiquities dealers. The House of Micheaux art galleries in Montreal, Quebec City, and Paris displayed some of the finest antiquities from Peru, Ecuador, Mexico, and Belize. In the end, the show palaces were nothing more than a façade to conceal their smuggling operations.

In Central and South America, the Micheaux brothers used a network of thieves to loot graves and tombs, archaeological sites, private collections, and museums. In Europe, they exploited poor families to do their grave robbing. In Italy, they used the Tombaroli, which were small teams of thieves responsible for robbing over 10,000 gravesites. The plunder was stashed in private warehouses from Switzerland to Canada. The French police raided one warehouse in Montpellier, recovering over $30 million in artifacts that had been stolen from Greece and Italy. The article also named the art dealers and auction houses that allegedly helped the twins create fraudulent provenance so they could sell the antiquities on the open market.

Iggy Vasilakis didn't know anything about art, but he was a proud Greek, and the story of the Micheauxs disgusted him. He rested the newspaper on the table and resumed eating his orange duck as the sounds of Puccini's *Nessun Dorman* flowed through the elegant room of lacquered woods, mirrored walls, and vintage ceiling fans. Under normal conditions, Iggy might have enjoyed himself aboard the 1930ish paddleboat, but tonight was about work.

He disliked spying—it was better suited for the salacious voyeur. Iggy was a detective or at least had been one before retiring eleven years ago from the Athens police. His government pension was meager, which made it difficult for him to support his family in a city as affluent as Lucerne. The only alternative left was to take whatever jobs he could get—even if it meant lowering his ethics, and taking work he didn't want—like this one.

He was following the couple sitting at the table across from him and he didn't even know their real names. His client referred to them only as Ebony and Ivory. They weren't lovers, but they were more than just friends. There was the occasional touching of hands, hugs, and the perfunctory peck on the cheek—but they also had a rhythm together. He noticed it when he first started tailing them three weeks ago. They moved as a synchronized team, instinctively assessing every situation, reacting, and watching each other's backs. A certain look in the eyes, a nod of the head, or hand on the arm or elbow meant something in their unspoken language. He also noticed something else. When they walked, the redheaded woman always stayed on the outside curb and the man on the inside. She was always the first in the door, and she never left him alone at the dinner table.

Iggy's eyes shifted back to the chamber quartet when Ivory glanced in his direction. The ethereal beauty was dressed in a black pantsuit, heels, and wore an exquisite heart-shaped diamond necklace with matching bracelet. She moved with the grace of a model, but Iggy knew she was a professional bodyguard. He was having a tougher time reading her companion.

Ebony was older than she was, maybe fifteen years or more—it was hard to tell. Iggy knew one thing for sure. The man was wealthy, evidenced by the costs of their rooms at the Lex Plaza Hotel, their nightly visits to the casino, and the little side excursions like this Sunday evening dinner cruise to Frullen. The mustachioed man with the salt-and-pepper hair was an immaculate dresser, probably a businessman, Iggy guessed. But there was also an edginess about him, a certain street savvy, and a swagger in his step that suggested more. Iggy was curious by nature, but his instructions were clear. He was only to follow, observe, and file reports. Nothing more.

Their daily routine seldom varied. Every morning they went jogging along the lake, followed by breakfast back at their hotel where they stayed until they left for the casino in the evening. Twice a week they took the short boat ride across the lake to the Burgenstock Hotel for brief visits before returning. Iggy never followed them to the mountain retreat for fear he would be seen. But he would have given up a month's income to know what they were doing up there.

At the end of each day, Iggy was required to call in his report to an anonymous answering machine in Norway. The job was easy and he was being well paid by his client, but he still didn't like the work.

* * *

The cruise concluded with the captain surprising the 400 passengers by steering the paddle steamer past the historic Chapel and Mill Bridges, which spanned the Reuss River. Soft amber lights glowed from the octagonal water towers and medieval gables as the steamer paddled by.

When the ship docked at the town center, Iggy saw a black sedan looming in the shadows of the buildings. He recognized the Chief Inspector's Mercedes and fell back as passengers began leaving the ship. Two men approached Ebony and Ivory, and minutes later they were whisked away in the Inspector's car.

The Mercedes crossed Chapel Bridge to old town and Haldenstr, and turned onto a deserted street littered with mural houses, flower boxes, and pastel-colored shutters. The car stopped in a narrow cobblestone square under a shingle that read: *Presslerlux Pub and Brew.* The former monk house was empty, except for a barmaid and the owner who were cleaning up. The men escorted the couple upstairs to the dimly lit room.

"May I see your passports, please?" the Swiss Inspector asked.

The black man reached inside his cashmere overcoat and pulled out his wallet, tossing it on the table. "You mind telling me what this is all about, Inspector?"

The Inspector carefully checked their passports before handing them back. "I apologize for my surreptitious actions, Mr. St. John—Miss Belleshota. I thought this would be a somewhat more pleasing environment to talk in than my spartan office."

"Why are we being detained?" Marcus asked.

"Detained? No, I merely would like to ask you a few questions."

"So, we aren't under arrest?"

"No, I only wish...."

"Good, then I'm leaving. Come on, Sydney, we're out of here," Marcus said, getting up from the chair. One of the Inspector's men blocked his path. "You want to move your bubble butt out of my face, or am I going to have to go through you?"

"Please, sit down, Mr. St. John; this will only take a moment of your time." The Inspector leaned his chair back against the wall.

Marcus stared at the small, bespectacled man as he weighed his options. Reluctantly, he sat back down. He pulled a cigar from his pocket. "May I?"

"Yes, of course. How rude of me."

A policeman handed him an ashtray. Marcus lit the cigar, and crossed his legs. "What questions?"

"What brings you to our lovely city?"

"Business."

"And Miss Belleshota?"

"She's a business associate."

"What kind of business?"

Marcus blew a thick cloud of smoke in the air. "I don't have to answer that."

"That is true. Let me be more direct. What business do you have with madam Micheaux?"

"That's between us."

The Inspector returned the chair to all four legs. "No, this does concern me. Any time someone of madam Micheaux's stature complains to my office about being harassed and threatened, it becomes my business. The Micheauxs are one of the most prominent and respected banking families in Lucerne, and I will not tolerate you or anyone else making threats against them."

"Hold on, Inspector Clouseau, or whatever the hell your name is. Don't lecture me on the Micheauxs. I know all I want or need to know about Sasha Micheaux. Anyone that kills her own family isn't entitled to any respect, at least not from me."

"I don't understand…"

"Ask Sasha what happened to her anal-retentive twin brothers."

"Philip and Pierre committed suicide in their car in Paris last month after they learned they were under investigation. Their driver witnessed the ordeal."

Marcus laughed. "Trust me, the last time the twins saw the inside of a car was in the trunk of their baby sister's Bentley, after she popped a cap in their butts."

"That's ridiculous, and you have no right to make threats against her life."

"I've never spoken to the woman, much less made any threats against her. She won't let me near enough for that."

"You have never threatened her?"

"No. I may have had a few choice words with some of her people, but then again, I've always had a problem when people try and get up in my face." Marcus exhaled more smoke. "Sasha's rattling your cage because she doesn't want to deal with me. I'm a patient man, I can wait."

The Inspector saw the determination on his face. "Why do you want to see her?"

"Sasha knows, ask her. But I doubt she'll tell you the truth."

The Inspector sighed. He wasn't getting anywhere with this man. He stood up and walked to the door. "Mr. St. John, if you or Miss Belleshota cause any further disruption or harm to Madam Micheaux, I will be talking with you again. It won't be in my brother's establishment, though, but in my jail. I don't want to hear of you being within a mile of the Burgenstock resort or Madam Micheaux. Is that understood?"

"I got the message, Inspector."

"Somehow I doubt that. You are sure there is nothing you want to say?"

"Yeah, there is something. You've made us miss our steamer to Vitznau, so which one of you is going to take us to the Lex Plaza Hotel?"

"It's closed for the season," the Inspector said.

"Not this year."

* * *

Lucerne is one of the most beautiful cities in the world, nestled between the hills where the Reuss River meets the lake, and surrounded by the towering Alps. It was hard to believe that anyone could tire of the captivating renaissance city of Baroque fountains and painted gables, but Marcus had had enough of the city. He had lied to the Inspector. He was not a patient man, and he wasn't going to wait forever to get an audience with Sasha Micheaux. But he also knew he couldn't afford another run-in with her men or another midnight rendezvous with the police. Three weeks in Lucerne was wearing on his nerves and he couldn't stay here another day.

He and Sydney took the boat to Alpenachstad Village, and caught the clog wheel railway to the top of Mt. Pilatus. It was sunny at the summit, but cold. Alpine horn players performed in front of the restaurant as visitors strolled around the scenic walkways and paths. Wildflowers and lichen-encrusted trees sprouted in snowy crevices on the side of the mountain. The Italian Alps were visible in the distance.

"Julian would love this," Sydney said, admiring the panoramic view.

"Knowing Doc, he's probably already been here." Marcus rested his arms on the railing as he took in the view. "This sure as hell beats the city."

19

"You're going to have to use that world-class jet of yours for travel instead of a tax write-off. You are missing a lot of the world."

Marcus laughed. "I'm a homeboy. Living and traveling in the tropical forests of the Virgin Islands and frigid Switzerland is not my idea of vacationing. I don't like heat and I hate the cold. If God wanted me exploring the hinterlands, he wouldn't have made five-star hotels, room service, and HBO."

"Didn't you enjoy your trip to St. Thomas last year?"

"It's okay, but I can live without it—just like this place. Once I deal with Sasha, I'm out of here. I only wish Doc were here. He would know how to deal with that schizophrenic prima dona."

"Asha is not going to let him leave her sight, so we may have to do this the hard way."

"Yeah, I suppose."

They had lunch, then took the gondola down the mountain and caught the train to Geneva, where they stayed for the weekend.

On Monday, they returned to Lucerne and spent the day in the city at the Picasso and Richard Wagner museums, before hopping on the steamer for the Lex Plaza. Rain drove the few passengers on deck indoors.

Marcus ordered drinks while Sydney searched for a window table.

"I should have ordered a double," Marcus said.

Sydney smiled. "This is the first time we've taken a break since we've been here. Try to relax. A little culture is good for you. Art is more than your video collection and the movies you've seen."

"At least those make sense. I'd rather look at Elvis on velvet than the crap I saw today. I can't believe people actually revere that kind of stuff."

"Some are even obsessive-compulsive about it, like your friends the Micheauxs. Maybe when you see Sasha, she can expand your appreciation for art," she said, chuckling.

"The only thing Sasha Micheaux can do for me is tell me what she knows about your father and where I can find him."

"You're wasting you're time trying to find him. Besides, Jason Worrick is the one you should be after. He's the one who deceived us and is responsible for Xavier and Aristotle Toussaint's deaths."

"Worrick and Andy Preston take their orders directly from your father. They're just the puppets he used against us."

"My father wasn't involved in any of this," she said emphatically.

"Your father is involved in *everything*. You know what a manipulator he is. I can't believe you can sit there and honestly tell me that Worrick or that dim-witted Andy Preston could have orchestrated this by themselves."

"All I know is that my father would not have had me kidnapped. That's insane."

"Your father does a lot of insane things that make sense to him."

"What possible motive would he have?"

"He wanted the Micheaux twins out of his way and he needed someone to do his dirty work for him. Doc and I just happened to be the ones with the word 'stupid' tacked on our foreheads. He picked us, and we fell for it."

"That doesn't make sense. My father doesn't have anything in common with the Micheaux family. Worrick might, but not my father."

Marcus sighed as he brushed his drink to the side. "Jason Worrick is a senile old man who couldn't lead a horse to the trough. Your father, however, is the devil incarnate and a greedy bastard that wants to own the world, just like those crazy Micheauxs and the other Merovingian families. That's what they have in common. And that's why your daddy went through all this crap, and why Cicero ended up shipping his brothers' home in boxes. The men who tried to kill us in France worked for your daddy—you said so yourself. If you're in so much denial that you don't want to accept that, then I guess you'll wake up when you hear it from Sasha's own mouth."

Sydney's face turned crimson. Marcus hated her father, and for good reasons. But that didn't make it any easier for her to accept. Talking about him was a sensitive subject. Every time his name came up, their conversation ended in hot words and recriminations, no matter how hard they tried to respect each other's feelings. Sydney desperately wanted to believe her father was innocent, because the alternative would mean that he had played her just like he did everyone else in his life. And she couldn't accept that.

"I hold no illusions about my father. I know who and what he is, but he's my father and I'll always love him—no matter what. I know you're still pissed because you blame him for your old girlfriend's death years ago and..."

"Pissed...I have a right to be pissed, Sydney. I gave him the benefit of the doubt when his men murdered her, and I let it slide. I would have even turned the other cheek for your sake when he tried to whack me in France. But when he killed Xavier and Aristotle...that was it. What kind of father uses his own daughter as bait to get rid of his enemies? He's a coward, and he thinks he's God. I'm sick of your daddy! He's been screwing with my life for the last six years, and I'm tired of it." Marcus was shouting as the words spewed from his mouth. A couple at a nearby table decided to find a quieter spot on the boat. "I should have taken him out years ago, and maybe if I had, some good people would still be alive. I'm through worrying about the next thing he's gonna throw in my life, and I'm about to turn this shit around. Let's see how he likes having someone on his ass for once. He's hiding out there somewhere, and so are his flunkies, Worrick and Preston. And I'm going to put the bunch of them to sleep."

Sydney finished the rest of her gin and pushed her chair away from the table. The handle of her holstered Beretta glittered in the light as she stretched across the table and snatched her overcoat off the chair. Her gray eyes bore down on him. "If by chance we find my father, don't make the mistake of thinking our friendship will stop me from putting a bullet in you if you even think about harming him." She stormed out of the bar and went out to the deck and pouring rain, where she stayed for the remainder of the trip. Marcus downed his drink in one gulp. He wished he had ordered that double.

* * *

The Lex Plaza Hotel sat at the base of Mount Rigi in the lakeside village of Vitznau. The Belle Époque-style, fairy-tale castle of gabled roofs and romantic balconies was a five-star resort with three restaurants, a piano bar, and a reputation for discretion. The hotel never kept a public register of their guests. Not that it mattered this time of year, since it was supposed to be closed for the winter, but Marcus needed a secure place to stay while in Lucerne, so he coaxed the owners into leasing him the use of the hotel. It wasn't cheap—$4,600 a night for him and his men. In return, they had free access to the one hundred and thirty room resort, a full-time chef, and all the food they could eat.

When the paddle steamer docked, Sydney rushed past the guard and went straight up the hill to the hotel. Marcus thought about calling out to her, but she was still mad and he was tired.

"Anything happening?" Marcus asked his guard.

"Quiet as a mouse around here, boss. How'd you guys enjoy your trip?"

"Could have been better."

The intuitive guard looked briefly at his employer. "You know, boss, sometimes this PMS thing is overrated. Women are just hard creatures to understand, you know?"

Marcus smiled and lightly patted the big man's shoulder. "I suppose. Goodnight, Sam."

"Goodnight, boss, see you in the morning," he said as he returned to his post.

There was a message waiting for Marcus in his room. It was from Benno Rood, a research historian who worked for him on special projects. Marcus called him back at his San Francisco office.

"Mr. Leon-Francis has not been seen in public since August. Mr. Worrick is on extended vacation somewhere in Europe and Mr. Preston left the company right after his last meeting with you in early October," Benno said.

"So if Leon-Francis' top men at Excalibur are gone, who's running his billion-dollar corporation—Santa Claus? What a bunch of crap. You think Leon-Francis is still in the states?"

"It's doubtful, it would be too risky. He likes being close to his business interests and most of them are overseas."

"Where?"

"Everywhere. It's impossible to get a handle on everything he owns. He has businesses in Rome, Versailles, Amsterdam, Vienna, Stockholm—just to name a few."

"How about real estate holdings—houses, townhouses...?"

"None, other than the house in San Diego and a penthouse at Excalibur. We could narrow our search area if his daughter could be persuaded to cooperate."

"Fleas running through hell in a paper bag have a better chance than me of convincing Sydney to help. What did you find out about Andy Preston?"

"He's the only child of an East Hampton attorney. His parents haven't heard from him since he went to work for Mr. Leon-Francis. A lot of that misinformation he passed to me was very convincing. I was so sure the Micheaux family was responsible for Ms. Belleshota's kidnapping. I'm..."

Marcus interrupted the Dutchman. "You don't have anything to apologize for, Benno, you were just doing your job. We all got sucked in by the deceit. Worrick and Preston will pay for it. I don't care what it takes or how much it costs, Benno...I want you to find these guys for me."

* * *

Marcus had a terrible night sleeping. All he could think about was Sydney and how they had left their last conversation. He was thankful when he saw the sun finally appear over the mountains. He put on his running clothes and took the stairs to the garden. To his surprise, Sydney was already there, warming up. Neither spoke as they went through their stretches on opposite benches.

"You ready yet?" she asked without looking at him or waiting for an answer. She started running down the road to the lake. They jogged in silence along their three-mile route.

Afterwards, Marcus showered, dressed, and headed downstairs for breakfast. Sydney surprised him again when he saw her eating at their customary table in the piano bar. He grabbed some fresh fruit, eggs, and a steak from the buffet and joined her. Again, neither of them spoke while they ate. It didn't take long for the guards and chef to realize something was wrong.

Marcus finally broke the silence. "Sydney, I'm sorry, for the things I said."

"Why? You were only telling the truth."

"Well, I could have been a little more considerate. You know how I am. Most of the time my mouth is running faster than my brain. I'm sorry."

Sydney looked up from her plate, but avoided his eyes. In many ways, they were mirror images of each other. Both were hot-tempered, overly opinionated, arrogant, and stubborn; but that is why they got along so well. They understood each other. Her eyes finally met his. She loved Marcus because there was no pretense about him. He was an honest man with a passion for family and friends, and he made no distinction between the two.

"You meant every word you said about my father, and you're piss poor at apologies. But, I'll accept it—under one condition. I want your word that you won't try and hurt my father if we find him. You do that and I promise not to take your head off." She was smiling, but her eyes conveyed the desperation and seriousness of the paradox they faced. Marcus knew she was torn between loyalties.

"I can't do that, Sydney—you know how I am. I'm sorry...."

She wasn't surprised by the answer. Marcus lived by a simple code of conduct: you respect his family and he would respect yours. Step over the line and you were in trouble. Her father had long since crossed the boundary. Marcus was not a forgiving man, and given the chance, he would take her father out in a heartbeat. She also knew that if that day ever came, she would have to choose sides. And Marcus would lose.

She got up from the table. "I'll be leaving as soon as I can get my things together."

Marcus felt like someone had punched him in his chest. He felt helpless as he watched her walk away. "Sydney, you don't have to do that. Let's talk some more. If you still want to leave after that, I'll have Tre' fly you home tomorrow."

She stopped, turned, and gave him an icy stare. "I don't want anything from you, Marcus. Goodbye."

That evening he stood by the window as one of his men helped carry her bags down to the waiting boat.

Chapter 3

Stamsund was just one of a string of connected villages that made up the Lofoten Islands, on the northern tip of Norway. The little fishing village was crammed with red buildings perched high on rock stilts rising from the sea. Fishermen swarmed the docks of the oddly shaped harbor, readying their nets and boats. This was the height of the fishing season. The Lofoten Islands were a byproduct of the Gulf Steam. As a result, the area was blessed with warm waters and bountiful cod, all surrounded by green fjords and cascading waterfalls. Jordan and a group of backpackers from the Stamsund Hostel stood in a line to board the coastal steamer. She was the only woman in the group.

Jordan's plans for traveling incognito were quickly dashed once she boarded the *SS Cutter*. She was the only black face among the two hundred and thirty-three passengers taking the excursion cruise of the Norwegian fjords. Traveling alone and being attractive only garnered her more unwanted attention. Two days into the voyage she had managed to avoid any meaningful conversation with the other passengers. That changed on the third day when the cruise ship pulled into Bergen and Lady Beatrice Wollford arrived.

Lady Beatrice boarded the vessel with full entourage and more luggage than Queen Elizabeth, her distant cousin—or at least that's what she told everyone. Technically, she was English royalty, but only because her husband was a cousin of the Earl of Wessex. She occupied the VIP stateroom across the hall from Jordan's suite. The women met in the hallway as they were heading to the dining room for dinner. While Lady Beatrice had a flair for exaggeration, she also had an excellent memory, especially for faces and those of England's social elite. She was convinced she had met Jordan before. Jordan spent the next two days in her room, trying to avoid the incessant, chatty woman. On the seventh night, she was invited to dine with the captain at his table, along with ten other guests, including Lady Beatrice.

Jordan spent most of the evening talking with the captain and avoiding Lady Beatrice. After she finished her meal, Jordan excused herself from the table. Lady Beatrice wiped a piece of peach cobbler from her mouth with her linen napkin as she watched Jordan leaving the dining room. "Captain, how much do you know of Mrs. Phoenix?"

The captain lowered the crystal goblet from his mouth. "A Brit like yourself. I believe she is a university professor. Apparently very bright, too.

My staff says she is fluent in several languages. Why do you ask, Lady Beatrice?"

"Curiosity. Her face seems so familiar to me."

* * *

Jordan grabbed the towel off the sink as she stepped from the shower. She dried her body and then used the towel to form a turban for her wet hair. Yellow scented candles filled the boudoir with the aromatic fragrance of Chardonnay while Liszt's *Dante Symphony* played softly in the background. Her silk robe fell loose around her shoulders, revealing a rock-hard body. Jordan sprayed her neck and breasts with expensive perfume as she watched her reflection in the mirror. She had her Scottish grandfather's Gaelic nose and round lips, and her mother's Nubian eyes and dark skin. The oval shape of her face gave her a youthful, and naïve appearance, even though she was thirty-nine and had an IQ that was off the charts.

The glint from her emerald and gold wedding band reflected a green hue off the mirror. She nervously twisted the band on her finger and thought about the sacrifices she had made to save her marriage. In the end, it didn't matter. She had wasted the last six years of her life on a man whose political ambition was greater than his love for her. Tears formed in the corner of her eyes, which she angrily wiped away with her hand. She had vowed never to shed another tear for a man that wasn't worthy of them. She pulled the expensive ring from her finger and flushed it down the toilet. She had more important things to think about.

Jordan curled up on the bed and tried to watch the news on television, but fell asleep before the weather forecast. A winter storm was creeping across Russia and the Barents Sea, heading south toward Scandinavia. If Jordan had been awake, she might have thought twice about what she was planning to do.

The following morning, the *SS* Cutter made an unscheduled stop at a remote port south of Fauske, Norway. The snow was falling and it was bitter cold. Lady Beatrice and the captain stood on the upper deck watching Jordan cross the ramp to the deserted dock.

"Where is she going?" Lady Beatrice asked.

The captain zipped his coat and held on to her arm. "I have no idea. She insisted that we drop her off here. She must be crazy—there is nothing out there but snow."

"I think not. She bears an amazing resemblance to a woman I once met at Buckingham, and she was far from being crazy."

Jordan made her way across the icy road to the waiting vehicle parked along the side of the road. The elderly Russian driver struggled to open the door against the strong wind. Jordan tossed her bag in the back and slid in the passenger seat.

The Russian smiled, showing his crooked teeth. "I am glad to see you again, Colonel. How was the trip?"

"Too long, Ziv. How is your wife?"

"*Zloy* and mean as ever. She has prepared your favorite dish."

"Is everything ready?"

"*Da*. The supplies you requested are waiting for you in the village."

"Good, let's go."

* * *

Jordan waited until evening before setting out from the village on her journey. A red-footed falcon followed her snowmobile as it streaked across the snow-covered mesa. Wild reindeer and wolves sought refuge from the heavy snow and wind that pounded the mountain. It was midnight by the time she reached the summit, but light as day, thanks to the northern lights showering the heavens with their kaleidoscopic colors.

The bird watched as she struggled through the inhospitable sanctuary of frozen tundra and dangerous glaciers. Wind-blown snow covered the tracks of the snowmobile as it disappeared into the forest. Jordan, dressed in a white snowsuit, Tossu overboots and a facemask, worked quickly in the subzero temperature. She hid the snowmobile under a white tarp and made sure her equipment was secure before trudging off through the thigh-deep snow.

It took her an hour to reach the edge of a wide precipice overlooking the canyon. The bottom of the canyon was as flat as a plate, due to sediment deposits from an ancient river that once flowed through the mountain. She checked her coordinates to make sure she had the right location. This was the place. She scanned the grounds with electronic binoculars. There were eight acres of pristine snow and woods below, marred only by a series of intersecting ski tracks circling the perimeter grounds. Two guards patrolled the woods directly below her, and another one stood on the road leading to the house chiseled in the side of the mountain. A white Apache helicopter sat on a twelve-foot high platform next to the house.

The snowstorm was getting worse and the temperature was dropping. Most of the guards abandoned their posts for the warmth of the inside. Jordan dusted the snow from her lens and stuffed the binoculars back into her pack. It was time to go.

The falcon watched her rappel down the side of the canyon wall and cross an ice bridge, before dropping down to the ground. She removed her backpack and set up a position 800 meters from the house. She dug a shelter pit to wait for the storm to pass. It didn't.

By 2:00 a raging blizzard howled though the canyon, forcing all but one man indoors. The loan guard stood on the road with his back against the wind and his hands wrapped around a cup of hot coffee. Jordan could not afford to wait any longer. She slithered down the bank and crawled along the ravine to the concrete culvert that supported the road, where she attached the explosives.

* * *

Devin Leon-Francis laid two more logs in the mammoth fireplace that was sandwiched between the floor-to-ceiling bookcases. He jabbed at the burning wood until the fire exploded into flames, shooting hot embers up in the belly of the mountain. Resting the poker against the fireplace, he stood up and straightened the crooked oil painting hanging over the mantel.

Jason Worrick was lying on the sofa in front of the window. "This damn weather is going to keep me up all night." He squirmed under the covers, trying to get his naked legs warmed by the fire.

Leon-Francis stood at the mirror, adjusting his tie and playing with his thick, perfectly coifed silver hair. He had a square-jawed face with a mustache that covered his thin lips. Bony fingers were the only things that gave away his true age. "I have to go," he said.

"You're going out in this weather?" Worrick asked.

"Yes."

Worrick sat upright on the couch. "You coming back?"

"I'll send for you in a couple of weeks or so, after my business is finished. I need you to stay here and wrap things up."

Worrick flinched as a burst of pain shot through his hipbone and down his legs. Leon-Francis watched the old man's wrinkled hand squeezing the edge of the couch in pain, but he didn't move to help. He passed Worrick the handkerchief from his breast pocket.

29

"Thanks," Worrick said, wiping his mouth. "You must have a hot date to risk your life going out in this weather."

"I do. With Sasha Micheaux."

"It's horrible out there. You sure this can't wait until morning?"

"The secret in the art of war lies in an eye for locality and not letting the right moment slip through your fingertips. Now is the right time."

"Whatever Chinese philosopher said that never met the Micheauxs or the other Merovingians."

Leon-Francis stroked the fire again. "Superior force never guarantees victory, Jason, especially if you don't know what to defend against. Sasha will soon discover that."

"You think you can knock off the queen bee without the Merovingians getting upset?"

"The other families won't interfere."

Worrick wanted to ask him how he knew that, but he had learned from thirty-five years of working with his boss not to ask certain questions, and this was one.

Leon-Francis survived by two principles: never tell anyone more than they need to know; and never trust anyone. He had an intelligence network superior to most third world countries, and always stayed a step ahead of his adversaries.

Jason Worrick was Leon-Francis' only friend and second in command, but like everyone else who worked for Devin Leon-Francis—Worrick was also kept in the dark about most things. Leon-Francis shuffled his personnel like pawns on a chessboard, in a game where only he knew the outcome.

"You've got Sasha's brothers out of the way, and now you have the media and authorities breathing down her neck. Let them finish her off. Why take extra risk?" Worrick asked.

"I am going to finish what I started. The Micheauxs had their chances to do business with me."

"So why do I have to stay here?"

"I need for you to take over the operation in Narvik until I find a replacement for Andy Preston."

"Why—what's wrong with Andy?"

"He's a drunk and he's chasing some skirt all around Europe. I don't need him anymore. He's out."

"He's still a kid, Devin. He's homesick, maybe a little love struck, but harmless."

Leon-Francis gave him a cool stare. "He knows too much about…this place…and my daughter. Woodberry will talk with him." He put on his overcoat and gloves. Worrick sighed as he rested his arms on his cane. Leon-Francis lightly brushed his hand across his felt hat. "You're taking this too personally, Jason."

"The kid was beginning to grow on me, that's all."

Leon-Francis smiled. "What's the update on my daughter?"

"She and St. John are still in Switzerland trying to get an audience with her Royal Highness."

"They're wasting their time."

"Tell that to St. John. That guy doesn't know when to quit. He's never going to give up searching for us. All he needs is a sniff and he will be all over my butt. I've been hiding up here for six weeks, ever since we put your plan into operation. This is getting ridiculous. Why do you insist on keeping that fool alive? He's dangerous." Worrick used his cane and tried lifting himself off the sofa. "This damn weather isn't good for my rheumatoid arthritis. You need to get me out of here to someplace warm…anyplace other than this frozen wasteland."

Leon-Francis helped him to his feet. "St. John is nothing without Julian Sebasst—and he's being taken care of as we speak. You're safe here. In a few weeks this will all be over and I'll send you back home, but right now…"

A bullet shattered the triangular window next to them, spraying the room with glass shrapnel. A second shot barely missed Leon-Francis's head and blew a chunk of granite from the wall. Leon-Francis fell to the floor. He opened his eyes and saw a golf ball-size hole in Worrick's neck. Pandemonium broke out as armed men swarmed from the house. There was another unheard shot, and a guard fell face down in the snow. Two more shots and more men fell. The guards fired their weapons into the empty forest until the whole canyon sounded like an erupting volcano.

Two guards found an abandoned sniper rifle lying next to one of their dead men. They followed the tracks for forty yards, before realizing the shooter had circled behind them. The noise from Jordan's shotgun blasts alerted the others. Five yellow snowmobiles shot from underneath the helicopter platform, followed by men on skies. They made it halfway across the road, before an explosion ripped the culvert apart, sending men and machines flying.

31

Jordan watched the carnage from the ridge—her finger still glued to the trigger. She took one last look down at the burning men before tossing the detonator in the snow, and continuing up the ridge.

It took her two hours to reach the foot of Nehemiah's Wall, and fifteen minutes to dig out the provisions and gear she had buried. She chewed her rations while changing out of her wet clothes. Jordan slipped on new thermal underwear, an Icelandic sweater, and a new snowsuit. The facemask was discarded for a ski cap and goggles. She shoved her service revolver in her holster, tested the tether line securing the skis to the backpack, and made sure her boot crampons were on tight. She had forty-nine hours to get over the wall, across the glaciers and down the fjord to Fauske to catch her ride home. Jordan looked at the immense wall of ice staring her in the face. She took two deep breaths, swung the axe deep into the ice, and lifted herself up on the 810-foot icefall.

* * *

A silver-headed man they called the Norwegian led his patrol up the mountain where they spent two hours hunting for Jordan on the summit. All they found was her snowmobile. As they returned to camp, the Norwegian passed a row of dead bodies spaced neatly apart covered in snow. The section of road that once covered the culvert was now a giant hole and repository of body parts. The Norwegian picked up a severed hand by his foot and threw it in the hole with the other parts. He looked for Woodberry. He found him standing in the riverbed with his hands in his pockets, barking out orders. Woodberry not only looked like a marine drill sergeant, he was as tough as one. The Norwegian knew it would be a long night.

Tiberius Woodberry inspected Jordan's snowmobile from the riverbed. "Where did you find it?"

"Up on the summit, a couple of kilometers from here," the Norwegian said.

"Which direction is he headed?"

"We didn't find any tracks."

"That doesn't make sense." The Norwegian grabbed Woodberry's hand and helped him up the slippery bank. "Put the snowmobile in the shed. I'll check it later." He grabbed the Norwegian by the shoulder as he was leaving. "And then I want you to send two more patrols back up to the summit and find me something…a body, a turd, something that tells me which way he went. You came highly recommended; let's see you earn your money."

The Norwegian nodded his head.

Woodberry headed back to the house. "Get these men out of here and bury them!" he said, passing the corpses and slamming the door behind him. The fire in the fireplace was out and men were nailing cedar planks over the shattered windows to keep the snow out. Jason Worrick's body was stretched out on the sofa under a blood-soaked blanket covered in snow. Woodberry ran up the steps to the loft and went down the hall to the master bedroom.

Devin Leon-Francis sat in his easy chair, reading. "I know you have some good news for me," he said, without moving his eyes from the book.

"There was only one shooter. We found his snowmobile on the top. He won't get far on foot in this weather."

"Why aren't you holding his ass in your hands?"

Woodberry shifted uncomfortably on his feet. "I don't…have his ass yet, sir, but I will. My guess is he is heading to Fauske. That's the nearest town from here."

Leon-Francis lowered the book from his face. "Let me see if I understand you so far," he said, tossing the paperback into the open suitcase on the bed. "Some maniac rolled up here, to my home that no one is supposed to even know exists…kills Jason…my boys, and you can't find him. Does that about size up the situation?"

"I believe we're dealing with a professional. The rifle we found was a British…"

Leon-Francis jumped to his feet. His voice was soft—almost a whisper, but his gun-metal eyes were red. "I don't care about belief, Tiberius, I only deal in fact. Let me give you the facts we're currently dealing with. First, your boys didn't do their jobs. Second, someone in this organization opened his mouth about this place. Third, I don't like people trying to kill me." He inched closer to his face. "I want this man, and I want you to get him now. There are only two ways off this mountain—across the summit and over Nehemiah's Wall. I want your boys waiting for him when he comes down the other side. Are we clear on this?"

"Sir, the road is destroyed. How are…"

"High jump over, or bungee across. It doesn't matter to me. Get him, and then I want you to go to Narvik and find out who Andy Preston has been running his big mouth to."

"Yes, sir."

Leon-Francis closed his suitcase. "I'm leaving. I'll get back to you and you better have some good news for me. Don't let me down again, Tiberius."

Leon-Francis walked through the tunnel leading to the helicopter platform. The helicopter lifted off the pad and hovered above the fortress that he knew he would never see again. "Get me out of here," he yelled to his pilot.

* * *

The anticipated storm hit the Norwegian coastline with hurricane force. The French freighter, *Vincien Micheaux*, sat disabled, bobbling helplessly back and forth in the blue waters of jagged ice. The French captain checked the ship's position again and took another look through the binoculars. He was searching for the tugboats, but he only saw the heavy fog and freezing rain that engulfed the pilothouse window. He was beginning to regret having destroyed the communications and radar equipment, but it was better to be safe than sorry. Two of the imprisoned crew had escaped and tried to radio for help before they were caught by his men. He didn't want to take any chances that something else could go wrong so he had the equipment smashed and tossed overboard. That was before the storm set in and twenty-foot swells pushed the ship off course. The captain had no idea of where they were, but he knew they couldn't survive the night in this weather. Suddenly, he heard a faint whistle off in the distance. He pointed the floodlights toward the sound. "There!" he shouted in French to his five deckhands waiting below. "Off starboard."

The captain blew the freighter's whistle once and then twice more. The first tugboat came into view and moved astern, followed by a second tug. Off the portside bow, appeared a third tugboat, but it dwarfed the other two. It was a huge yellow 300-foot salvage tug with a floating crane, divers, and a crew of eighteen men dressed in red-clad Columbia raincoats. They jumped off the boats and secured the lines to the freighter.

Floodlights burned as the men transferred the cargo from the freighter onto the tugboats. Men in red wet suits worked underwater securing the explosives to the hull and propeller shaft of the freighter. After they finished their work, they waited for the boss. An hour later, a white helicopter landed on top of the salvage tug.

The French captain hustled up the platform steps to get what he thought was going to be his final instructions from Devin Leon-Francis. Instead, Leon-Francis' men shot the captain and his deckhands and threw their bodies overboard. Ten minutes later, Leon-Francis and his helicopter were gone.

Leon-Francis' men cast off the lines and two of the tugboats disappeared back into the fog, leaving the wounded freighter at the mercy of the salvage tug. The tug pushed the larger vessel 144 miles north of the Arctic Circle, and detonated the explosives. The *Vincien Micheaux* sank to the bottom of the Barents Sea, along with the thirty-one Knight Guardians locked in the cargo hold.

Chapter 4

Andy Preston did not get word of Jason Worrick's murder until two days later while ordering dinner. He finished his drink, crushed his cigarette out, and handed the menu back to the waiter. The seven-minute gondola ride down the mountain seemed like eternity in the crowded car. Everyone looked suspicious, including the old man hugging the rail next to him. Andy's damp hand slipped from the pole as the gondola came to a quick stop. Embarrassed, but unhurt, he let the old man help him back to his feet. He wiped his perspiring hands across his trouser legs and looked for a taxi.

He was a nervous wreck by the time he got back to the office. Andy had two drinks in quick succession and poured another one before sitting the bottle down on his desk next to him. He raised the glass to his lips, but hesitated. If St. John's people could get to Worrick in one of the most remote and inaccessible areas of the world, what chance did he have of staying alive? He'd warned Jason Worrick for weeks that they were underestimating St. John's abilities and resources. With his money and tenacity, he was as dangerous as a rabid dog and just as hard to stop. Andy had reason to be afraid.

Jason Worrick had recruited Andy for a special job a year ago. He was hired to pose as a private investigator working for Leon-Francis to find his daughter. His real job was to feed Marcus and Doc a trail of lies and create a false paper trail implicating the Micheauxs in Sydney's kidnapping.

Andy let the sting of the vodka linger in his mouth before swallowing. Then he poured another. Soon his mind was as dull as the dreary landscape his eyes seemed riveted to. The weather had changed from rainsqualls to a torrential downpour, throwing cold rain against the grotesque, orange-colored machinery littering the docks. A sea of yellow tugboats anchored in the harbor bobbed in the water like corks in a tub as the wind increased.

From the east, the Malmbanan train from Lapland rolled into the yard and workers began unloading the boxcars filled with high-grade iron ore from the LKAB mines in Kiruna, Sweden. The train made thirteen daily runs hauling its precious cargo. It was so valuable during the war that the British and German navies decimated Narvik for control of the port. Now, the town's inland harbor was nothing more than an underwater graveyard of sunken war relics, like the *Georg Thiele*, whose bow thrust proudly from the water. Narvik was a dreary town and twenty-four hour days of darkness and miserable weather made it even more depressing for Andy.

He opened the utility cabinet and used the satellite phone to call Devin Leon-Francis' mountain retreat. One of the men told him Leon-Francis had left the mountain. Tiberius Woodberry had also vanished, and the rest of the men were out tracking Jason Worrick's killer. Nobody on the mountain knew a damn thing about anything. He tossed the phone back in the case. Andy was afraid to do anything, but his real fear was that he might have compromised Leon-Francis' security. He poured himself some more vodka.

He left his office the same way he did most nights—drunk. He staggered down the steps and made his way through the shipyard. Worrying about St. John and Leon-Francis had taken a back seat to the real cause of his despair and the reason he was turning into a twenty-four-year-old alcoholic. He was a fool in love, which was the worst kind to be. Jordan Phoenix consumed his thoughts when he was sober, and that's why he drank. He really thought she loved him; but now that his blinders were off, he could see that he created his own reality. Andy had been stupid from the very beginning when he first met her at a baroque concert at the college, weeks ago.

She told him she was a visiting professor of literature on sabbatical from Oslo University. She was petite, dark as ebony, with an engaging smile and personality that instantly made him feel at ease. She wore an evening dress that hugged her body like a glove. They talked for hours after the concert, about the great books of literature, the opera, classical music, and the New York Mets. They had so much in common, he thought. But that was because his heart blinded him from the truth. The signs of her transparent love were everywhere, from the distant and sorrowful look in her brown eyes to the enigmatic expression on her face when they made love. They spent every day together, but her heart was somewhere else. One morning he woke up and she had vanished as quickly as she had entered his life. No note, no goodbye. Nothing but an empty closet where her clothes once hung. When he contacted Oslo University he discovered they never heard of Professor Jordan Phoenix.

* * *

Andy found himself walking in the opposite direction of his hotel. He ended up in the lobby of the Grand Royal, soaked to the bone. The manager recognized him as the frequent visitor to room twenty-two, and gave him the key in exchange for fifty dollars.

The room of brass and flowered wallpaper reeked of Pine Sol. He half-heartedly searched the empty closets and drawers, and leafed through the pages of the hotel directory and room service menu. He would have been happy to find a piece of lint—anything that was a part of her. He unabashedly threw back the bed covers and sniffed the sheets for her scent, but of course, there was none.

Andy knew that Jordan had used him, he just didn't know how. Her disappearance and Worrick's death was too much of a coincidence. He racked his brain trying to remember their conversations and any slip-ups he may have made, but he knew he hadn't. If there was one thing he was good at, it was keeping his mouth shut. He never talked about his work or what he did, and she never asked. But still, he knew something was wrong.

He stood on a chair, popped a ceiling tile out, and stuck his head up in the crawl space of the suspended ceiling, but found nothing but metal and wires. He dropped to his knees and ran his hand underneath the bed until his fingers hit the wooden box frame. He shoved the corner of the mattress off the box. A neatly folded black military uniform with a nametag embroidered across the breast, lay in the middle of the box. His knees buckled.

* * *

Andy wandered the streets of Narvik for an hour, before he found himself back on the docks. Another train from Kiruna sat idle in the station. The pungent odor of wet charcoal made him vomit as workers splashed through pools of slimy black resin. He wiped his mouth with his coat sleeve and picked up his glasses. The cap he was wearing was lost to the wind.

He took a shortcut through the station and ran across the marina with Jordan's uniform safely protected under his coat. He gave up trying to outrun the rain and walked the rest of the way back to the harbor. His office was over the side entrance gate to the tow yard. Halfway up the stairs he stopped. Andy stared at the gaping hole in the middle of the yellow tugboats where the giant blue and red freighter had been anchored. "Whaa...where's the ship?" The night guard on the ground looked confused. "*Angela's Storm*...where did it go?"

The guard shrugged his shoulders.

Andy went up the stairs and unlocked the door to his office. This was the very reason he hated working here. Ships came and went in the dead of night, and no one told him anything. There were already three missing tugboats that had not returned after being dispatched to the Arctic Ocean two weeks ago. Now the *Angela's Storm* was gone and the only person who knew where they all went was Devin Leon-Francis.

He went in the office, finished off the corner of vodka and threw the empty bottle in the trash. It was time to leave. He didn't care about Devin Leon-Francis—or Jordan—anymore. All he wanted to do was get out of this hellhole. He turned the light out, opened the door, and found Tiberius Woodberry staring him in his face.

Chapter 5

Sunday morning while half of Europe was digging out of the snowstorm, St. Thomas islanders woke to balmy weather. Men in shorts and women in white linen and cotton dresses streamed into the old basilica cathedral located in the heart of Charlotte Amalie.

The original window shutters that protected the historic structure against nature's harsh weather were rusted in place. Chunks of crusted coral stone and brick were missing from the badly cracked foundation. The Romanesque pillar capitals were deteriorated beyond repair, and the west wing of the church had been closed for years. Nevertheless, the 400-year-old structure stood proud, casting its shadow over the harbor.

Parishioners strolled along the stone walkway passing through the church garden that had been a slave market. Tower bells that once rang the alarm of Napoleon's ships entering the harbor, now tolled as a reminder that morning services at the Baptist church were about to begin.

Service began sharply at 10:45 with an opening prayer and scripture reading, followed by the praise and worship service. The African-American pastor stepped up to the rostrum just before noon. He wore a traditional Italian catholic cassock—his way of paying homage to the old culture that had once occupied the cathedral before the Vatican abandoned it in 1899. The tailor-made robe with French cuffs enhanced his tall frame, giving him a rakish, yet elegant appearance. He moved slowly across the floor with his hands clasped behind his back as he spoke informally to the crowd.

He welcomed the new visitors to the church, and the safe return of a family from their vacation in the states. He teased an embarrassed deacon caught napping on the front pew, and a church mother whose floral hat seemed more suited for a bird's nest than something to adorn a woman's head. After he led the congregation in prayer, he opened his bible and began his sermon.

"The major reason many of us have failure in our lives is because we've become distracted by the fears of life, which keeps us from realizing our full potential and the destiny God has planned for us. We suffer from the fear of decision-making, because we're always afraid of making the wrong choices for our families and ourselves. We worry about our finances because money plays such an integral part of our daily existence, and there never seems to be enough to meet our needs. We fear loneliness, both the physical absence of being connected, and a spiritual loneliness when our daily actions conflict with our Spirit. We have a fear for the safety of our kids every time they leave the house, and a fear of taking risks, because we are afraid of ultimate failure or embarrassment. Then of course we fear the future, because it's the unknown and uncertain. But mostly we fear death, because it's the ultimate cheater of life itself. Our mortal bodies are always in some state of paralysis brought on by our fears. Just when we think we've conquered one fear, it metastasizes itself and attacks us in other parts of our lives. Life is hard work that takes perseverance and a resolute determination to push through to the end, no matter what."

"Speak the word, pastor!" and a sprinkling of "amens" resounded through the church encouraging the pastor to continue. For the next forty-five minutes he quoted a plethora of scripture verses from memory and preached to the congregation on the virtues of prayer and perseverance, modulating his voice to emphasize key points, and finishing in a crescendo pitch that brought the 340-member congregation to their feet with applause.

A white man wearing tinted glasses remained seated and finished picking his fingernails with a toothpick. He took a long look at the preacher and then slipped out of the back pew.

Doc was sweating as he stepped from the pulpit.

His wife, Asha, smiled and gave him an affectionate hug. "Beautiful message," she whispered.

After the service, he retired to his chamber office located in the rear of the church. Iridescent colors reflected off the walls and ceiling from the rays of sunlight flowing through the stained glass windows. He hung his robe in its customary spot behind the large oak door and poured himself a drink of cold lemonade from the pitcher on his desk. His oversized recliner seemed to swallow his large frame as he relaxed and closed his eyes. A soft knock on the door interrupted his moment of solitude.

Asha peaked her head in the door. "Are you okay?"

"Just a little tired, that's all." Doc moved the recliner back to its upright position.

She sat on his lap. "You're not getting enough rest." She stroked his face and gave him a kiss. "Go back to sleep—I'll see you tonight at the restaurant."

* * *

41

After a short nap, Doc showered and went down to the harbor to have lunch with his partner at their restaurant, the *Seawolf Cove*. Later, he took a boat shuttle out to his seaplane and flew across the bay to St. Croix.

The taxi dropped him off in front of the old administration hall at the University of the Virgin Islands. Doc entered the building and took the steps up to the second floor. The hallway was as quiet as a tomb. He walked down the long corridor until he reached his corner office. Most of the university faculty had already relocated to their new offices in the Research and Extension Center next door. But Doc preferred staying in the old building, which was more spacious and private, and had a great view of the 130-acre campus.

A desk full of work was waiting for him, but that was the furthest thing from his mind right now. He changed into his shorts, Addidas, and gloves, and went over to the heavy bag hanging in the corner. He peppered the leather bag with light jabs as he warmed up. His chest ached with every punch he threw. The pain was an everlasting reminder of his close encounter with death. By all medical reasoning, he should have died along with the Toussaint brothers in France. For some reason, God had chosen to bless him by sparing his life. He wasn't confident that his friend would share the same fate.

Doc hadn't heard from Marcus in weeks. His only contacts were through Sydney, and those were infrequent. The little she told him only caused him more concern. Marcus was on a mission and he wasn't coming home until he dealt with Leon-Francis, Jason Worrick, and Andy Preston. Marcus was no match for someone like Devin Leon-Francis, and Doc knew it. The reclusive billionaire was as allusive as Howard Hughes and as ruthless as Pablo Escobar. He was a Jekyll and Hyde, a chameleon—a man who controlled both a global business empire and the largest criminal network in North America. None of that mattered to Marcus. He wasn't afraid of him or any other man, and he never ran from a fight. It was that kind of insane thinking that would get him killed. But he also knew there wasn't anything he could do. His first priority was to his wife and soon-to-be newborn baby. After the anguish he caused Asha, he didn't have the courage to ask her to make any more sacrifices for him. Doc punished the 200-pound bag for thirty more minutes, before finishing with a flurry of combinations that rattled the rafters. Releasing his aggression didn't accomplish anything other than tire him out and make him late. He took a quick shower and left to meet his wife for dinner.

* * *

The French Quarter restaurant was located high on the hills overlooking Charlotte Amalie and the harbor. Asha was waiting for him at their private table on the terrace. The lights from the city glimmered below as a cool breeze gently stirred the palm trees and hibiscus. They ordered a rack of lamb with green peppercorn sauce and caesar salads. After dinner, Asha went to the kitchen and made two tropical fruit milkshakes. She handed one to Doc. Doc stared at his wife who was wearing an off-white wrap jumper/dress and white ankle boots. Her long braided hair and rainforest green eyes made the Cuban beauty even more alluring.

"Julian, what are you looking at?" she asked, playing with the straw as she slurped the milkshake.

"An incredibly beautiful woman sitting at my table, and wondering how fortunate and blessed I am to have her in my life," he said, sipping his shake.

She flashed him an ivory smile. "That's why I married you. You always say the right thing at the perfect time." Her brown hand stretched across the table and clasped his fingers. Asha and Doc had been married for three years and she loved him even more now than when she first met him seven years ago. She looked lovingly at him as he continued talking. She loved hearing his voice, especially when he was impassioned about something as he was now, sharing his plans for restoring the church. He was an inspired leader with strong convictions and a talent for persuasion.

"Honey, you're preaching to the choir. You don't have to sell me on the merits of restoration. It's long overdue, and I think it's a wonderful idea. How much will it cost?"

"Two million dollars will correct the major structural deficiencies in the main sanctuary. We can concentrate on the repairs to the west wing later."

"Julian, the foundation alone will cost more than a million by itself. The west wing—probably two more, and at least another four or five million to do the rest of the repairs."

"We can't afford to restore the whole sanctuary."

"Honey, if you're going to do it at all—do it right. And do the whole thing."

"You're kidding, aren't you? We don't have that kind of money."

"I can raise eighty percent of the funds. Have the church pick up ten percent, and we cover the balance including any cost overruns."

"How are you going to raise that much money?"

"I built this place, didn't I? Have some faith in me," she said, smiling, as she resumed her milkshake.

"Restoration of a 400-year-old church is not that simple."

"I didn't say it was. I just said I can raise the money."

"Okay, if you're sure you want to take this on?"

"I'm sure." Doc didn't say anything.

That was too easy, she thought. She had broached the subject of repairing the church before, but Doc was always ambivalent about spending so much money. Now he was eager to start the project along with everything else he was juggling in his life. Asha knew it was only because it helped keep his mind off Marcus. His heart was here with her, but his mind was in Switzerland.

Doc waved his hand in front of Asha's blank eyes as she sucked on the empty straw. "Where was your mind?"

She gave him a weak smile.

* * *

Asha went downstairs to see Jamal, while Doc finished his drink. She found the 30-year-old Cuban at the bar wearing his customary white tuxedo and bow tie. The French Quarter was the most popular restaurant in the Caribbean, and Jamal Calderon was its manager. Any night of the year you had to have a reservation to get a table, and tonight wasn't any different. A cruise line had reserved most of the tables for their corporate executives who were in town for one night.

"How's business tonight?" she asked.

"See for yourself. We've got them packed in like sardines. Things should be better after the new section is completed, which we're still on schedule to have finished by this time next month. With a little luck we should increase seating capacity by forty percent." He looked at his boss. She hadn't heard a word he'd said. He smiled. "You look lovely tonight, as usual, Ms. Panther." She kissed him on the cheek and encircled her arm in his.

They walked together through the crowded restaurant, greeting guests as they went. Asha played the gracious host as she talked with some of the executives. Jamal watched her work her magic as the table of men and women roared with laughter at something funny she said. She signaled one of the waiters to bring over some French champagne from her private stock, and then excused herself from the table.

She searched for Jamal and found him in the vestibule talking with some of the waiting guests. She went outside to wait. The harbor was beautiful at night, and there wasn't a better place to view it from than the place she was standing. Asha turned around and gazed at the church she had resurrected and transformed into a five-star restaurant. The monastic marvel looked radiant as it basked in the ambient light being cast from torch-lit sconces, with flames flickering against the white stucco façade.

Twenty-two years ago, local islanders thought she was crazy when she bought the dilapidated structure that clung desperately to the hillside. She lived like a pauper in a friend's garage until she had saved enough money from her modeling and hostess jobs to purchase the property. She had the building gutted, added two intersecting wings, and a second story with a bell tower. Asha decorated the interior with imported oak and madrona wood, Italian wallpaper, and the finest china and crystal from Europe. There wasn't a place or thing in the restaurant that didn't hold special meaning to her.

Jamal came outside and saw her standing by the cliff. "Are you okay?" he asked as he joined her.

She grabbed his hand as they headed back to the restaurant. "You've done a wonderful job with this place, Jamal. I'm going to miss coming here every day."

"Does Dr. Sebasst know you're doing this?"

"I haven't told him yet, because I know he'll try and talk me out of it. I'm going to have my attorneys draw up the sale papers."

Jamal was at a loss for words. He'd been with her and the restaurant for the last nine years and loved it as much as she did. Asha had received several purchase offers over the years, but never once considered selling the restaurant until now.

"Do you already have a buyer?" he asked.

"I want you to own it."

"Me? Ms. Panther, I can't afford a restaurant like *this*."

"Jamal, you've poured your heart and soul into this place and you deserve it. Knowing the restaurant is in your capable hands makes my decision much easier. Don't worry—I'll sell it to you at a reasonable price. You're like the brother I never had—enjoy it." She hugged him and left before he had a chance to speak.

"Oh, there is one condition. My husband and I get to keep our table and you pick up our tab." She smiled and went back upstairs.

45

* * *

Doc and Asha left the restaurant after midnight. It was a beautiful night for a drive around the island. The sky was full of diamond-shaped stars and the yellow moon was set against the backdrop of the Atlantic Ocean. Doc took the long way home along the western side of the island. He maneuvered the Wrangler down the twisty roads, stopping momentarily to appreciate the vista view of the Caribbean. Asha sat next to him, slumped down in the seat with her naked legs hanging out of the window. She cuddled against his shoulder as they silently watched the dark blue waters roll in. A tropical shower came and went before Doc had time to raise the top on the jeep.

Their villa was perched 700 feet above the Atlantic Ocean on the Peterborg Peninsula, sandwiched between the ocean and Megen's Bay. Doc parked the Jeep while Asha made a beeline to the answering machine.

A few minutes later, Doc entered the house and tossed his keys on the sofa table before heading to the bedroom. "Any word from Marcus?"

"No, but Sydney called, and she didn't sound very good. I tried calling her back, but she's not answering. It sounds like she had another fight with Marcus," Asha said as she let her dress slip to the floor before entering the wardrobe closet.

"Marcus is fooling around with the wrong man and he's going to wind up getting himself killed," Doc said angrily.

Asha yelled from the other room, "You don't really believe that, do you?"

"Yeah, I know how the boy thinks. When he's angry, all reason goes out the window and he's running on guts and emotions. It's even worse now with Leon-Francis."

Asha reentered the room wearing a heather gray satin chemise. "He really hates that man, doesn't he?"

"Yeah, ever since his ex-girlfriend, Anna Mateo, was murdered years ago while researching a story on Leon-Francis. He's convinced himself that Leon-Francis had her killed. Since then, Marcus has been looking for an excuse to go after him and now he has one."

Asha slid underneath the covers of the four-poster bed and pushed the lighted button on the headboard. The giant sunblind covering the windows began to slowly retract, revealing a panoramic view of the ocean. "Are you coming to bed?"

Doc saw Sabu and Taurus sleeping by the pool. "I forgot to let the dogs in, I'll be right back," he said. He slipped on his pants and shoes and went downstairs. The dogs were at attention—and growling at the woods. Doc turned on the floodlights. The two Great Danes started barking.

He knelt down and rubbed Taurus's head. "You smell something, boy?" he whispered. Taurus barked. Sabu raced to the other side of the pool. The dogs waited for a command.

Doc's property covered six and a half acres of lush tropical trees and foliage, protected by a five-foot-high wall to discourage trespassers. Something was out there. Doc gave a hand signal and the dogs raced into the woods. Light rain began falling. Fifteen minutes later, the dogs returned. Sabu had blood on his mouth.

* * *

"I'm sure it was just some wild animal that wandered onto the property," Asha said, petting the giant dogs curled up on the floor next to her. They licked her hand.

Doc smiled at the exchange of affection. "You've spoiled my dogs rotten. I remember when you couldn't stand to be around them."

"They grow on you." He held his wife close as they gazed out at the ocean.

Asha caressed the scar on his chest. "How's the wound doing?"

"Fine."

She playfully slapped his stomach. "Nothing bothers you. You wouldn't complain if you had a hole in your head."

Doc kissed her on the forehead as she continued caressing his chest. "That's not true."

"How would you feel if I sold *The French Quarter*?"

The question startled him. "Why in the world would you want to do that? You love that restaurant."

She drew imaginary circles on his midriff. "Now that we're going to have a family, I intend to spend most my time with the baby and working on the church."

"I hope you're not selling it to help finance the church."

"No, it's not the money. It's just time to let it go. I'm selling it to Jamal for $500,000."

Doc shook his head in disbelief. "I think you've really lost your mind. You're giving away your restaurant?"

"I told you I'm selling it for $500,000."

"You say that as though you actually think that's a good deal. I hope at least you didn't offer him a payment plan." She laughed. "Okay, if that's what you really want to do."

She gave him an affectionate kiss. "You're being very agreeable tonight. There must be something wrong?"

Doc laughed. "I'm always easy—you just have to get me at the right time."

Asha propped herself up on her elbow and looked at him. As much as he tried to pretend everything was fine, she knew her husband. "You're worried about Marcus aren't you?"

"He's out of his league with Leon-Francis, and if he keeps messing with Sasha Micheaux like Sydney says he has, he going to box himself into a corner he can't get out of."

"Sydney said Sasha Micheaux is ruthless."

"And smart, which is a wicked combination. The information we took from her brothers' home in Quebec implicates her in some of their shady business dealings. She's been running the family's banking empire since she was twenty-one, and she's built it into one of the most prestigious banks in Canada and Europe. By the world's standards, the bank is fairly small, but it serves some of the wealthiest people in the world."

"You mean the Merovingian families?"

"Yeah. The Banque de Micheaux is the bank of choice for the families. Many of them are either limited partners with her or serve on her board. Sasha has made them a lot of money by moving and hiding funds in her banking network. She shrouds her activities in a coat of armor that's tough to crack. And because she's French-Canadian with her permanent residence in Quebec City, she's exempt from following Switzerland's stringent banking laws, which means she can pretty much do anything she wants without disclosure."

"Lovely. Do you think she knew about her brothers' art thefts?"

"It wouldn't surprise me if this whole thing was her idea. The twins didn't impress me as being that bright."

"So these Merovingian families are all related to each other?"

"Not just relatives. They share the same bloodline, and claim to be the direct descendants of Jesus Christ."

"Good grief, Julian, are you serious?"

"As serious as a heart attack. And believe me, so are they. They believe that Jesus never died on the cross, and that he and Mary Magdalene escaped to France where they married and had a child. Their offspring supposedly married into the royal family of the Franks and sired a son named Merovee, who later became king. The Micheaux's think they're the direct descendants of Merovee, and are therefore bearers of his 'holy bloodline'."

Asha shook her head in disbelief. "Do Caitlin and us a favor. Go to Switzerland and drag her husband home before he gets himself hurt fooling around with these crazy people. I'll call Sydney in the morning and tell her to pick you up."

"Are you sure?"

She kissed him. "He needs you more than I do right now." Doc pulled his wife closer and kissed her. She rested her head on his chest. "Just don't get involved with Sasha Micheaux. I understand she is quite a beautiful woman."

"Who told you that?"

"Sydney. She also said she noticed how Sasha Micheaux looked at you. Apparently you made an impression with her."

"That's ridiculous. I've only met the woman once. I'm the last person she wants to see again."

"Well, I trust Sydney's assessment. We women know how other women think. You're probably the only man to stand up to her."

Doc laughed. "More likely the only one to live to tell about it. The woman has issues."

"It's your charisma," she said.

"Then why doesn't it work on you?"

"It's not supposed to—I'm your wife." He laughed. She rolled over on top of him and gave him a passionate kiss. "So—is she?"

"What?" He wrapped his fingers in the straps of her chemise.

"Is she beautiful?"

"She's a flawed diamond—you're a rare gem. Does that answer your question?"

"You always know the right words." She kissed him as he slid the chemise from her back. "This is how I got in this situation, remember?"

"We may as well try for twins."

* * *

Doc was too restless to sleep. He kept thinking about the bloodstain on Sabu's mouth when he came out of the woods. He quietly slipped out of the bed and got dressed, without waking his wife. The wind was blowing harder and heavy rain fell from the windows. Doc grabbed a jacket from the hall and ran to the guesthouse with the dogs. He took one of Sydney's guns off the wall.

Asha would have thought he was paranoid, but Doc knew there was no animal on the island that could scale a five-foot-high wall—except a human one. Doc followed the dogs along the edge of the cliff to a trail on the north end of the property. There was a boot print in the mud next to a fallen tree limb. He followed the tracks with his flashlight until they reached the back wall. The white stucco surface was marred with bloody fingerprints. The barrel of a Remington automatic lay in a mud pool next to a piece of torn flesh and tinted sunglasses. Someone had come to kill him.

A sudden gust of cold air off the Atlantic blew across the steeped hillside, followed by monsoon-like rain. Treetops swayed, and branches cracked as the ocean waters crashed against the rocks. Doc watched the dark clouds smother out the full moon. A storm was brewing and it wasn't the kind you could see. Devin Leon-Francis was invisible and more lethal. Doc tucked his gun in his waistband and headed back to the house.

Chapter 6

Monday morning, Aero flight 332 from Geneva was delayed for ninety minutes while workers cleared snow off the runway. It took an additional hour for mechanics to de-ice the wings of the plane. The jet finally lifted off the ground before noon, only to have the pilot announce that the airplane was returning to the terminal. The passengers released a collective groan.

The blonde American actor sitting in first class swore as he jerked the sunglasses from his face. "What the hell is going on?" he shouted to the flight attendant.

"A VIP passenger is coming aboard, sir."

"What kind of airlines are you running here? I can't believe this!" He cursed some more and ordered another drink, which the star-struck flight attendant was happy to serve him.

The articulated bridge swung out from the terminal and locked on to the airplane, and the flight attendant opened the cabin door. A man dressed in black leather and wearing a beret entered first, carrying two bags, followed by a raven-haired woman in black sheer nylons, three-inch heels, and sunglasses. She occupied the vacant seat next to the actor and her companion sat across the aisle. Her fragrance was as expensive as the French dress that clung to her body like latex. She crossed her long legs and brushed the corkscrew curls from her eyes as she pulled a magazine from her bag. The actor almost spilled his drink gawking at her.

Sasha Micheaux wasn't interested in anyone on the plane, especially the narcissistic actor she had the misfortune of sitting next to. The man could have avoided a wounded ego had he known she didn't associate with people she didn't consider her equal, which was practically the entire world. She had enough to deal with right now, and was not about to spend the next two hours with this man leering at her body. She leaned across the aisle and spoke to her bodyguard, Enric Bourbon. He disconnected his seatbelt, came over, and whispered in the man's ear. The actor sat quietly staring out the window for the remainder of the trip.

Her chauffeur-driven Bentley was waiting for her when the airplane landed in Carcassonne. She handed her coat and gloves to the driver as she entered the car. The Bentley eased out of the restricted area and traveled southwest toward the mountains.

Sasha had not been back to France since the death of her brothers, nearly two months ago. Many things had changed since then, and all of them were bad. The discovery of her brothers' art smuggling business led the Canadian government to close the family's art galleries and insurance company in Montreal and Quebec City. The French and Italians had seized their hotels in Canne and Milan; and the United States was pursuing legal action against her brothers' holdings in New York. The investigations and litigation could last for years, neither of which Sasha could afford. The longer she was under public scrutiny, the more vulnerable she was on the Merovingian Council.

The death of Sasha's brothers created an unprecedented problem for the all-male council. The Micheauxs and their cousins, the Bourbon family, selected Sasha as their representative to fill her brothers' seat on the council, but no woman in the history of the 253-year-old organization had ever been allowed membership. As much as the council members wanted to exclude her, Sasha was too powerful to ignore.

She controlled the Merovingian treasury, worth billions of dollars, and had two hundred loyal Frenchmen at her disposal to protect it and her family. The treasury of plundered gold and priceless artifacts was buried in the caves of Languedoc-Roussillon in southern France, where the Merovingian's ancestors had successfully hidden it for centuries.

* * *

Sasha woke from her nap just as the car climbed the mountain road to the castle. The estate had been in the Micheaux family since her ancestors, the Knights Templar, lived there when they were not off protecting the pilgrim routes to the Holy Land during the Crusades.

Sasha's first cousin, Carlos Bourbon, met her as she stepped from the car. The other council members had arrived and were waiting for her in the tower. She walked through the inner court and up the back stairs. The large iron door squeaked as it opened into a two-story room, with small stained glass windows and arrow slots. Seven members of the council sat at the large octagon table in the middle of the room. She gave a nervous smile as she occupied the last chair. Sasha was humbled as she gazed at the old men—some of whom were the most prestigious investment bankers in the world. This was her first meeting before the full council, and she knew it might be her last once she told them what she had to say. She dug in her pocket for her eyeglass case.

"I would have assumed you would have already been prepared, Mademoiselle," said the rude German.

She laughed softly, as she slid the black frames on the bridge of her nose. The half-glasses accentuated her almond-shaped hazel eyes and full brows. She peered at her enemy as she laced her fingers together on the table. "I just wanted to have a clearer vision of you, Herr Eisenstadt, do you mind?" She gave him a provocative smile as their eyes met. The uncomfortable German was at a momentary loss for words and was thankful when the chairman interceded.

"Madam Micheaux was gracious enough to allow us to meet in her home. I think we can allow her whatever time she needs to adequately prepare. I understand that you had some travel complications, nothing serious I hope?" Anthony Chiapetta asked.

"Nothing that cannot be resolved with new mechanics or new *avion*." Some of the members chuckled.

The German was not amused. "With your permission, Mr. Chairman, I would like to ask Madam Micheaux some questions."

"Meinhard, there will be plenty of time for that," Chiapetta said, dismissing him with a wave of the hand. "We must first properly welcome our newest, and unquestionably, loveliest member to our council."

The members stood and applauded her. The surprising gesture caught her off guard as she sat, embarrassed, but also stunned by the reality that she was now part of one of the most powerful organizations in the world.

The Merovingian Council consisted of the two French-Canadian families, Micheaux and Bourbon, and seven of the most influential families of Europe, from Italy, Germany, Switzerland, Austria, Spain, Denmark, and England. They were the fallen aristocracy—descendents of the Hapsburg Dynasty that ruled Europe for over 300 years. But, they were more than usurped royalty. They were Merovingians by blood—families that believed they were part of the holy bloodline of Christ, and unified in the common purpose to re-establish their rule in Europe. Until that time arrived, they were content to continue being the behind-the-scenes financiers of wars and rebellions that promoted their financial interests.

"Let me begin by saying that your brothers, Pierre and Philip, will be missed. While their loss deeply saddens us, we realize they could have been an embarrassment to the whole body. We are deeply indebted to you for the courageous and unselfish steps and actions you undertook to protect this body, and the financial interests of our families. This council will always remember the personal sacrifices made by the Micheaux and Bourbon families. Your leadership of the families during this time of crisis has only served to confirm what other council members and I already knew—your family has made a wise choice in their selection of a new leader. The Micheaux family has always been held in the highest of esteem by this body, and we welcome the wisdom, vision, and leadership qualities you bring to this council as its newest member. Congratulations," Chiapetta said.

The men applauded again. Eisenstadt could not bring himself to look at her as the men reseated. He was seething inside. There was nothing illustrious or prestigious about the Micheauxs. Sasha's great-grand father, Jean-Reni Micheaux, was Europe's greatest art thief. Unfortunately, for him and the family, he was caught and hung by the Russians in 1872. Now, her brothers had almost exposed the council again by their greedy exploits and desire to assume their ancestor's role. As far as Eisenstadt was concerned, the entire Micheaux family was a disgrace. He hated Sasha especially, because she controlled the Knight Guardians. The Knights were supposed to be the protectors for all the Merovingian families, but Sasha had wielded them into her own personal security force. That much power in the hands of a woman was unacceptable, and the fact that she was a Micheaux made it worse.

He watched her playing with her hair as she waited for her laptop to boot. Her lips, ripe and moist, etched a perfect smile on her face. She was a maddening temptress who knew how to use her body as well as her brain to get what she wanted.

Eisenstadt was anxious to get right to business. "If we are through coddling Madam Micheaux, perhaps we can continue. I for one am very interested in hearing your explanation about what happened to the shipment we entrusted to you, and the breakdown in your security that allowed our possessions to be stolen from under our very noses?" Chiapetta rested his hand on the old German's wrists, but Eisenstadt wasn't about to be diplomatic. "I warned the council from the beginning that her plan was pure lunacy, and that it would not work. I warned you of the logistical security problems associated with the transferring of such a massive amount of artifacts, and I warned you that it would fail. Madam was most persuasive in convincing this council that her family and our Knights were up to the task of adequately protecting our interests. Perhaps she could explain to the members why we have not heard from her captain since he left the Black Sea three weeks ago, and what has happened to our cargo of $200 million."

Sasha's nervousness gave way to her boiling anger. "The treasures you so reverently speak of were the sole possessions of the Micheaux family, and none other. Any losses will be our loss."

"How can that be?" Chiapetta asked. "We gave you full authority to begin moving all of our assets from Languedoc-Roussillon."

"I felt it prudent to proceed cautiously, since this was our first shipment. What was lost was only a portion of the wealth my ancestors and brothers acquired. They were some of the assets the authorities are desperately searching for and, therefore, the most vulnerable to my family and the council. I have suspended further shipments until we determine what has happened to the *Vincien Micheaux*."

"You are mad if you believe we will allow you ...," Eisenstadt said.

"I believe our financial future is in North America, Herr Eisenstadt. This incident only reaffirms what I have so strongly believed for a long time. Historical lore and fairy tale myths of our treasure are legendary, and the reasons why thousands of fortune hunters flock to our mountains seeking our riches. We have successfully protected what we have had for centuries, but the world today is different from the world of our fathers. Today our activities are being monitored closely by governments that have the resources, technology, and will to relentlessly pursue and recover what has taken us centuries to acquire. The United States, Israel, Greece, and most of the countries represented at this table, including mine, will never relent. If we are to continue to prosper, it must be in an environment that is safe and free from prying eyes. We fool ourselves if we think the caves and tunnels of Languedoc-Roussillon will be safe forever, or that our lips will always remain sealed and not give up the secrets our forefather's swore to keep sacred."

"No one would dare break the oath of silence," the Spaniard said.

"Someone has already. My freighter has vanished without a trace, along with my crew and guards. It is inconceivable to believe that this was an accident of any sort. I must admit that it was with much pain that I had to conclude that this was an orchestrated theft that could have only been accomplished with the assistance of my personnel. Accepting this fact, the only logical conclusion is that someone on this council passed vital information to the thieves about my shipment."

"This is ridiculous. You are attempting to transfer blame for your ill-conceived plans, inept security, and losses to the council?" Eisenstadt asked. "You think one of us had a momentary lapse in memory and accidentally divulged your plans? This is preposterous."

"No, Herr Eisenstadt, I think one of you is a traitor. A traitor to your family, and a traitor to all the Merovingians and what we hold sacred."

"This is outrageous! I demand that she be expelled from this council...immediately!" he shouted, pointing his knobby finger at her.

Chiapetta rapped the gavel several times, trying to restore order as accusations flew. "Please, gentlemen…please take your seats. This is a serious matter we must undertake."

"I will settle for nothing less than this woman's removal from our sight and the relinquishing of our Knights," Eisenstadt said. The Englishman and Spaniard joined him in his denouncement.

Sasha sat quietly, unnerved. Her fiery eyes burned as she waited for an opportunity to speak. "Perhaps before you attempt to crucify me or burn me at the stake, you will want to hear the rest of what I have to say."

"We have heard enough, Madam," Eisenstadt said.

Chiapetta gaveled the table again. "You may continue, but remember, Madam, you have already burned your bridges, and you should be mindful and careful of what you say and to the body of whom you are addressing."

Sasha nodded in acknowledgment. She had to control her anger. "I took the liberty of checking the bank records of my crew, and discovered that sizable deposits were made to their accounts prior to my freighter leaving Gruissan." She turned the laptop around so they could see the screen. "Five of my Knights, including the captain, were paid a total of five million dollars. I pay my people extremely well, but not a half million dollars a man and one million dollars to my captain. It has been difficult to accept and acknowledge what I know to be true in my heart. I have treacherous men in my family. Men whose evil and lust for riches have no doubt resulted in the deaths of good and loyal Frenchmen who will never see their families again. And for that, I assume full responsibility. The Micheaux and Bourbons are merely two branches of nine connected to the body. If two branches are infected with traitors, then we must also admit that the body as a whole cannot be well."

"Ludicrous, all of our members have been on the council for years. To assert that any one of us would betray our family is crazy," Eisenstadt said.

"I agree," said the Swiss banker, Frelinghuyen. "It has to be someone outside this organization—and I believe it is the Americans, Sebasst and St. John. They are the ones that created our current dilemma with the authorities, by exposing your brothers. They have extensive knowledge of our business, and St. John continues to spout his venom upon you in Lucerne."

"He is a pest, a nuisance, but nothing more," Sasha said. "Monsieur St. John is upset that his people were killed, but neither he nor Dr. Sebasst has any reason to steal. If we want to find the guilty person, we must look within for the accomplice that helped perpetrate the theft. I have taken the liberty of making some inquiries." She touched a key on the computer. "The provenance of the money deposited into my captain's bank account came from a tugboat company in Narvik, Norway, known as Tow-2-Tow International. Unfortunately, the owner's identity is still unknown, but we will find him and regain what has been stolen. I already have men in place in Norway waiting to act on my orders, unless of course, the council has lost complete faith in my abilities to protect our interests. If so, I willingly relinquish my position on the council and my Knights to whomever the council deems more suitable for the task."

* * *

Sasha stood with her arms folded with Carlos Bourbon by her side as they watched the last limousine cross the drawbridge and leave the castle.

"How did it go?" Carlos asked.

"As I expected. The members will use the theft as an opportunity to try and destroy us."

"And Anthony?"

"He suspects nothing. He skillfully manipulates the discussion to reveal Eisenstadt's ignorance, and to cast suspicion away from himself. Meinhard Eisenstadt is stupid and senile, but loyal. Anthony Chiapetta is not. The Italian's love for money has always been greater than his love for family, and he has always coveted our wealth."

"He's not stupid enough to try something crazy."

"He has no fear as long as his god, Devin Leon-Francis, is his source of power and his protector."

Sasha's father had warned her about Anthony Chiapetta. He was an obstructionist and a cancer on the council. He and others were content to keep what they had and wait for the inevitable day the European markets collapsed. Sasha on the other hand, was a businesswoman first, and a Merovingian second. Her only interest was in increased profits and more wealth for the families, which meant moving and diversifying into more lucrative endeavors like the family's art smuggling business.

"I think I should go back with you to Lucerne," Carlos said.

"No, you must protect our interests here. Others may have been corrupted by Leon-Francis' blood money. We cannot afford to have our own men sabotage us, so I am trusting you to find any and all traitors and to deal with them appropriately."

"And Chiapetta?"

"The Italian has no patience. He will be anxious to get his reward from Leon-Francis for his betrayal to us. We follow him and he will lead us to our treasure and Leon-Francis."

"How much time do we have?"

"The council intends to meet again before the New Year."

"It's not enough time."

"That is all they have given us, cousin. We fail and we lose everything," she said.

"What do we do about Leon-Francis?"

"I have avenues available for finding him. Anthony is the important one right now. He will lead us to our treasure." Sasha extended her hand. "Come—go with me to visit Philip and Pierre."

* * *

The Bentley drove through the village and turned off onto a private dirt road leading to the valley. Sasha's heart beat faster as the car meandered through the emerald green pastureland and up the steep grade to the top of the hill, where it stopped. From the crest, they could see the family abbey on the other side of the creek. A black pickup truck was parked next to the bridge.

"What is that truck doing here?" Sasha asked.

Enric Bourbon drove slowly across the narrow road and pulled the Bentley up behind the truck's bumper. Carlos got out of the car and told his brother to stay with Sasha. He went over to the truck, where he noticed the rental sticker in the corner of the windshield. He checked the visors and the glove box, but didn't find any papers or registration. The abbey and cemetery grounds were private property, and no one, including curious tourists, was permitted beyond the main road. Carlos crossed the bridge and swung open the large courtyard doors. He motioned to Enric to bring the car across. The courtyard was empty and quiet, and there were no signs of the trespasser. Carlos leaned in the car window. "Enric, find the owner of that truck and get them out of here."

The muscular bodyguard checked the abbey and cloisters, but couldn't find anyone. He walked around the building to the family cemetery and never came back.

Sasha leaned forward against the front seat. "What happened to him?"

Carlos got in the car and locked the doors. "I don't know." He placed his gun on the seat and made a phone call.

Sixteen minutes later, a carload of Knight Guardians arrived at the abbey.

* * *

They spread out and began searching the property. Carlos was on the phone talking with the car rental company. He closed the phone and tossed it on the car seat.

"What's the matter?" Sasha asked.

"The truck was rented by the St. John-Sebasst Security Force."

"Monsieur Sebasst is here?"

"No, the truck is registered to his partner, St. John." The news erased the smile on her face. Carlos grabbed his gun and locked the car door behind him.

Sasha lowered the car window. "Cousin, be careful." Carlos gave her an affectionate smile and reassuring pat on her hand before leaving. She relaxed and poured herself a glass of wine, as her thoughts drifted to Dr. Julian Sebasst. Her mind and heart played tug-of-war trying to sort out her feelings about him. She hated him because he almost destroyed her family, yet she later found herself defending him before the Merovingian council when they wanted to have him killed. She had never met a man she couldn't control with either her power or beauty. Doc was the one exception. Sasha drank the rest of her wine and tried to think about something pleasant.

Ten minutes passed and the men were still not back. Sasha was bored and got out of the car to stretch. A Knight tried to talk her back into the car, but she ignored him. She walked toward the chapel, where her family and ancestors had worshiped for centuries. Two of the men followed behind.

Ornate sandstone carvings of the angel of St. Matthew and the lion of St. Mark stood intact at the entrance to the chapel. She picked up a rustic goblet off the floor and lightly brushed the dust away, before reverently setting it on the wooden table. From the side window, she saw remnants of the elaborate corbels that once supported the stone vaulting of the transept to the church. To her left, she saw her men crisscrossing through the cemetery. All of her ancestors were buried there, including her father and mother. And now Philip and Pierre. In happier times, she remembered coming with her brothers here and spending hours playing in the back woods. She wondered if the old tree house they built as kids was still visible from the tower.

* * *

One of the Knights found a broken watch lying on top of a gravestone and handed it to Carlos.

"It's Enric's," Carlos said, with a frown. Where was he—they had searched everywhere. He looked back across the field at the row of buildings. His eyes locked on the tower. "Has anyone checked up in the chapel tower?"

* * *

Sasha refused to let her men go with her as she climbed the eighty-four winding steps to the top. She ducked under the archway and onto the tower platform. Enric Bourbon sat in the corner with his mouth bound and hands tied. He had a gash above the right eye.

"You are a hard person to get an appointment with."

Sasha spun around at the sound of the voice. At first, she didn't recognize the woman sitting on the tower wall holding the firearm at her side. "You are Monsieur Sebasst's ward Mademoiselle Belleshota."

"I wouldn't go that far," Sydney said.

"You have cut your hair since the last time we met. It is very becoming. Now, please tell me what you are doing here. What is it that you want?"

"To talk with you, nothing else."

Sasha folded her arms and gave her a cold stare. "Are you the woman my men spoke about that was with Monsieur St. John when he tried to force his way into my home in Switzerland?"

"All we wanted to do was make an appointment to see you, but your people are a little overprotective. We never tried to force ourselves past them."

"And Enric—I imagine that his wounds are self-inflicted?"

Sydney slid off the wall and walked toward her. "Sorry about that. He's a little too tempestuous for my taste. He's okay; we just had a little disagreement. I traveled a long way to see you, and I wasn't planning on letting anyone stop me."

"How did you know I would be here?"

"Lucky hunch. When I found out you were coming to Carcassonne, I thought you might stop by to see your brothers' graves. Anyway, if you hadn't shown up pretty soon, I was going to make a house call over at that castle of yours."

"You are as mad as that lunatic you work for."

"I've heard that a few times in my life."

Sasha gave her a contemptuous look. "What is it that you want?" Footsteps were heard coming up the stairs.

"I want to have a civil conversation with you, and I don't want to hurt anyone else to do it. Now, you better stop whoever is flying up here from showing their heads or I'm not going to be able to keep my promise."

"Let Enric go first."

"Fine, he can go."

Sasha unbound him and pulled his beret from his mouth.

Sydney called to him as started down the steps. "Hey, man in black. You forgot this." She tossed him his empty revolver. "Remember to work on those communication skills of yours." Enric stared coldly at her.

"Enric will see that we are not disturbed. Now, tell me what is so important that you and your colleague have to say to me."

Sydney slid her gun back in the holster and sat down on the bench. "I want to know what is between you and my father."

"Your father...what are you speaking about?" she asked with a puzzled look on her face.

"You have business with my father, Devin Leon-Francis, and I want to know what it is."

"I have never heard of him. This is what you have been so anxious to discuss with me?"

"And I suppose you never heard of Jason Worrick either?"

"No, I have not. Who is he?"

"I think you know, but I'll play your little game if you want. He works for my father, and he had me kidnapped to implicate your family and destroy your brothers. And it worked, the minute you put a bullet in their heads." Sasha's face reddened. "Your family was set up from the beginning and so were my friends." Sydney saw the confusion on the French woman's face as she tried to assimilate and assess the newfound information.

"And you say that this work of deception was planned by Monsieur Worrick and not your father?"

"Yes. He hired Antonio Jaillet to kidnap me to make it appear that your brothers were responsible."

"Why?"

"I don't know. I thought you could tell me."

Sasha's brow rose. "I have nothing to say to you except leave my property while you still may. Otherwise I will have my people drag you from this place."

"I'm not through talking with you."

"I said leave!" Sasha said as her whole countenance changed. Her eyes were black as coal. Sydney started to speak, but Sasha lashed out with her hand, slapping her hard against the face. "*Whore*—leave!" she screamed.

Sydney hit her with a left cross, knocking her off her feet. "You must have lost your damn mind. Don't you ever put your hands on me again! Understand one thing. I'm not leaving you alone until I get the truth and if that means coming to see you again, I'll be back. If you thought Marcus St. John was a pain in your ass, you haven't experienced real pain, lady. Now, I'll trust that your men in black down there are not going to take my visit personal, and will let me pass without any trouble."

"You may go," she whimpered as she struggled to her feet.

"Good. You need to work on that temper of yours," Sydney said as she walked to the stairs.

Sasha turned her back and gazed at the tree house. "How is Monsieur Sebasst faring?" Sydney ignored the question and started down the steps. Sasha continued staring at the trees.

A man in a white gabardine overcoat blocked the stairway with is body so Sydney couldn't pass. She found herself staring at the handsome man, who bore an amazing resemblance to Sasha Micheaux. "Ahh…Valentino. Do you want to step aside so I can leave, or is there something on your mind?"

"You are either a very brave or very foolish woman for coming here alone," Carlos Bourbon said. He braced his arm against the stone wall to block her from going around.

"I've never been accused of being stupid or foolish, and I certainly don't need anyone to protect me from you. Now, I'm going to ask you one more time to please move out of my way."

He leaned forward, inches from her ear. "I could kill you right now, and no one would ever know."

"You could try," she said calmly, staring into his turquoise eyes. She whispered in his ear, "Is this your way of telling me you want a date?" The smell of her fragrance and the touch of her soft hand caressing his face were overpowering. He felt an overwhelming desire to kiss her. Sydney was struck with an impulse also, but unfortunately for Carlos, it wasn't the same one. She pushed him and he flew backward down the steps, landing hard on the floor.

He lay spread-eagle on the rotten floorboards, shaken but unhurt. Strangely, Sydney found herself extending her hand and helping him to his feet.

"I suppose I deserved that," he said with a sly smile as he dusted off his coat.

Sydney was amazed at his calmness. The fall could have easily broken his neck. "I asked you nicely, remember?" She walked out into the courtyard.

He caught up with her. "I was told you had a quick tongue and temper."

"Your men could benefit from better manners and more training." She kept walking.

Carlos grabbed her arm and they stopped. "Perhaps you would like to teach them?"

"Not likely." She gazed into his eyes again. "Now, take your hands off me." She started walking again. Carlos opened the truck door for her. She turned on the ignition and rolled down the window. "What's your name?"

"Carlos Bourbon."

"I'll try to remember that."

* * *

Sasha clung to Carlos' arm as they watched the fading dust from Sydney's truck. She touched her bruised cheek. "This is why we must deal with these people like the dogs they are. They have no respect for us, and they continue to try my patience."

"If she is Devin Leon-Francis' daughter, she may be useful to us," Carlos said.

"No, she has not been in contact with him or she would not have risked her life to come here and ask me such foolish questions. She has no idea where he is, and I am not interested in dealing with her ever again. Do whatever is necessary to see that neither she nor her companion ever bothers me again."

"Yes, it will be taken care of."

"Good, now ride with me to the airport. There are other matters I wish to discuss with you."

* * *

Sydney drove out to the highway and headed east to Carcassonne. Eleven miles later, she pulled off to the side of the road, got out of the truck, and slammed the door behind her. She realized she had taken a big risk in revealing her identity to Sasha, but that was the only way she knew to get at the truth. And the truth was beginning to hurt. Sasha's face confirmed what Marcus had been telling her all along. Her father used her just as he did everyone else in his life.

Chapter 7

Andy Preston was scared to death when Tiberius Woodberry showed up at the tug yard. Woodberry was Leon-Francis' hatchet man, and he was in Narvik to find out what he knew about Jason Worrick's murder. Andy's first mistake was not telling Woodberry about Jordan Phoenix. The second mistake was not leaving Narvik while he still could. Wherever Woodberry went, people usually ended up dead before he left. But that was yesterday, and now he was gone—and Andy was still alive.

They had dinner together last night where Woodberry grilled him for hours. Andy was convincing in his denial. By the evening's end, Woodberry seemed satisfied. He told Andy to stay close to the telephone in case they needed to talk again. Then he disappeared.

Andy rested on the bed, thankful that Woodberry had not looked in the briefcase. He reached under the bed, pulled out the case, and opened it. Jordan's military uniform was still neatly folded. He knew he should get rid of it, but he couldn't. Something compelled him to hold onto a piece of her. He stuffed the starched shirt under his nose and inhaled, before carefully folding it again and putting it away.

Woodberry's sudden arrival sabotaged Andy's plans for leaving town. Now, the snow had moved in, the airport was closed—and he was stuck for at least another day. He dressed and went to work, where he watched television, read the newspaper, and waited for Woodberry's call. The only call he got was from a stranded Russian trawler. Andy dispatched a tugboat.

He moved the colored marker for the *King's Way* tugboat onto the laminated status board to mark its destination point. The status board contained markers for all the ships in Tow-2-Tow's fleet. The markers for the three missing tugboats dispatched to the Arctic Ocean were still in place, although Andy knew they weren't still there. And then there was Devin Leon-Francis' missing freighter. He lit a cigarette and fondled the green-striped pin for the *Angela's Storm*. He had no idea where the freighter had gone, but he felt a strange sense of obligation to do something with the pin. He closed his eyes, and placed it on the map. "Greenland," he said.

By mid-afternoon, he gave up trying to find creative ways to entertain himself, so he left the office and started back to the hotel. The snow had stopped and he was hopeful the airport would be open by tomorrow morning. All he needed was to pack a few clothes and purchase his ticket. The whistle of the Malmbanan train from Kiruna, and the loud clanging noise of the large orange cranes were heard in the background. Half a dozen men raced by him

65

in the black slush. He turned his coat collar up, trying to muffle the sounds as he ran away. *I'm getting out of this place even if I have to walk.*

* * *

Andy hurried to his room. He unlocked the door and stepped into the entryway. The lights were on and Jordan's uniform was lying on the bed.

Woodberry sat in the corner chair with his legs crossed. "I'd say she's a size seven, what do you think?"

Andy felt nauseous. He ran to the sink. Woodberry waited for him to finish vomiting before handing him the towel. Andy wobbled over to the bed and flopped down. Woodberry slowly washed his hands.

"Mr. Woodberry, I would like to explain what…what happened."

Woodberry wiped his hands on the towel, and said, "Sure, go ahead, kid. But if you want to talk to me, you better be looking at me and not the damn floor."

Andy raised his head, half-expecting Woodberry to be shielding a gun under the towel.

"You've been looking at too many movies, kid." Woodberry tossed the towel on the floor and reoccupied the chair. "You said you wanted to talk…then talk. I'm listening."

Andy told him everything he knew about Jordan. "Up until I contacted Oslo University, I had no idea Jordan had been lying to me all along," he concluded.

"Why didn't you tell me this last night?"

"You wouldn't believe me, just like you don't believe me now."

"Don't tell me what I believe, kid, I'll tell you," Woodberry snapped. He uncrossed his legs and leaned over, resting his forearms on his legs. "All you've been doing is running your mouth about how stupid you've been to think a beautiful woman would lay with your puny ass. What you haven't told me is what you gave her in return."

"I swear, I didn't give or tell her anything."

"Then how did she find out about Mr. Leon-Francis' mountain retreat?"

"I don't know!" he shouted, more out of frustration than anger. "I didn't tell her anything—and she never asked. How do you even know for sure that she was involved in Jason's death?"

"Let me tell you something, Preston. She didn't have to ask you a thing after she got your stupid ass in bed with her. Your nose was so wide open; you wouldn't have noticed a thing unless it was stapled to her butt. That black uniform you're coveting says it belongs to a Colonel J. Bloodstone. If that's your ladylove's real name, you can stop asking yourself if she was capable of murdering Worrick. She is."

"How can she…" Andy felt himself getting nauseous again. He ran to the bathroom.

Woodberry stood in the doorway watching Andy wipe his mouth. "Am I going to have to bring a chair in here to finish this conversation with you?"

"No, I'm alright." He sat on the stool with his head in his hands. "What else do you want to know?"

Woodberry didn't know if Andy was just stupid or naïve, or a little of both. But he was beginning to feel sorry for him. His glasses were askew on his round face, and his thin hair looked like it had been spiked with electricity. "Look, Preston. As much as it may hurt your ego, this woman didn't spend three blissful weeks with you just to kill time. Think. What did you tell her?"

"Nothing."

"Did you ever take her to the office?"

"No."

"Are you sure you never brought anything home from the office that would have given her a clue about Mr. Leon-Francis' location?"

Andy stood up and flushed the toilet. "I told you, no. You've checked my room and you've been to the office. Did *you* find anything?"

Woodberry snatched him by the neck with his left hand, pinning him to the wall. "Don't get loud with me, kid. You're about one second away from getting your wish to leave this place. I'm trying to give you the benefit of the doubt here, but smart-ass remarks like that don't help your case." He released his grip and straightened Andy's glasses. "Now, tell me some more about this woman."

The questioning went on for an hour, with Woodberry asking variations of the same questions repeatedly, and getting the same answers. The kid didn't know anything other than what he had told, but the truth didn't make Woodberry feel any better. Unless he knew how the information was leaked, he was out of a job, and he wouldn't have to worry about applying somewhere else. He decided to take a different approach.

They walked down the hill to the office, where Woodberry painstakingly went over everything, including listening to Iggy Vasilakis's recorded tapes of his reports of St. John in Switzerland. Next to the answering machine was a locked brush chrome case.

"What's in here?" Woodberry asked.

"The satellite phone Jason gave me to stay in touch with him." Woodberry opened the box and pulled out the laptop-sized telephone. A small black metal object the size of a watch battery was attached to the back of the unit.

"What is that?"

* * *

They left the office and Woodberry walked him as far as the railway terminal near the south quay. Andy continued up the hill with Woodberry watching him from the corner. Any notion of running was now out of the question. Woodberry believed his story, but that didn't mean he was out of the woods. The last thing he needed was to do something stupid that would make him look guilty.

Andy got to his room and took the first shower he had in two days, and then ordered room service. Later, he went back to the office to catch up on the work he had neglected for the last two weeks.

He opened another bottle of vodka and had a quick drink before starting. He picked up the day's mail and opened the company's monthly bank statement. Andy blinked twice, adjusted the glasses on his nose, and re-read the statement. Five million dollars had been deposited from an offshore account into the company's account—and transferred the same day to a French bank in Marseilles. Andy folded the statement and laid it on the desk. He didn't know what any of this meant—missing tugboats and freighter, and now phantom money. But then again, if you worked for Devin Leon-Francis you weren't supposed to know anything.

* * *

Woodberry had a message waiting for him when he got back to his room. He dialed the toll-free number and a monotone voice answered. The operator switched his call over to another number, which began ringing.

Devin Leon-Francis was on the other end of the telephone. "Tell me some good news, Tiberius."

"You were right, sir, Preston dropped the ball. His girlfriend planted an electronic triangulating device of some sort on his telephone that allowed her to get a fix on our location."

"A woman killed Jason?"

"Yes, sir, a black Englishwoman named Jordan Bloodstone. She's British Royal Navy. I'm having her checked out."

"She must be working with Marcus St. John. Are he and my daughter still in Lucerne?"

"St. John is, but your daughter left two days ago."

"Where?"

"The Greek, Vasilakis, thinks they may have had a falling out. She could be headed back home."

"Good."

"What do you want to do about Preston?"

"Has he told you everything?"

"Yes, sir."

"Then dump him. I want you in Fauske by morning to help the Norwegian track Bloodstone."

* * *

Woodberry knew everyone working for Devin Leon-Francis was expendable. Andy Preston had served his purpose, screwed up, and now would pay the price. Woodberry wasn't planning to have the same obituary written about him. He called the Norwegian and told him about Jordan Bloodstone and that he would join him tomorrow on the mountain. After the telephone call, it was time to pay a final visit to Andy Preston.

Woodberry twisted the silencer on his Smith & Wesson and tucked it back in his waist. He used the stairs to go down to Andy's room on the next floor. He picked open the locked door and entered the dark room. Light streamed from underneath the bathroom door. He opened the door, but Andy wasn't there. *He probably stepped out for some smokes or a drink.* Woodberry crossed his legs and sat on the bed with the gun on his lap, but Andy didn't return. Woodberry got nervous. He got up and went to check the clothes closet. When he opened the accordion doors, Andy smashed the edge of a leaded-glass ashtray into the side of his head. Woodberry fell back, hit the bed, and bounced to the floor.

Andy left through the service entrance and walked as fast as he could without drawing attention. When he got to the office he rummaged through his desk and found the key he was looking for. He hurried down to the boats in the harbor and leap-frogged over four of the tugboats to get to the *Nordic*. She was a seldom-used tugboat with a galley and sleeping quarters.

He decided to stay there until it was safe to leave.

Chapter 8

The Sulitjelma region was 900 square miles of wilderness with high mountain peaks and dangerous glaciers. The Norwegian had set up base camp on a promontory over the frozen lake, twenty-six miles from Fauske. High winds and snow beat against the sides of the tent as he tried to keep warm inside.

He and his men had tracked the killer for three days, without any success. The woman was proving to be totally unpredictable. When they thought she would cross the summit, she didn't. When they expected the weather to slow her down, it didn't. Now, the Norwegian had guessed she was traveling west through the fjord to Fauske, but he was wrong again. *She should have been here yesterday if she was heading to Fauske.* The blowing snow obliterated all traces of her on the mountain. There were several routes off the mountain, but in this weather most of them were impractical. Fauske was the most logical, because it was the closest city and easiest to reach. The other possibility was that she was headed toward Sulitjelma and the Swedish border.

Of course, she could already be dead from hypothermia, or have fallen off any number of ice cliffs, bridges, or crevices. All of these scenarios presented problems. If she was dead, Woodberry was going to want to see the body. If she was alive and heading east, she would have to cross Slajekna Glacier and take the trail down to the Swedish outpost of Kvikkjokk. The total distance was over sixty miles. Even in the best of circumstances it would take a hiker or skier days to travel the rough terrain.

The Norwegian grabbed the map and ducked under the tent flap where his men were waiting for him outside, next to the helicopter. "We are going to split up this time. I believe the woman is heading east. Team A will be dropped off at this lake, east of the glaciated massif," he shouted, pointing to the spot on the map. "You will then follow the trail on the south side of Lake Langvatnet toward Sulitjelma. Team B will drop near Sulitjelma, and you'll work your way toward the lake and Team A. We must stop her before she reaches Sulitjelma and the mountains." The men grabbed their rifles and bags and climbed in the helicopter.

The Norwegian stayed at camp to wait for Woodberry's arrival, and to ensure that Jordan didn't slip by him. He poured another coffee and went over his maps again. The more he studied them, the more he was convinced he had made a tactical mistake.

This woman was too smart to allow herself to be trapped in the remote settlement of Sulitjelma, which was surrounded by dangerous glaciers. The Norwegian marked other possible escape routes on the map. All of them were further north where the terrain and weather were the worst. Anyone venturing that far north in this weather had to be an expert survivalist. His men weren't that good. To catch her, he was going to need someone who knew the mountain, and he knew just the right men for the job.

* * *

Team A made its way along the ten-mile trail through the woods to a small frozen lake. The temperature dropped another three degrees, and the men found themselves in the middle of a sleet storm. When they finally reached the outskirts of Lake Langvatnet, they were covered in ice, disoriented, and lost. They made their way along the lake, only to discover too late that they were on the wrong side. The trail they were on was not listed on their map, and they ended up in the middle of a white wilderness. They collapsed in the snow. One of the men tried to use the radio, but his fingers were frozen. His partner curled up in a fetal position as violent shivers racked his body. A moment later he stopped breathing. The other man was propped against a tree trunk, paralyzed by the cold, and slipping into semi-consciousness.

A woman in white appeared from nowhere, moving toward him with the suppleness of a cat. He didn't know if she was real or a hallucination. She removed her mittens and knelt down in the snow to check the pulse of the dead man. Then she turned to him. Their faces were a foot apart. The woman's angelic face was black as opal and smooth as glass. She watched him in silence. He struggled to speak, but his mouth wouldn't open. She reached over and closed his eyelids.

* * *

The severe weather grounded the helicopter in Sulitjelma and knocked out all radio communications to the mountain. The Norwegian was stranded in camp until the weather cleared, which also meant he had no way of transporting more men to join in the search. He was stuck for at least the night, and maybe for another day, depending on the storm. The Norwegian had never seen a snowstorm of this intensity and duration, anywhere. He was cold and miserable, but at least he had a propane-heated tent. He couldn't imagine being outside. *Woodberry had better show up tomorrow or I'm leaving without him.* He rolled over in the sleeping bag and turned off his lantern.

* * *

Jordan kept moving east toward the border until she found herself standing at the edge of a wide expanse covered by an ice-encrusted suspension bridge. She carefully stepped on the old planking and slowly moved across. The bridge bowed under her weight and began to sway. She stopped to peek down at the dangerous glacier stream below. Each step she took was tentative and measured. Twenty feet from the end of the bridge, a strong crosswind knocked her off balance and she slipped over the side. She reached out, caught hold of the rail, and hung on. Her body swung in the air as she looked down at the glacier, one hundred and thirty feet below. Jordan struggled to maintain her grip, but she was losing the battle. She tried pulling herself up, but her backpack and rifle weighed her down. She reached for the knife at her waist, cut the straps from her shoulders, and watched the backpack fall. She managed to swing her body over and grabbed onto the bridge post. With the last remaining strength in her arms, she pulled herself up onto the landing. Jordan sagged back against the post and caught her breath. Everything was gone: food, radio, and dry clothing. She checked her jacket to make sure she still had her GPS and revolver.

In all the weeks of meticulous planning, she never counted on the weather being a debilitating factor. If anything, she expected the snow to work in her favor. She was miles from where she needed to be and at her current pace, it would take another five days. All the endurance and stamina in the world wouldn't help her survive another two days in this cold. She pulled out her last dry facemask and slipped it over her head. She stuffed her hands in her coat pockets and marched into the strong headwind across the snowy plains.

By morning, the snow had stopped and the sky was clear, but it was still cold. Team B had wisely sought shelter during the night in a communal hut outside Sulitjelma. They went out at first light, searching the trails north of the village. The Salajekna Glacier loomed in front of them as they skied down the slope near the glacier stream. They found Jordan's insulated backpack wedged between the rocks on the bank.

Chapter 9

Marcus was tired of waiting for Sydney to return his telephone calls and he was sick of sitting around doing nothing. Enough was enough. It was time to get busy. Marcus left the hotel, and took the boat over to Burgenstock. He entered the Hummerstrassen Hotel, where he quickly found the maintenance room and stairs leading up to the roof. He searched until he found an unlocked skylight large enough to fit through. He disconnected the window from the frame and lowered himself down to the hallway. Marcus heard the voices of two men around the corner heading in his direction. He ducked into a restroom as the guards passed. He quietly opened the door, checked the hall, and then ran across the hallway to Sasha Micheaux's office. The door was unlocked.

Sasha's office was immaculate and not too large, which made his task easier. He worked the office as efficiently as any cat burglar, quickly moving through the desk, locked files, and wall paintings. But there was no safe, which he thought was unusual. He turned his attention to the maple wood bookcase against the wall, and ran his fingers along the book spines until he stopped at a blue, soft-leather diary with ribbon markers. Marcus read through several of the pages before carefully sliding it back into place.

All he had to show for his hard work were some phone records and the memoirs of a frustrated woman. He thought about climbing back up to the roof, but changed his mind. He was convinced Sasha had a hidden safe somewhere. He searched the hall until he saw the private elevator leading to Sasha's penthouse. A guard spotted him. Marcus ran into a conference room, locked the door behind him, and ran out one of the side doors. Two women screamed as he ran through their workspace toward the hallway. The burly janitor tried to tackle him, but Marcus dropped him with a punch.

He took the back stairs down to a balcony that overlooked the main lobby. Two men rushed him. He leapt over the banister and sprinted for the front door. Another guard foolishly tried to stop him and ended up being thrown through the glass window.

Marcus hit the plaza running as fast as he could. Once he was safe in the woods, he discarded his body suit and put on the clothes he had hidden under a tree. He straightened his tie and walked to the elevator that took him back down the mountain to the station.

He missed the paddle steamer to Vitznau by three minutes, so he ordered some coffee and called the hotel for messages. He had one message, but it wasn't from Sydney. Tre', his pilot, had left a message that he had to make a short trip and would be back by tomorrow night. Marcus cursed, and tossed the phone on the table. *I'm going to kill that boy when I see him. He thinks my plane is his own personal property.* He pulled Sasha's telephone bills from his pocket, but they didn't reveal any clues. Most of the calls she made were to her bank in Geneva and a few to Quebec City and Bergen, Norway. *What the hell am I supposed to do with this?* Marcus balled up the paper and smashed it on the table in frustration. His elbow accidentally tipped over his hot coffee. He jumped out of the chair to avoid the spill.

A plump man sitting in the corner quickly averted his eyes back to his newspaper. Marcus saw him. The man's odd behavior only heightened Marcus' sense of paranoia. He tried to see the man's face, but he stayed hidden behind the newspaper. There was something peculiar about the little man in the black derby. Marcus had seen him before and always in the same shabby blue suit, scuffed shoes, and old hat.

The *D.S. Stadt Luzerne* arrived fifteen minutes early. Marcus paid for another drink and hurried across the sky bridge to the steamer.

Iggy Vasilakis didn't lower the newspaper from his face until the steamer was out of view. Even then, his hands still trembled. He tucked the paper under his arm and hurried across the street to the market to pick up some groceries for dinner. Somewhere between produce and canned foods he decided he didn't want any more of the spy business. The extra money he was getting wasn't going to do his family any good if they had to spend it on his medical bills, or a funeral. He decided that today's report to the mysterious man who hired him would be his last.

He paid for his food and went to the bus stop on the corner. Iggy placed the bag of groceries on the bench beside him and pulled out his notepad and pen. He scribbled a few words of what he would say when he called in his final report. The bus turned the corner and stopped. Iggy fumbled with his notepad as he went to pick up his groceries. The bag tore and the contents fell out into the street. A head of lettuce rolled in the gutter until Marcus stopped it with his foot.

"Hey, old dude, let's take a walk," Marcus said.

Iggy thought he was going to have a heart attack. "My food—I must get my…"

"Forget the groceries; I want to talk with you." Marcus helped him to his feet and they hailed a taxi.

"What do you want?"

"Where were you going?"

"Home," Iggy said nervously.

"Good, let's go. Give the cabby your address."

* * *

Iggy's flat was in a warehouse on Salistrasse Street, just outside the downtown area. They took the freight elevator up to the third floor, and walked down the hallway to his apartment.

"Sir, I plead with you, may we go somewhere else? My daughter..."

"I'm not going to hurt your family. I just want some answers."

Iggy stuck the key in the door. The flat was spacious, with light streaming through the large windows that stretched from one end of the room to the other. They passed through a small kitchen with an undersized refrigerator and vintage stove. Marcus noticed the too few rugs that were used to try to cover the cold cement floor. He stuck his head in the bedroom and saw a bed that barely fit in the small room.

"That is my daughter's and granddaughter's room."

Iggy folded the sleeper in the living area for Marcus to sit on. The cushion springs dug at his butt as he tried to find a comfortable position. When he did, he still felt like he was sitting on the floor.

"Ignacious—right?"

"Yes, but you may call me Iggy."

"Okay. You're Greek?" Iggy nodded as he sat in a straight chair with his hands clasped. "Relax, I told you I just want information. Who hired you to follow me?"

"I don't know. A man contacted me by telephone and asked if I wanted the job. He told me to watch you and the young lady while you were here in Switzerland."

"And this number you gave me, this is who you report to each day?" Marcus asked, holding the scrap of paper in his hand.

"Yes. They also told me to call whenever you left the city."

"Did you ever speak with a person?"

"No, just the recorder."

"I can't believe you've been following me all these weeks and I hadn't noticed before," Marcus said, sucking on his toothpick.

"I was a detective," Iggy said proudly.

"Well, if you had changed up your wardrobe a bit, I might not have caught you." Iggy fidgeted with his jacket button embarrassed that it was his only suit. Marcus pointed his toothpick at him. "Were you with me when I went to Burgenstock?"

"Only as far as the station—never to the hotel."

"What do you know about Sasha Micheaux?"

"Only what I have read in the newspaper."

"What's your general impression?"

"Her brothers are responsible for the pillaging of many of my country's cultural treasures. I don't have any respect for criminals, even if they are women."

"I'm beginning to like the way you think, Iggy. How would you like a job?"

"Not if it involves following Madam Micheaux or anyone else. I won't do this kind of work anymore. I have a daughter and a 16-year-old granddaughter I must support. I must think of them."

"They don't work?"

Iggy seemed insulted by the question. "My daughter is legally blind, and Agalia is still in school."

"Okay, those are even better reasons to come to work for me. How much were they paying you to follow me?"

"Three hundred dollars a day."

"Okay, I'll pay you $500 and expenses, and you won't have to tail anyone."

"I don't know anything about you."

"What do you need to know? I own a security company in San Francisco, I pay my taxes, I'm not a criminal, and I won't ask you to do anything illegal. Unethical, maybe, but not illegal. The people that hired you are the bad men, not me."

"What do you want me to do?"

"Nothing right now, but one of my people will contact you if and when we need you."

"How long will my employment be for?"

Marcus heard the anxiety in his voice. "I'll pay you for a month and then we'll see."

Iggy wobbled to his feet with a grin, showing his yellowed teeth. He squeezed Marcus' hand and helped him off the sofa.

"Damn, Iggy, you're as strong as a bull." Marcus rubbed his right hand.

Iggy excused himself to go to the bathroom. When he came out, Marcus was gone, but there was a check for $6,500 and a note on the table. *Consider this your retainer.*

* * *

Marcus decided to stay in the city tonight. He packed a bag, caught the steamer back to Lucerne, and checked into the St. Claire. He worked out at the hotel gym for a couple of hours and had his hair trimmed. Afterwards, he got dressed and took the shuttle to the Monte Cristo Casino.

The eaves of the two-story villa-style casino were flooded in yellow lights as the stylishly dressed crowd made their way down the green carpet to the casino. Marcus's first stop was at the restaurant. He hadn't eaten all day and was starving, but nothing looked particularly good on the menu. He ordered the first item on the menu and handed it back to the waiter.

A brunette at the other table stared at him as he toyed with the centerpiece, but he ignored her and tried to get Sydney on the phone again. *Damn, where was she?* He had done some stupid things in his life, but this had to be near the top of the list. He hated her father, but he had no right to take his frustrations out on her. He didn't blame Sydney for getting the hell away from him. Marcus ordered a scotch and his mind drifted to Doc. He hadn't spoken to him in five weeks. He pulled his cell phone from his pocket, touched the speed dial, but then quickly closed it before it rang. Marcus tossed the phone on the table. He wasn't in the mood to hear Doc's preaching.

* * *

The thirty-something brunette followed the black man to the roulette table. She had her eyes on the handsome caramel-colored man the minute he entered the gaming room. The manicured fingernails, tailored tuxedo, and expensive but non-ostentatious jewelry on his finger and wrist told her he was wealthy. He'd barely touched his roast duck during dinner. Perhaps he was sad because of a lost love or a sour business deal. She didn't care—he was ripe for the picking.

He'd wandered through the casino watching others play, in no particular hurry to lose his money. Finally, he finished off the glass of scotch he had been nursing for the last half-hour and found his way to the Baccarat table next to hers. His modest one hundred dollar bets kept him entertained, but he was obviously just killing time. His mind wasn't in the game at all. Now was the time to strike.

She stopped the waitress and ordered two more scotches. The drinks arrived just as the chair next to him became vacant. The Latino woman couldn't believe her luck. She slid in the seat and waited for the dealer to finish. The dealer pulled the last card from the box and then collected the chips from the table.

"You never were any damn good at this game," said the woman standing behind Marcus. The Latino woman glared at the provocative-looking redhead in the black, low-cut gown. "He's taken, senorita, so don't waste your time." The woman was embarrassed and at loss for words. Sydney reached over and took the glasses of scotch from her hand. "These can stay, but you have to go."

Marcus watched the voluptuous woman storm away. He scooped up his chips. "Let's get out of here."

* * *

They arrived back at the St. Claire Hotel as the bar was closing. Marcus slipped the manager two hundred dollars to fire the grill back up. They sat in the captain chairs in the lounge with their drinks, watching the cook prepare their dinner.

"How did you find me?" Marcus asked.

"You're pretty predictable. Where else would you be except the hotel or casino?"

"You okay?"

She forced a smile. "I'm working on it."

Marcus laughed as he took the handkerchief from her hand and wiped the corner of her eyes.

"You know, I don't know what's worse, finding out that my dad used me or having you see me cry."

Marcus stirred his drink with his finger. "Everyone gets used in this world, but it doesn't mean you aren't loved. Sometimes we just don't think of the consequences until it's too late."

She wanted him to keep talking, to say something that would distract her from the pain she felt, but he didn't have any words of comfort. They both watched the young cook flip the steaks on the grill.

"Naw, you have to cook mine better than that," Marcus yelled. I don't want to see any pink when I cut it."

The cook rolled her eyes at him and turned the meat back over.

Sydney's fingers touched Marcus's hand on the bar. "I...I don't understand. How could he do this to me?"

He held her hand. "Your dad is a lot of things, but one thing he isn't is a bad father. Don't ever question his love for you. He's spent his entire life sheltering and protecting you from his world, and he wouldn't blink to kill anyone he thought might hurt you. Who the hell knows why he did what he did. But I bet if he was here right now and you asked him, he'd probably have a damn good reason—as sick as that might sound."

"When did you become a defender of my father?"

"I still hate the old bastard, but I give any man credit where credit is due." He put his glass back to his mouth. She kissed him on his cheek. "Don't be doing that in public, you'll mess up my game."

Sydney smiled. "Your game was played out about twenty years ago. Be thankful Caitlin still puts up with you."

"I'm still sweet. I don't know what you're talking about. You saw that fine filly trying to run up on me at the casino, and you're trying to tell me I'm not smooth? Get outa here, girl. You're just jealous."

"The filly was a slut, *and* old, *and* obviously in need of glasses."

Marcus laughed as he watched the chef out of the corner of his eye. He leaned over the counter. "Hey, let it cook some more. I don't want that thing trying to bite me when I cut into it."

"If I cook it any longer, there won't be anything worth cutting at all," snapped the woman. "You old guys never learned to appreciate the flavor of the meat. If it doesn't look like shoe leather, you don't want it."

"Old? I don't know what you're talking about, but I'm anything but old." She put the steaks on the plates, and laid them on the counter. Marcus poked his fork at the T-bone as if he was expecting it to move. "Are you sure this is dead?"

She sliced a piece of the meat and picked it up with a fork. "Open," she commanded. Marcus opened his mouth and she fed him.

"I guess it's okay, but I still see a little red." He cut off a larger piece and jammed it in his mouth.

"Is he always like this?" she asked.

"Worse, just give him some time. By the way, this food is excellent," Sydney said.

"Thank you." The young woman propped her elbows on the counter and watched Marcus devour his food. "Are you two together?"

"I'm just his chaperone to make sure he stays out of trouble," Sydney said.

The cook wiped her hands on her apron before reaching over and removing Marcus's glasses from his face. "For an old man, you aren't bad looking at all—nice hair, white teeth, and great tux. Yeah, I'd say you could give a few younger guys a run for their money around here." She gently placed the wire frames back on his nose.

Marcus grinned. "Damn, I like this girl, Sydney. You want to come to work for me?"

She patted his hand. "My father might not approve of that, Mr. St. John."

"How do you know my name?"

She picked his credit card off the bar and handed it to him. "I heard my father mention your name the other night after he picked you up."

"Your daddy is Inspector Clouseau?"

"The last name is Desjardins," she said, laughing.

He stared at the young woman with the inviting smile. "Glad to see ugly doesn't run in the family."

"My father says you're unstable."

Marcus choked on the steak trying not to laugh. "Only when I eat red meat."

"What do you have against Sasha Micheaux?"

"You obviously haven't met the woman or you wouldn't be asking."

"Everyone knows who she is. Her family is one of the richest ones in Lucerne. I followed the news about her brothers. My father says you think she killed them. Is that true?"

"As true as me sitting here trying to enjoy my food."

"So why did she do it?"

Marcus laid his fork down. "Damn, you're as nosey as your old man."

"Please—tell me."

"Sasha Micheaux's brothers were punks. They would have sold her down the river to avoid prison. She's the brains and power in the family, and she wanted to protect her own butt."

"I can't believe that."

"Believe it," he said, picking up his fork. "She is about making money and protecting what she has. She'd kill the Pope if he got in her way."

* * *

It was dawn when they hailed a taxi to take them to Vitznau. Both of them had too much to drink, but it was nice to forget their problems, even if it was only for a night. Marcus wiped the condensation from the side window. It was still snowing. The morning sun crept over the Alps, casting its golden rays on the blue water. The cabby paid more attention to the winter wonderland than his driving. He hit the "dead end" sign on the corner as he turned, going up to the hotel driveway. *That's not the only dead end around here*, Marcus thought. He knew he wasn't any closer to finding Devin Leon-Francis or his men than he was three weeks ago. His only hope was Sasha Micheaux. He nudged Sydney with his shoulder.

"Wake up, Sydney. Tell me some more about Sasha's cousin."

She grunted and rolled over, facing him. "Not much to tell. His name is Carlos Bourbon, he's prettier than me and speaks better English." She moaned and closed her eyes again.

"Any idea what Sasha was doing in France?"

"Lamenting the loss of her brothers, pining over Julian...I don't know. The woman is psychotic."

Marcus chuckled. "Yeah, I know what you mean. The girl is seriously conflicted. You ought to see all the stuff she wrote about Doc in that diary of hers. She doesn't know whether she wants to jump his bones or crush them. But I'll say one thing for her, she's a whole lot smarter than her brothers were. I couldn't find anything in the diary about your father."

Sydney's eyes opened. "I can't believe you read her diary."

"I'd sniff her crusty feet if I thought that would help me find your father."

"And you really thought there would be something about him in her diary?"

"It was worth a try, what else do you expect? You won't help me."

Sydney yawned, and then pushed herself up in the seat. "Marcus, this obsession of yours is going to get you killed if you don't find a way to let it go. You're right; I'm not going to help you get yourself killed, because that's what will happen if you keep this up. Let me tell you a few things about my father that is not in that little dossier you have on him. His only permanent residence is a yacht that is constantly on the move and protected by an army of men. He travels in a fully armed Apache gunship, and he has three of the best bodyguards in the business. No one, and I mean no one, has ever come close to beating him, but somehow you've convinced yourself that you're going to be the exception."

"I know what I'm doing," he said, looking out at the snow.

"You're honestly going to sit here and tell me you've given this some serious thought? I mean—on the other side of all this anger and hate, you've actually got a plan?"

"My *plan* is to deal with Worrick, Preston, and your father, in my own way. That's my plan."

She sighed and sank back against the seat. "You know, Marcus, the only reason I've stuck it out with you these weeks instead of going home with Julian, was because I thought you'd wake up and see how stupid this was. I figured that time would help soothe the pain, but you've gotten worse. This ridiculous need of yours to uphold your moral code and dispense justice has overridden your good common sense. I admit I was just as guilty, but in the last twenty-four hours, I've come to realize that I can't change anything. That little revelation came to me in the flash of a moment when I was with Sasha Micheaux. It finally hit me that I can't make people do jack they don't want to do, no matter how much you try to intimidate them. All my little stunt accomplished with her was to piss her off, just like your crusade against my father is going to get you killed. Nothing we do will bring back the Toussaints, and my father and the Micheauxs will continue to do whatever it is they do. We've worn out our welcome here, let's go home."

"You can go home if you want. I've got unfinished business to settle. The cabby pulled the taxi up to the hotel. Stop the cab!" Marcus said. He pulled out one of his guns.

"What's wrong?" Sydney asked.

"Where's Sam and the other guards?" Marcus paid the cabby and the car sped away. "I don't like this." Music was coming from the hotel. "I don't believe this. I pay these guys good money and they think they can slack off just because I'm supposed to be in the city for the night. I'm about to hurt somebody up in here."

"Come on, Marcus, the men deserve a little R&R too," Sydney said, trying to keep pace with him.

"Not at my expense they don't," he said, running up the steps.

Tre', his pilot, was in the lobby on the phone when Marcus burst through the door. "Boss, I was just trying to reach you at the hotel, I..."

"Well, you found me. You're fired, Tre'. He didn't break stride as he continued down the hall to the bar. Three guards were sitting at table playing cards and listening to the music blaring from the stereo.

Sam was the first to see him. "Hey, boss—you're back." He had a big alligator grin on his face.

"Yeah, and all of you are gone. If you want to get drunk and party all night, do it on your own dime and time, not mine." Sydney and Tre' came in the room. "I told you to pack your stuff, Tre', we don't have anything else to talk about."

"How are you going to fire your own nephew?" Doc asked, standing up from behind the bar. He wiped dust from his slacks and handed a bottle of ginger ale to Marcus. "Sydney was right about you, you're getting pretty cranky in your old age, Marcus."

Chapter 10

Doc hopped back over the bar. "I wouldn't have hurried had I known you were having such a good time," he said, fingering the satin lapel on Marcus's tuxedo.

"Having a good time is not exactly the way I would describe my experience here," Marcus said.

"Good, you should be ready to go home, then."

"I can tell Sydney has been bending your ear about me. I am not going home."

"Is this worth losing your family for?"

"What are you talking about?"

"Your wife, Caitlin, and your daughters—remember them?"

"That's not funny, Doc."

"You're right. Running around Europe trying to catch the invisible man instead of being home taking care of your family *isn't* funny, Marcus. I would never have thought you would desert your family over this."

Marcus stood up out of his chair. Sydney stopped dealing the cards at the other table.

"Okay, you've said your piece. Let it alone, Doc. I don't turn the other cheek and I'm not about to let this rest. I don't want to hear one of your sermons, or you telling me how I abandoned my family. I don't appreciate the comments," he said, raising his voice.

"Look, if hurting your feelings is what it takes to get your attention, then I don't care if you don't like what I have to say. Someone has to tell you the truth to keep you from doing something stupid."

"Don't push it, Doc."

"Sit down, Marcus, we're too old for this. We haven't fought since we were in grade school, but if kicking your butt again is what it takes to get through that hard head of yours, then I'm going to do it."

Marcus straightened his tie. "Okay, but no more comments about my family." He sat back down.

"When was the last time you spoke with Caitlin?"

"Doc…"

Doc grabbed his forearm. "Come on, man—when was the last time?"

"I don't know."

"This is what I'm talking about, Marcus. This place has made you crazy. Sasha Micheaux must have the patience of Job to put up with you, because no reasonable person would allow that kind of behavior. I wouldn't and you certainly wouldn't. We just buried two of our friends, and I'm sure not planning on going to your funeral. At least not until you're an old man and you've had a chance to see your godchild's children."

Marcus's face lit up. "Godchild? You and Asha?" Everyone in the room broke out in laughter. "You're lying just to get me home, aren't you?"

Doc grinned. "Asha is pregnant. She's expecting in July."

Marcus let out a wolf whistle and jumped to his feet.

"Damn, you hear that, guys? We're going to have a son!" He started dancing to the music.

"We already know, boss," Sydney said. She collected her poker chips as the guards threw in their cards.

"Now, can we finish our talk?" Doc asked.

"Yeah, yeah, we can finish—but I don't know how you can stay so calm about this, Doc, we're finally going to get that son we've wanted! You should be celebrating, too."

"First of all, I don't think you had anything to do with getting my wife pregnant, and secondly, who says it's going to be a boy?"

"It's gonna be a boy. I feel it in my bones."

"What you're feeling is the arthritis in your joints. By the way, they stopped doing the robot about twenty-five years ago, so I think you can take a break from it for a few minutes to talk with me."

Marcus plopped in the chair, out of breath and with a wide grin on his face.

"Your family misses and needs you with them—not out here playing Supernegro. We want you and Caitlin to be there when the baby is born."

"Not a problem. We'll be there—you know that."

"Afterwards, we're taking a vacation cruise to Monte Carlo. Caitlin's excited about going. All we need is you."

"Cruise! Naw, Doc, you know I don't do boats, and I'm certainly not into coming back to Europe after all we've been through over here."

"Think about it. Monte Carlo is your kind of city—bright lights and more casinos than you can count. You can even wear this cute little suit of yours."

"I'll think about it."

"Okay, fair enough. So, let's get out of here."

Marcus pushed his chair next to Doc. "Look, Doc, I'll make you a deal. Stay with me for one week—seven days—and help me find the bastards that did this to us, and I promise you I will leave with you and Sydney whether we find them or not."

"You must be smoking crack. I'm not helping you hunt down anyone so you can kill them. Do you hear yourself? I can't believe you. You can't go around serving up your brand of vigilante justice. People like Devin Leon-Francis and Jason Worrick will have their day of reckoning, and believe me, their punishment will be a lot worse than anything you could ever do to them."

"Doc, you know I can't let this pass. You of all people should understand that. For all the hell we went through I want to know why. That is not asking a whole lot. How could I face momma Toussaint and tell her that her son's lives were wasted on some crap I don't even understand?"

"No one is blaming you for what happened to them. The Toussaint brothers knew the risk when they agreed to help us. momma Toussaint understands that, too. She hoped you'd be at the funeral."

"I just couldn't do that. No way. I can't go home until I get some resolution to this. I'm a helluva security specialist, but I can't find the nose in front of my face. But you can. I'm asking you as my best friend to help me. One week, that's all I'm asking you for."

"Marcus, I'm not tracking down..."

Marcus leaned over in his chair. "No, nothing like that. Just help me out a little."

"Doing what?"

He paused for a moment and sat upright. "Talk with Sasha Micheaux and find out what she knows."

"Now I know you're crazy. That woman will put a bullet in my head faster than she can sneeze."

"Trust me, she won't. Sydney and I have tried everything, but she'll talk to you—I know it. You get her to tell you what she knows, and I'm outa here with you. That's all—I swear. What do you say?"

The card party was over and the guards had left, leaving Sydney alone playing solitary. She stretched her arms, yawned, and looked at her watch. "Hey, are you guys going to fight or go to bed? It's 4:35." Doc and Marcus were still in the heat of discussion.

"That's all you want me to do—talk with her?" Doc asked.

"Just talk, and find out what's cookin' between her and Devin Leon-Francis," Marcus said.

"And then you'll give this up and go home with me?"

"The jet will be ready to go when you get back."

Doc grumbled as he got up from the table and started for the hall.

Marcus caught up with him in the hallway. "Just to set the record straight, you never kicked my butt in the sixth grade."

Doc smiled. "Yeah, I did. You're just too old to remember."

* * *

Sasha's return trip from France was delayed a day because of bad weather. When she arrived back home in Burgenstock, she was informed of the deaths of two of Leon-Francis' top men. His bodyguard, Tiberius Woodberry, was found dead in a downtown Narvik hotel and Jason Worrick had been murdered. The Narvik police were seeking a third man, Andy Preston, who was also linked to Leon-Francis' organization. Sasha listened to the rest of the tape before burning it. She drummed her fingernails on the desk. She had never heard of Tiberius Woodberry or Andy Preston, but she knew Jason Worrick.

Worrick tried to negotiate the purchase of some artwork from her brothers last year in Quebec City, but the sale fell through when Sasha discovered that he worked for Leon-Francis. Six months later, Worrick popped up again off the coast of Pescara, Italy, on the Adriatic Sea with Anthony Chiapetta. Sasha became suspicious when she received reports of the men's clandestine meetings onboard Leon-Francis' yacht. If Jason Worrick was doing business with Chiapetta, that could only spell trouble for the Micheaux family.

Underneath all the pomp and smiles, Anthony Chiapetta was not a friend of the Micheaux family, especially in matters concerning money. The Chiapetta family once owned one of the largest shipping companies in Italy, but Anthony managed to squander most of the fortune on bad investments, four ex-wives, seventeen children, and a lavish lifestyle. They lived like royals at the expense of the Micheauxs. While the German, Eisenstadt, had never made any bones about his covetous desires to strip the Knight Guardians from the Micheauxs, Chiapetta's agenda was more subtle.

The Merovingian Council operated by what Chiapetta called his Dumas Principle, which was a sophisticated revenue-sharing plan where all the families shared in the collective profits of the whole. While the "all for one and one for all" agreement seemed fair, it wasn't. The Micheauxs made billions of dollars through their illegal art smuggling business and Sasha's shrewd investments. Consequently, they contributed a disproportionate share of their profits, much of which ended up subsidizing Chiapetta's lavishness.

Chiapetta was a leach and a greedy one at that; but he was also the council's most powerful and respected member. Sasha knew he and Leon-Francis were behind the disappearance and theft of her ship, and that it would be an uphill battle to prove it. The only way she could convince the council members of Chiapetta's deceit was by finding her missing freighter or Leon-Francis, both of which were daunting tasks. To make matters worse, the council had given her only a week to accomplish the task.

Sasha turned on the computer and opened a file showing the cargo manifest of the *Vincien Micheaux*. The eclectic collection of impressionist art, pre-Columbia artifacts, and Egyptian sculptures was valued at $200 million, but the monetary loss was paltry compared to the Degas, Cezanne, and Renoir collections she hadn't included in the shipment.

Recovering her brothers' collection was less important than letting her enemies get away with it. It was a matter of honor—and preservation—both of which she intended to maintain at any cost. She turned off the computer monitor and went to take a shower.

* * *

Doc waited in the hotel lobby while the Frenchman called Sasha's suite. Two stoned-faced guards stood on opposite sides of her private elevator. Doc removed his gloves and shook the wet snow from the hem of his overcoat. Another storm front was moving in this evening and this was the last place in the world he wanted to be stuck. He had taken the risk of coming here unannounced, hoping she would see him.

The stares from the beret-wearing Knights made him uncomfortable. Especially those from two of the men he remembered seeing at the abbey. Doc shoved his gloves in his pockets and sat down to wait. The guard hung up the telephone and motioned to him to approach the counter. Doc raised his arms as a guard scanned the metal detector over his body before sending him in the elevator. The paneled and mirrored elevator rose slowly to the top floor. When the doors opened, Enric Bourbon met him in the foyer.

Sasha stood behind the frosted glass doors, watching Enric methodically searching Doc's body again. The American looked taller than six-five, as he stood with arms stretched out, wearing a white mock-neck sweater and black dress overcoat. She pulled opened the double French doors to greet him. Sasha's penthouse was covered in frosted green glass, white furniture, and pastel-colored pillows. Doc felt like he had just entered Delilah's den.

"Monsieur Sebasst, welcome to my home."

"Thank you for seeing me on short notice."

She offered him a seat on the sofa across from her. A maid brought in a tray of herbal tea and placed it between them on the coffee table.

"I understand you appreciate excellent tea?" she asked, making it sound more like a comment than a question.

"How did you know?"

"I recall madam Belleshota mentioning it."

"You have a good memory."

"I am blessed with some of papa's extraordinary abilities. Like him, I have the memory for details—and for every transgression, no matter how slight." Doc poured their tea while she watched him as she played with the crucifix necklace on her tanned neck. She sat barefoot on the couch in white slacks and sleeveless turtleneck. She picked up her towel and continued drying her hair. "I hope you have sufficiently recovered from your injuries?"

"I'm fine." Doc wiped his mouth with the napkin during the awkward pause that followed.

Sasha twisted her necklace some more. "Why have you come to Lucerne?"

"I came to get my friends and take them home."

"They would do well to have your manners. Perhaps in their next lives they will be more fortunate." She leaned over to pick up her tea. "What do I have to do with this?"

"Don't you think you owe us an explanation for what's happened to us?"

She looked at him in disbelief. "An explanation? I owe *you* an explanation? Monsieur Sebasst, you and the vermin you choose to call friends have destroyed my family, desecrated the things we most cherish, and nearly destroyed everything my family and I have fought so hard to acquire. No, I owe you nothing. You are the one that must answer to God for what you have done. You deceived me to secure the release of that witch of a friend, and then betrayed my family. My brothers would be alive today, if you had not interfered in business that does not concern you."

Doc was convinced she was nuts—or just anxious for a fight. "I am not going to argue with you, and I am certainly not going to defend myself for doing what was right. Your brothers were murderers, plain and simple. So are you for killing them. What is it about the sanctity of life that you Micheauxs don't get? If you have a disagreement with someone, you don't kill them, *especially* your family. Don't blame your family's misfortunes on me—they were headed for disaster long before I showed up." Doc placed his teacup back on the tray and folded his napkin. "I am not your enemy. None of this would have happened and a whole lot of people would still be alive if it hadn't been for Devin Leon-Francis. So if you're going to assign any blame to anyone, you're picking on the wrong person. Devin Leon-Francis wanted your brothers out of his way and he used both of us to get what he wanted."

"I have never heard of this Devin Leon-Francis."

"You're a poor liar. I frankly don't care what you two are up to. I just want to know what my friends and I got dragged into, that's all."

"My men did not kill your people."

"I know that. It was Devin Leon-Francis. He planned this whole scenario, like a scriptwriter. Everything he did was calculated with the end result being the elimination of your brothers. I never blamed you for the deaths of our friends, but I would appreciate an explanation."

Sasha placed her cup on the table, got up from the couch, and walked over to the desk. She picked an object off the desktop and returned to her seat. "I know little of this Monsieur Leon-Francis, or his vendetta against my family. I will tell you that the man who works for him, Jason Worrick, has been dealt with in an appropriate manner."

"What appropriate manner?"

"An assassin killed him a few days ago."

"One of your people?"

"A very clever *woman*," she said proudly, as she returned to the couch.

"Are you going to tell me what this is all about?"

"Monsieur Worrick used his friendship with my brothers to betray my family. He and others were merely advancing a plan by his employer to steal what does not belong to him." She sipped some more of the lemon tea, and pulled one of the sofa pillows close to her breast.

"And that would be what?"

"A very valuable shipment of mine disappeared as it was being transported on one of my freighters from France to Quebec City. It is missing and so are my men that were on board."

"And you think that Leon-Francis is behind this?"

"I know it was that pig as surely as I know that you are sitting here," she said, flinging the pillow on the floor. "My freighter was last heard from when they entered the Arctic Ocean, and had mechanical difficulties during a storm. They made a distress call and a tugboat company owned by *that* pig sent out boats to assist them and none have been seen again."

"What was on the ship?"

"It is all on this." She handed him a CD disk.

Doc flipped the gold disk over in his hand. "What's on it?"

"An inventory of the items stolen. Take it with you. It will be useful in locating the missing pieces."

"What are you talking about?"

She flashed him a wicked smile. "You will find my missing cargo and return it to me, and then you and your friends will be permitted to leave and go wherever you wish, unharmed."

Doc couldn't believe what she had just said. He stood up to leave. "You're either delusional or you've sniffed too much of the synthetics on that pillow of yours," he laughed.

"Monsieur Sebasst, the people I am associated with are very anxious to have what was taken, returned to them."

"I don't care about the Merovingians, or your treasure, or any of your craziness. I want to get back to what you just said. I don't take threats lightly, and I certainly don't take orders from you. You've told me what I needed to know, and I thank you for that, but now it's time for me to go."

Sasha jumped off the couch and blocked his path with her body. "Monsieur, I don't make frivolous threats. Your friends have made enemies with their meddlesome prodding into matters that do not concern them. Certain measures have been taken to ensure that they do not interfere in my affairs again."

"What does that mean?"

"Let's say that their destiny is in your hands. I am powerless to interfere, but if you are successful in your retrieval of my goods, the council may reconsider their opinion and regard you as a friend rather than a foe."

"I want you to get on the phone right now and call whoever you need to and…"

"As I have said, I cannot do that. As unfair as this must appear, do you not see the irony in it? You gave me a similar impossible task. I had no knowledge of madam Belleshota's kidnapping, but nonetheless did as you requested only to discover that you were not a man of your word." She reached out and stroked Doc's smooth face, and then brushed an imaginary spec from his coat. "While I admit a certain fondness for you, I care nothing for your barbarian friend and his Valkyrie bitch. You have an opportunity to correct a wrong with a right, and I assure you that, unlike you, I am a person who keeps my promises."

Chapter 11

Sydney wished she had gone with Doc to Burgenstock instead of shopping. At least the resort village was heated. She was in downtown Lucerne trying to survive the blowing winds and icy sidewalks. Even the most ardent shopper was forced indoors. She sought temporary shelter in the Ingénue Cinema Complex, where they were passing out free lattes in the upstairs café. She grabbed one from the counter and sat by the fire. Water dripped from her boots as she laid them upside down next to the open flame. Her shopping adventure was over although she hadn't bought anything. She found a week old *New York Times* in the reading room, and read a small article in the business section that mentioned Marcus's acquisition of Cornerstone Global Insurance Investigations.

Marcus's aggressive pursuit to amass wealth reminded her of her father. The men were opposite sides of the same coin, separated only by the thinnest of margins. Marcus occasionally bent the law to get what he wanted, but her father didn't respect the law at all. There were no moral absolutes. Right and wrong were just two points on the same continuum, which made it easier to cross over when it was convenient.

Sydney waited for her boots to dry before going downstairs to the cinema. A handful of people were in the theater to watch *The Professional,* the story of a unique love and parental bond between a lonely hitman and a precocious 12-year-old orphan, named Mathilda. Sydney had seen the violent film several times — each time moved by its poignancy and the unconditional love and loyalty between the two characters. She identified with Mathilda, because both of their destinies had been altered by the death of a mother.

Sydney was only six when her mother died, but some memories of her were as vivid now as they were when they were together. She remembered her mother's exquisite hands as they moved the bow across her cello or softly played the piano as she entertained them. Angela Lia Belleshota was a woman of culture, who took delight in the simplest pleasures of life. She loved reading to her as they lay in a hammock on the beaches of the Mediterranean, having snowball fights in the Alps, and making kettle corn by bonfire at night. She remembered her mother's vibrant smile and radiant face every time Sydney's father entered the room.

The family was nomadic with no permanent home and no particular desire to stay in one place too long. Her mother loved living on the Mediterranean Sea, so they usually spent their summers in small villages on the coast of Spain, France, or Greece. They spent the winters in the mountains of Luxembourg or Austria. During those days, Devin Leon-Francis was constantly by their side. Any time they forged outside their protected environs, an entourage of his men accompanied them. The intrusive guards were a normal part of the family's everyday life, and a necessity.

Following her mother's death, Leon-Francis became more protective of his daughter and more reclusive. He disappeared for several months at a time, but he always kept a watchful eye on her, no matter where she lived.

Sydney sat in the empty theater staring at the closing credits rolling off the screen. It suddenly dawned on her that she was looking at the world through a child's eye, like Mathilda. There was a god, and he did have a higher moral standard that even men like her father were going to one day be held accountable to.

* * *

Doc finished his reuben sandwich and salad, and went for a walk around the outside terrace of the restaurant. The wind was strong and crisp, but felt good against his face. He leaned back against the building. The last thing in the world he wanted was a showdown with Devin Leon-Francis, but now he didn't have any other choice. Sasha was crazy enough to make good on her promise to kill Marcus and Sydney, unless he cooperated. *How do you find a person who spends his whole life being invisible?* He extinguished his cigar and headed back to the hotel.

The taxi dropped him off in front of the Lex Plaza Hotel as the boat from Kristerin arrived. Sydney stepped off the boat empty-handed.

"It doesn't look like you had much success in town," Doc said.

"It was horrible. How did you fare with prima diva?"

"I should never have listened to Marcus." He held on to her elbow as her boots tried to grip the slippery ice.

She laughed. "Julian, I don't know what it is about you that sets that woman off, but I knew you would regret the day you ever got involved with her again."

"You were right."

She saw his gloomy face. "Is it that bad?"

"Worse. Let's find Marcus." They found him in the bar having dinner.

"It's about time you got back. I was starting to worry about you guys," Marcus said. He pointed his fork at the empty chairs. "Have a seat, we can talk while I finish my dinner. On the other hand, maybe you two should sit over there. The depressing looks on your faces are making me lose my appetite." Doc stared at him. "So, are you going to say anything or just watch me eat?"

"I'm waiting for you to take your face out of that plate so I don't feel like I'm talking to the top of your head," Doc said.

Marcus tossed the fork on the table and sat up straight in the chair. "Okay...talk. I'm listening." Doc sat down and told him about his meeting with Sasha Micheaux. "Doc, how in the hell are we going to find Leon-Francis in five days?"

"We're not hunting for him. It'll be easier trying to find the missing ship."

"How are we going to pull that off?"

"I'm working on that. The first thing we need to do is pay a visit to Leon-Francis' tugboat company in Narvik."

"What about Leon-Francis?"

"Forget about him, Marcus. I guarantee you he'll come looking for us if we get anywhere near him."

"Maybe Sasha's avenging angel will find him first," Marcus said. Sydney flashed him a scowl. "Sorry."

Doc looked at them both. "You know, this is going to get worse before it gets better. "We better lay out some ground rules before we begin so there is no miscommunication. I am *not*, and I repeat, *not* going on a turkey shoot for Devin Leon-Francis. This is about finding the ship and the art so we can go home and not be wondering if those crazy Merovingians are after us."

"Okay—I got it," Marcus said, drawing his toothpick from his pocket.

"Good, then that's settled." Doc turned to face Sydney. "I don't feel comfortable asking you this, but I have to. The only way we stand a chance in succeeding is with your help. If you can't do that, we might as well pack it in now and take our chances with the Micheauxs. I'm not interested in your father, but he's not the kind of man that's going to roll over and open the welcome gates. If you can't be with us, we won't go. We're either in this together or we're not."

Sydney looked at the two black men she had spent more time with than her own father. They were as different as night and day, but they had two things in common—their love for her, and their honor. They were on the right side. No matter how she tried to justify or ignore the things her father did, the bottom line was he was wrong. "What do you want me to do?"

"Any idea where your father is?" Marcus blurted.

"Pick any place on the map. I have no idea. Julian is right. If my father did steal what Sasha says he did, he won't be within a thousand miles of it. He's too clever for that."

"You still don't think he took it, do you?" Marcus asked.

"Weapons, drugs—maybe. Not art. He's never been impressed with it, and I can't believe he is now."

"Oh, you can bet the boy had a reason," Marcus said.

"We could speculate forever on the possibilities, but Sasha says he took it, and I believe her," Doc said.

"What's the deal with the warrior princess in Norway that whacked Jason Worrick. Does she work for Sasha, and are we going to have to worry about her, too?" Marcus asked.

"I don't know to both questions. Don't worry about her, worry about finding the shipment. We need to leave here by tomorrow. The clock is ticking," Doc said.

"So, where is this Narvik place?" Marcus asked.

"Northern coast of Norway."

"You mean the North Pole?"

"Not that far north."

"Same thing," Marcus mumbled as he returned to his dinner. "I suppose I'm going to need warmer clothes?"

"Especially if you were planning on wearing that tuxedo. What are you all dressed up for anyway?"

"I thought we we're going to the casino tonight."

"Sorry, some other time. I have to make some calls," Doc said.

Marcus looked at Sydney.

"Not tonight, boss, I've been out all day and I'm tired," she said.

Marcus dropped his fork on the plate. "I can't believe you guys. I've been stuck in this hotel all day long waiting for you, and now you just want to leave me hanging by myself?"

Doc pushed his chair back from the table. "If you want something to do, call your wife. I'm sure she would appreciate hearing from you."

"Man, I've been on the phone with her for half the day already. Why do you think I'm trying to get the hell out of here?"

"Well, you better call her back and tell her you won't be home for Christmas."

Tre' was sitting at the bar and overheard part of the conversation. "We're going home, boss?"

"No, but get the plane fueled up. We're going to the North Pole."

97

Chapter 12

A millionaire businessman was dead, an ex-DEA agent was murdered, and Andy Preston was still on the loose. The Chief Inspector of Narvik Central Police tossed the empty antacid bottle in the garbage, then ransacked his desk until he found some old Tums in the corner of the bottom drawer. They tasted like wet chalk, and he spit them into the garbage can. He elevated his feet on the desk, and groaned as his sour stomach continued firing bursts of hot acid up his throat. The Chief was scheduled for surgery in the morning, but that would have to wait. Right now, he was in the middle of the biggest police investigation in Narvik history.

The more rocks he turned over, the bigger mess he found. Jason Worrick was listed as a victim of a hunting accident, but he was too old to walk, much less be out hunting. Tiberius Woodberry's DEA records were sealed, and Andy Preston was a preppy Ivy Leaguer with the common sense of a bat according to people who knew him. The seemingly dissimilar men had two things in common. They were Americans and they worked for the same man—someone named D.L. Francis, who nobody seemed to know. The Chief lifted the latest fax from the tray and read it:

Colonel Jordan Bloodstone: United States Marine Corp. assigned to British Royal Marines; intelligence and mountain reconnaissance specialist; expert in linguistics, light weapons and demolition. Status: AWOL.

He popped more of the tablets in his mouth and washed them down with warm water from his sports bottle. He needed to be home in bed, but that wasn't going to happen until he found out what was going on. He ran his hand across the embroidered Kings badge proudly displayed on the sleeve of Jordan's military uniform. This belonged to the same woman seen in the company of Andy Preston, and she had disappeared just as mysteriously as he had. He turned off the office lights and signed out at the front desk.

A car from the American Embassy sat across the street with its lights off. A black man in the back seat puffed on a cigarette as he watched the Chief unlocking his car door. "Let's roll," Mallon Jefferson said. The driver drove into the deserted parking garage and screeched to a halt in front of the Chief Inspector's Volkswagen.

* * *

Andy Preston had been hiding out on the tugboat for two days. But now he was out of food and time. He saw a police officer interviewing a worker on the harbor. Eventually they would get around to searching the rest of the tugboats in the harbor.

He swung the heavy telescope to the side, and sank to the pilothouse floor. He pulled a pack of cigarettes from his back pocket and thought about his dilemma. Part of him wanted to surrender to the police, but he was scared. What was he going to tell them? That Woodberry was trying to kill him and that he had only been protecting himself? Or that it was an accident and he really didn't mean to kill him? The police might believe his story, but he was more afraid of what Devin Leon-Francis would do. The fact of the matter was he couldn't explain any of this without implicating Leon-Francis, and that was suicide. He lit his cigarette. He had to get out of the country. If he was going to escape, he needed to do it now. But to do that he needed his passport, which was in the office safe.

Andy waited until the tug yard closed before venturing outside. The police were gone, but he knew they were still patrolling the area. He walked quickly up the boat ramp and crossed the wharf over to the tug yard. It was close to midnight. There wasn't much time left. The gate was unlocked. He ran through the smelter shop, and up the back stairs leading to his office. At the top of the landing, he wiped soot from the window and looked outside. The docks were clear.

He grabbed the Tow-2-Tow dispatcher's vest hanging on the wall and slipped it over his head. He used his cigarette lighter to see the tumbler as he dialed the combination to the safe. The passport was still there. He heard the distant whistle of the Malmbanan train making its way down the mountain.

A man in an anorak jacket watched the movement of light coming from the office window. Andy exited the building the same way he entered and headed toward the south quay and the railway terminal. The Malmbanan pulled into the terminal as workers stood ready to unload the cargo. Andy disappeared in the crowd. The man dropped his binoculars, jumped down from the roof, and ran after him.

Workers were already moving the iron ore from the conveyor belts to the storage silos on the waiting ship. The man climbed up on a shipping container, looking for the red and green dispatcher's vest Andy was wearing. But all he saw were men, crates, and machinery. He searched the quay, but didn't find him. Finally, he ran outside to the freighter, but was rebuffed by the captain when he tried to board the ship. From the ramp, he heard the sound of a whistle as the train pulled out of the station.

The Malmbanan seldom ran two locomotives, but on this trip, they were hauling one back to the LKAB processing plant in Sweden for repairs. Andy rolled his vest into a ball and made a pillow. The trip would be long. The train would travel fifty kilometers north to Lake Torne and sixty kilometers along the shore, before finishing the last fifty kilometers through mountain tunnels. With luck, he would be in Sweden in six hours, and by tomorrow, he would be on the coast where he would find a ship for home.

* * *

The Norwegian heard the faint echo of the Malmbanan as it made its way over the mountain to Sweden. He had moved the base camp further up the mountain, near the Swedish border. The weather was colder, but at least the snow had stopped, and he could communicate with the ground.

"Where are you now?" Devin Leon-Francis asked.

"Above the Aberzidan Trail, about thirty kilometers northwest of Kiruna," the Norwegian said.

"And Bloodstone?"

"She's on the trail headed toward Kiruna."

"You're certain of that?"

"Yes, sir. We found her pack downstream, and we spotted tracks up on this side of the glacier wall by the old suspension bridge. She's moving due east toward the border."

"She won't make it that far."

"I know. If she's not dead already, she soon will be."

"I want her alive long enough to tell me how she found me, and who sent her."

"Alive?"

"Alive. Bring in as many men as you need, but get her. There are a lot of small villages out there she could hide in. Check them out."

"I've already taken care of it."

"Good. What else are you doing?"

"I have another helicopter coming up with some ex-military men I know. They'll search the six-square-mile area above the fjord, which is pretty rugged ground. That's where she'll come out if she makes it that far."

"What's the status on Andy Preston?"

"He's on his way to Kiruna right now. We will be waiting for him." There was a pause on the other end of the radio.

"You get me the woman and Preston, and Woodberry's job is yours. Keep your radio on. I'll get back to you." The telephone went dead.

The Norwegian poured himself some coffee. Leon-Francis' final words had become his signature signoff. At least when Moses was on the mountain with God, he caught a glimpse of him as he passed. Devin Leon-Francis had a better act. You never saw him.

The Norwegian and Leon-Francis had never met, and until Leon-Francis called him to tell him the news of Woodberry's death, he was beginning to wonder if the man actually existed. "Keep your radio on" was a constant reminder of Leon-Francis' omnipresence. The Norwegian was used to working with powerful and eccentric people like Leon-Francis. They were demanding perfectionists, but so was the Norwegian. Now he had an opportunity to take Woodberry's place. There was no way he was going to let the opportunity slip through his fingers.

* * *

Team B stopped to rest for a minute, before continuing. They had been on her trail for three days, but couldn't catch up with her. She was like a machine that could run forever. For the last few miles, the men noticed shorter strides between the snowshoe tracks. Further along the trail, they saw a knee imprint in the snow. She was tiring. The team of four men found her first snowshoe near the entrance to the woods. A half-mile further, they found pieces of torn fabric and the second snowshoe. Trails of dropped salmonberries led them further into the dense forest. One of the men spotted the cut tree limbs lying at the bottom of a huge spruce tree. The men removed the branches covering the top of the six-foot diameter shelter pit, but it was empty. A man jumped down in the five-foot-deep hole to inspect the burnt moss and scrub willow. It singed his hand.

"She's close," he whispered. Bullets sent three of the men reeling backwards into the snow. The man in the pit ducked down in the hole for cover and returned fire, but it was useless. He couldn't see his target. He tossed his rifle and pistol out and raised his hands in surrender. Staring at Jordan's face was more frightening than the barrel of the gun she rested against his forehead. Her snowsuit was covered in mud, and the hood was torn and frayed. An improvised facemask of tattered fabric covered her face. The narrow slits revealed deep-set chocolate eyes and severely chapped lips. Part of her pant leg was missing and she showed signs of frostbite. She slid the chamber back on her .45.

"Toss," she said, barely audible. It took a moment for the man to understand what she was talking about. He unbuckled the pack from his back and held it out to her. She stepped aside. "On the ground."

He laid it by her foot, and raised his arms again. Jordan stood silent as she kept the gun pressed to his head. Her eyes were glazed and wild. She looked like a trapped wolf with no place to go and nothing to lose. The man trembled. She used her free hand to rustle through the pack until she found some beef jerky, which she shoved in her mouth as fast as she could chew, without taking her eyes or gun off him. "Get out." She moved back and gave him room to climb out of the hole. "Go!" He faced the open white plains she pointed to, and saw nothing but miles of more snow. He hesitated and she pointed the gun at his face. He took off running as fast as he could in the snowshoes. She kept her eyes on him until he disappeared in the snow.

Jordan retrieved the guns and stripped the dead bodies for dry clothes before tossing the corpses in the pit. She cut the shrunken socks from her swollen feet, put on the larger socks and boots, and then scavenged through the other backpacks for anything useful she could take with her. She unclipped the laminated sheet of coordinates sewn on the inside of her old snowsuit, and stuffed them in her pocket along with the GPS. If she was going to save her leg and life, she couldn't afford to make any more mistakes. Having a GPS and the coordinates to two-dozen communal huts was worthless if she got lost again. As near as she could estimate, the closest hut was seven miles away near the village of Kaitum on the Swedish border, which was east of her position. Only seven more miles and she could rest. They were probably waiting for her there, but that didn't matter anymore. Dying a soldier's death amidst a hail of bullets was infinitely more heroic and painless than the alternative of a slow, miserable death in the snow. She heaved the heavy backpack over her shoulders and headed east.

The shortcut to Kaitum took Jordan across the roughest terrain and glaciers on the mountain. The remote area had snowdrifts covering dangerous crevasses, all of which were too wide to jump. She couldn't cross here. She knelt in the snow and caught her breath. There had to be another way across. She backtracked down the trail.

She lost an hour traveling over razor-sharp rocks and ice to reach the base of another icefall, where she searched for an alternate route. There was none. The vertical ice in front of her was her only way to the fjord, but she didn't have her crampons. Without the spiked boots, it was suicide. Every part of her body ached, but she knew the men chasing her weren't going to stop because she was tired. She was trapped unless she could scale the ice.

She scanned the icefall looking for natural footholds, edges, and angularities she could use to her advantage. Climbing was all about energy management and having the right equipment. She had little of either one. If she moved slowly, and conserved energy, she might have a chance.

The extreme cold made the ice brittle and more difficult to hold onto with an axe. Jordan chopped at the hard ice and drug herself up on the wall. Her feet were numb and her hands bled through her mittens, but she kept moving. Crevices and cracks were few and far between. Every time she reached one, she pounded in an ice screw, attached her rope, and prayed the screws and ice would hold long enough for her to rest. She had to fight for every foot she gained. Most of the time her blade and energy were wasted, pounding away at ice that shattered more than it held. When the axe did sink, it was deep, requiring even more strength and energy to remove.

Jordan repeated the arduous task until she reached a sheet of sheer ice she could not get around. She tested the ice with her axe. It seemed solid. Screws were strong enough to support a thousand pounds, but they were only as good as the ice that held them. She inched her way higher looking for an optimum spot to plant another screw. She found one, just over her head to the right, but it was just out of reach. She cinched the rope tight around her shoulders, griped her left hand on the screw, and slowly pulled her body up. The ice broke off and slammed down on top of her, slicing a deep gash in her head.

Her body plunged sixty feet down the mountain before her safety line engaged. The rope held her unconscious body as it swayed back and forth in the air. She banged against the icy mountain for an hour, before the loud sound of whirling blades woke her up. She struggled to open her eyes. A black military helicopter hovered over her with a man holding a high-powered rifle. She was as defenseless as a beached whale on shore, and just as easy a target. Her body stiffened when the soldier leveled the rifle and took aim, but didn't fire. The helicopter continued hovering. *What is he waiting for?* She looked down and saw the answer.

Six men dressed in white with yellow and green patches on their sleeves, scaled the ice like a precision acrobatic team, using state-of-the-art equipment Jordan had never seen before. The elite force of Swedish Arctic Rangers attacked the ice like spiders on a web. They were trying to capture her alive, and at the rate they were moving, that wouldn't take long. The men were fresher, stronger, and faster than she was. She tried to think as her head pounded with pain.

The soldier in the helicopter watched her sink an eight-inch serrated screw into the ice, and then another one. He grabbed his binoculars. "What is she doing?" Jordan pulled out two more rings and fastened them to her rope, double-looping the rope around her shoulders. She held on tight with her right hand. With the left, she reached for her handgun. "Take it up! Take it up!" he shouted, but the pilot was too slow.

The sounds of gunshots echoed in the air, followed by a thunderous roar from the mountain as it unleashed an avalanche of 130,000 cubic yards of white death. The snow swept down the side of the mountain at one hundred ten miles an hour looking for victims.

* * *

Jordan couldn't remember how she made it over the icefall, or what happened to the men that were following her. She had a concussion, but still managed to drag her bruised and tired body two miles, before dropping to her knees in exhaustion. The ground suddenly moved under her knees—she was sinking. The south-facing glacier bowl was a victim of the glaring sun. Everything was beginning to melt, including the snow covering the crevice under her knees. With all her might, she swung the pick into the face of the rock as the ground gave way. The pick held long enough for her right foot to find a ledge. She hugged the mountain, terrified that the ledge would bow to her weight. She tossed her bulky backpack over the side, and stretched her leg across to solid ground.

A quarter of a mile down the mountain, a nomadic Saami family moved across the tundra. But they were too far away to hear her faint cries for help. Jordan was delirious and spent, but found a way to keep her feet moving. She stumbled and found herself on the ground again, staring up at the sky. She couldn't move a muscle. Then she remembered the look on the face of the man she watched freeze to death. She didn't go through all this hell just to die a few miles from her destination. She struggled to lift her right leg over her left, which rolled her onto her hip. The green meadows of the fjord were just a few hundred meters beyond the last remnants of snow.

She raised herself up slowly on her feet, clutching the GPS in her hand. She tried focusing her eyes on the coordinates. Just down the fjord. That's as far as she had to go, just down the fjord. She ripped the facemask off and breathed the crisp air. Right foot, left foot…right foot, left. That's all she had to do. Right foot, left foot…"

The mantra got her as far as the isolated shack that looked like an oversized outhouse. The building was a communal hut, one of several hundred provided by the Swedish government for weary hikers. There was a key in a box attached to the side of the building, along with a reminder to sign the guest book in the room.

The small room had a bunk bed and a wood stove. She wrapped the bed blankets around herself and collapsed on the floor. Sweat covered her body and delirium wracked her brain as she shivered. She saw the faces of the men she killed, and the horror on Leon-Francis' face as her bullet missed his head. Worse, she heard the sounds of death: men yelling and screaming, explosions and gunfire.

Men moving, searching, always searching for her, and more men. Closer, always getting closer. Then death. She heard footsteps—outside the door.

She raised the revolver off her chest and emptied the gun in the men storming through the hut door.

Chapter 13

Carlos Bourbon flew alone, 30,000 feet over Germany. He could see the coast of Denmark off of his left wing. He adjusted his heading two degrees and switched on the autopilot. If the weather held, he would reach Bodo, Norway in two hours, well ahead of St. John's jet. Carlos relaxed and returned to his poetry, a passion he acquired as a Jesuit in Montreal. He had a particular fondness for the great Chinese poets, like Han Shan, but tonight he preferred the simple eloquence and clarity of Longfellow.

The Oxford educated scholar with the Hollywood looks was serious about everything he did. Although the youngest of three brothers, he was the Liege of the Knights—a title bestowed to him as leader of Sasha's Knight Guardians. The thirty-one-year-old philosopher was smart, cunning as a general, and uncompromisingly loyal to the Micheaux family. Most of all, he was the best at what he did, which was protecting Sasha's interests.

A purple-reddish haze punctuated the sky. Nothing in the world was more satisfying or solitary than flying. He picked up *Songs of Hiawatha* again, but soon lost interest. Sydney Belleshota was on his mind.

His encounter with her left an indelible mark. She was a beautiful woman, but there was more than just a sexual attraction. He felt an immediate connection, even if it was brief. It was an intuitive feeling like the one he had when he first met his cousin, Sasha. He knew that they were right for each other. There was a soft quietness behind Sydney's mask of bravado and confidence, which he admired.

Carlos couldn't afford any distractions; they could get him killed. He had a job to do, and that was to recover the stolen shipment of art and kill Leon-Francis—and anyone else that got in his way. As much as he tried thinking about something else, his mind kept flashing back to Sydney and the bright smile she had on her face as she waved goodbye to him at the abbey. He pushed her from his mind as he banked the plane hard to the right—passing over the Rhine River. If he had looked to the east, he would have seen Meinhard Eisenstadt's mountaintop retreat, Agippa's Palace, off in the distance.

* * *

Agippa's Palace was a billion-dollar Roman spa and bath resort with all the opulent amenities of ancient Rome, complete with lush green courtyards with terraced balconies, olive vineyards, and gold fountains.

Eisenstadt was in deep meditation as his leathery body absorbed the hot steam of the sundatorium. The steam room was part of his daily regime and he always made sure the underground wood-burning stoves ran at full capacity. The heat was too intense for most, so Eisenstadt usually had the sweatbox to himself.

An obese man entered the room and quickly stripped from his terrycloth robe. He put on the special thick-soled shoes to protect his feet, and joined the German on the bench. Water seemed to squirt from every pore in his body. "This place is worse than hell, Meinhard. I cannot believe people pay your exorbitant rates for this kind of treatment," Anthony Chiapetta said.

Eisenstadt smiled. "You would do well to spend some time in this place, Anthony. The therapeutic benefits might cleanse your blood of all those pollutants you complain about."

"I would rather die from a stroke." Chiapetta wiped his face with the towel. "This had better be important. I don't know how much of this I can bear."

"I will not take much of your time, but I felt compelled to voice my anger and disappointment with you, and the way *that* woman is clearly forcing her agenda on the council—apparently with your blessing. Sasha Micheaux…her family, they are a total disgrace to all that we stand for, and you know that. Yet, you do nothing to stop her. Frelinghuyen and the others, I understand. But I can't believe you have fallen under her manipulative spell, too. Perhaps the heat in this room will melt the wax from your eyes so you can see just how destructive she can be if we let her continue."

Chiapetta coughed. His lungs felt like hot coals. "I agree…" He coughed some more.

Eisenstadt bent him over and slapped him on the back. "Take a few deep breaths."

Chiapetta complied and the coughing spasms stopped. He felt his lungs accept the hot air.

"Is that better?"

"Much. I agree, Sasha Micheaux is a problem."

"Then why didn't you stand with me to denounce her instead of embracing her?"

"As you said, Frelinghuyen and the Dane have always supported the Micheauxs. And I cannot risk polarizing the council over this matter. For this body to remain effective, we must be united as a group—as it has always been since our inception."

"So you intend to sit blindly by and do nothing while this woman weaves her evil?"

"I will not openly oppose her on the council, but I assure you that her tenure will be short. Her fate was sealed with her absurd accusation that one of us has betrayed the group."

"So you didn't believe her lies?"

"No more than you, old friend."

"Then you should have denounced her. That would have been the perfect time to deal with her."

Chiapetta wiped the sweat from his bald head. "The Micheauxs and Bourbons are a powerful collective force. We must be wise in how we proceed against them, and we must have the support of the entire council membership to sever them from the body. That is crucial to our success."

"Sever?"

"My interest goes far beyond removing Sasha from the council. We must expunge the entire Micheaux and Bourbon families, and ensure that they will never occupy a seat on the council again." That brought another smile to Eisenstadt's face. "The Micheaux family has been abusing its power for years, and Andre Micheaux's offspring have permanently tarnished all that he worked so hard to achieve. They have destroyed their own legacy with their corruption, murder, and now lies. I can simply no longer ignore the harm and risk they pose to the other families." Chiapetta had Eisenstadt's full attention. "Frelinghuyen is an optimist who presumes that mediocrity will rise to the occasion. But Sasha will fail like her brothers. None of them could shine as bright as their father. With that said, I was still willing to afford her an opportunity to prove me wrong, but she has proven to be an even bigger disappointment than her arrogant brothers. I supported her in her plans to move our treasury from France to Quebec City, hoping she would succeed, never thinking she would use her cleverness against the council."

"What do you mean?"

"The missing freighter that she so fervently accused one of us of stealing was never lost, and there was no theft. She orchestrated the whole affair, including the murder of her Knight Guardians. She deliberately sank her own freighter along with the collection of rubble art, which has little or no value. All this to help authenticate her lies so she can lay the blame on you or me. The freighter is resting on the bottom of the Arctic Ocean with our men shackled like slaves in the boiler room."

"That is preposterous, are you sure of this?"

"As sure as I know that she perceives you and I as her only opposition. An honorable Knight has come forward to expose her plans. Sasha will attempt to incriminate one or both of us, but this time she has gone too far. The very scheme she devised to ensnare us will be used to bite off her poisonous head. It will be impossible for her to recover what she has already destroyed, and then we will have proof to show the other families."

Chiapetta moved closer to Eisenstadt and whispered. "With the Knight Guardians securely in your possession, we will purge the Micheauxs from our ranks, and reclaim our treasury at Languedoc-Roussillon and the Micheaux's assets."

"Carlos Bourbon will never let that happen. Why not strike now? Let's convene the other members immediately and inform them of this news. Once they are presented with the facts and can speak with the Knight to confirm this, they will be forced to act."

"Patience, my friend. We must allow her enough time to sufficiently tighten the noose around her neck. Then we will cut off the head."

* * *

After a refreshing cool shower and breakfast, Chiapetta took the shuttle back to town where his car was waiting for him. He called a toll-free number and left a message for Leon-Francis to call him back. He grabbed an apple from the tray and waited. Everything had gone as expected. Eisenstadt had been so easy to deceive. He was so blinded by his hatred for the Micheauxs that he would believe anything Chiapetta told him. Chiapetta's plan was working better than he'd hoped for. He agreed to give Eisenstadt the Knight Guardians, in exchange for the German's support to seize control of Sasha's bank. The only issue left unresolved was what to do about Carlos Bourbon. Carlos and his brothers were dangerous and fiercely loyal to their cousin. Eisenstadt wanted Carlos dead, but Chiapetta thought it too risky. Besides, he prided himself on his civility. Murder was archaic and better left to barbarians. He could achieve his goals through artful subterfuge, a skill Sasha Micheaux had yet to master.

Chiapetta read the paper as his car traveled east on the autobahn to Berlin. He would stay there for the night before returning home to Florence. The limousine telephone rang forty minutes into his trip.

"Where are you calling from? I can barely hear you," Chiapetta said.

"Is that better?" Leon-Francis asked.

"Yes, it sounds like you are having a great party. Where are you, my old friend?"

"You know better than to ask me that, Tony." Chiapetta laughed until he started coughing. "I'd have that cough of yours looked at by a doctor if I were you."

"It's nothing. A recent affliction acquired from a beastly hot steam bath. If you have never tried one, don't. I feel as though I've aged another five years. Where did you say you were calling me from?"

"I didn't."

"Some things never change, old friend, and you are one of them. It is good to hear your voice again. I was sorry to have missed you on your boat, but Jason Worrick did a masterful job in assisting me with the details. Make sure you give him my regards."

"Jason is no longer with me, but I'm sure he'd appreciate the comment."

"It will be good to see you again after so many years. I am anxious to see what you have for me. Tell me, will I be disappointed?"

"Let's just say it will keep you and your family in caviar and wine for a very long time."

"Excellent, excellent! When will I be able to take possession?"

"I'll pick you up on Friday morning. We'll have dinner together, and on Saturday, my ship will transport your merchandise to your port of choice. If you want, you can sleep with it."

"I may do just that, my old friend. It may be the only time I have an opportunity to enjoy it before it is sold. I am deeply indebted to you for your generosity to me and my family."

"Forget it, I owed you."

"Did you find what you were searching for?"

"Yes."

"Excellent, we are both winners. I received what I wanted and you recovered the piece you had been searching for. This is the way it should be. I am curious. What item is so valuable that you would take such risk, only to give everything away to me?"

"It was a good business deal. I got what I wanted."

"What was on the ship that was so important?"

"The piece you gave Angela for a wedding gift."

"That relic I found in Egypt? It is certainly a fine piece of craftsmanship, but of no intrinsic value."

"It's valuable to me."

"I suspect this is more than sentimentality?"

"How's your brother?"

Chiapetta bellowed out a hoarse laugh. "You are still the old, sly fox I remember from our youth. You suspect everyone and trust no one. The devil will have his hands full when you arrive, Devin." He released another wheezing cough. "As for Ernesto, he is an old senile man that still hates the mere mention of your name."

"Like you said...some things never change. I'll see you Friday, Tony."

* * *

Devin Leon-Francis hung up the telephone after talking with Chiapetta. Everything was proceeding according to schedule. Everything, except one little detail he needed to deal with.

He watched the *Emerald Queen Holiday* cruising Lake Washington as a large crowd of beer-drinking revelers stood cheering from the shore. A procession of University of Washington students followed the ship in kayaks and canoes as it made its way past the cluster of expensive floating homes on Portage Bay. Neighbors from the adjacent deck waved their champagne goblets to the reclusive man they knew only as Mr. Lawrence, a wealthy retiree who rarely resided at his houseboat. The cool chill from the water sent a shudder through his body. Leon-Francis wrapped the wool blanket tightly around himself. "Morgan!"

The bodyguard muted the television and opened the sliding glass door to the deck. "Yes, sir?"

"We missed Sebasst in St. Croix. And now he thinks he has nine lives. He and St. John are on their way to Narvik. "I want you and Fisher to take some boys and deal with them once and for all."

Chapter 14

Marcus sat in the co-pilot seat listening to music and relaxing as the luminescent cockpit lights glowed in the dark. Stars filled the night sky as the jet streaked into Norwegian air space. "Man, I tell you, if you have to fly, this is the only way to go."

"Boss, you should learn to fly. Then you wouldn't have to depend on me," Tre' said.

"I hate flying as much as I hate putting up with you, but I tolerate both. Besides..." He stuffed a cigar in his mouth and lit it. "Keeping you employed is a small price to pay not to hear your momma's mouth." The door opened and Sydney entered the cockpit. Marcus removed his headphones. "What's up—Doc's snoring wake you up?" he asked, peeling a piece of loose tobacco from his tooth.

"In case you forgot, it's Christmas." She handed him a wrapped gift.

"I thought you didn't celebrate Christmas."

"I made an exception this year."

He opened the package to find a miniature digital camera. "This is *sweet*, thanks." He gave her a kiss. "I'll take some pictures for Caitlin."

"Download a picture of yourself and send it home so she can remember what you look like."

"Yeah, that was funny," Marcus said sarcastically.

"Actually it was," Tre' cackled.

"How about I take a picture of you, so you can remember what your job looked like?"

Tre' looked at his uncle. "That's not funny, boss."

"I thought it was hilarious," Marcus said, slapping his knee. "Sydney, I have a little something for you, too—but it's in my bag in the back. And I wrapped it myself."

"I'm impressed."

"Just trying to be a little more genteel like Doc. Speaking of the sensitive one, is he asleep?"

"No. Do you want to see him?"

"Yeah, tell him I'm sick of looking at Tre's face. I need some comic relief."

Sydney left the cockpit and picked up a package off the front seat as she walked to the back of the cabin. Doc was lying on the couch, watching a movie.

She mixed herself a drink at the bar. "How's the movie?"

"The popcorn is better." He swung his legs off the couch to make room for her. "For a guy that prides himself on his good taste, Marcus's selection in movies is horrible."

"He could still learn a few things from you." She laid the package in his lap.

"What's this?"

"Your gift. I'm sorry I didn't have time to have it gift-wrapped. Open it," she said anxiously.

"You know you didn't have to do this."

"Just open it, Julian."

Doc meticulously untied the white string and brown paper. His eyes lit up in surprise.

"Merry Christmas, Julian." She gave him a hug.

"I can't believe this. Where did you find it?"

"A book store in Geneva. I couldn't believe it, either. Look inside, it's even inscribed." Doc gingerly opened the first edition of *Harlem: Negro Metropolis*. The slightly tanned book was still in excellent condition.

"You know how long I've been trying to find this? I don't know what to say."

Sydney held onto his arm. "I wish Asha was here."

"Me, too. She's going to love this book. Our kid is going to be the best educated in the world." Doc gently re-wrapped the paper over the book.

"And he's going to have the best dad in the world. You're going to make a great father, Julian—you're so good with children."

"Are you okay?"

"Of course. Why?"

"Adulation saturation isn't your style."

"You just have a tough time with compliments, that's all. It's your only weakness."

"Asha would argue that point."

"She's fortunate to have a man like you in her life."

"Okay…" He laid the book on the seat. "What's going on?"

"You know I don't do holidays very well. I tend to get more introspective as I get older," she said, laughing. "Sometimes I think it would be nice to have what you and Asha have."

"You have another ten to fifteen years before you begin lamenting your life. Are you still worried about your father?"

"I try not to think about him much. It only makes me feel worse." She sipped her drink.

"Then what is it?"

"It's my life and what I'm doing with it. There has to be something more than this."

"The average person would envy your lifestyle. Adventure, traveling the world, meeting new and interesting people. I thought this was the kind of life you always wanted."

"It is—sort of. I love my work and I wouldn't trade it for anything. But sometimes it feels routine. My father taught me how to live alone, and sometimes that bothers me."

Doc studied her face. "Have you ever been in love?"

"Why would you ask me that?"

"Because I want to know. Have you?"

"No," she said uneasily.

"Have you even been in a serious relationship with *anyone*, male *or* female?"

"No," she laughed. "Where are you going with this, Dr. Sebasst?"

"Do you really want to know?"

She rested her head against his shoulder and closed her eyes. "Yes, give me your prognosis."

"You're young, beautiful, *and* rich. But you live with a married man and his wife in their home. Your life is exciting, but you don't really have an exciting life. And the only special men in your world are Marcus, your father, and I. Are you beginning to see the little hole you've dug for yourself?"

"Continue," she said.

"I understand what you're going through because I've been there before. You're a casualty of your occupation. And you've been conditioned to accept loneliness as being virtuous, which is fine until you wake up one day and discover that it's a lie. Excitement is no substitute for living a real life, Sydney. I didn't realize how incomplete and messed up I was until I met Asha, and vice versa. Therefore, I'm giving you the wisdom of a person that's been where you are now. Don't throw away your life on some illusion based on how your father lives his life. You have far too much love to offer someone to waste it. The first thing you need to do is fall in love with someone, *anyone*—then you can get the heck out of my house." He playfully nudged her shoulder, and she smiled.

"How did you and Asha know you were right for each other?"

"I don't know. We just did. One minute she was my best friend and the next, I found myself in love with her. I imagine she can tell you the exact day and time she was smitten by my charm, but the bottom line is, life has a whole lot more to offer you when you can share it with someone you love."

"No fast heartbeats or fireworks exploding in the head?"

"There's truth to the axiom that you will know when it's the right person."

"I don't make a good first impression with the men I'm attracted to."

"You're kidding."

"Nope. I have a habit of opening my big mouth or doing something stupid like…like pushing them down a flight of stairs…" She yawned.

"I could see where that would be a problem. What kind of guys are you hanging out with?"

Sydney mumbled a few unintelligible words and drifted off to sleep. Doc lifted her legs up on the couch, and pulled a blanket over her. He placed his book on the bar and poured himself a glass of ginger ale. He leaned on the bar watching Sydney sleep. She was indeed beautiful, but she was also too intimidating for most men. Her toughness was one of her greatest assets, but also her greatest liability. Her life was her work, and she paid for it at the expense of relationships. In all the years he had known her, he had never seen her with a man. Asha's attempts at matchmaking met with dismal failures. Sydney was too much like her father. She had a restless independent spirit that kept her from forming lasting relationships. It was pretty obvious to Doc that she had met someone special, and for that, he was happy for her. He finished his drink, and headed for the cockpit.

"It's about time. I thought you jumped out," Marcus said as Doc entered.

"I didn't know you were waiting for me. What's on your mind?"

"Just wanted to wish you Merry Christmas, that's all."

"Thanks, you too. Where are we?"

"Over the Norwegian Sea. We'll be touching down in Bodo in a few minutes. You want to land her, Doc?" Tre asked.

"No, but thanks."

"Hey, Tre', you want to keep your hands on that stick. I don't want my wife identifying me through a vial of my DNA," Marcus said. He swiveled around in the seat and faced Doc. "How much of a finder's fee do you think the insurance companies will pay us for recovering the Micheaux's pottery?"

"You're not serious." One look at Marcus's eyes told him he was. "You are out of your mind, you know that? Sasha Micheaux has plans to kill you, and you're thinking about double-crossing her?"

"I'm not afraid of those lunatics. We ought to be doing what is right. The Micheauxs have stolen everything they own. I can't believe you would even consider turning the ship over to them. They're a pack of thieves. The only ethical thing to do is to return the pieces to the rightful owners."

"This has nothing to do with ethics, Marcus, it's about money. Is that all you ever think about?"

"Don't be silly, of course not. But I can't afford to look a gift horse in the mouth and not see the possibilities. Besides, I have Tre' and a bunch of other kinfolk and so-called friends to think about. With Sydney back, my payroll is swollen larger than this jet. I've got expenses to meet, Doc."

"If you're so broke, why are you still buying new companies?"

"What's that got to do with anything? That's a different deal. This is this deal."

Doc shook his head, laughing. "I'll never figure you out, Marcus. Instead of thinking about a reward, you should be thinking about finding that shipment."

"That's your job—I'm just backup. What do we do when we get to Narvik?"

"It will take us about five hours to get there from Bodo. We'll check out Tow-2-Tow, and then pay a visit to the local police and see if they know anything."

Marcus passed him a cigar. "I doubt anyone up here including the police, if they even have any, is going to want to help two *brothers* recover a cache of stolen pottery. They aren't going to care a rip about us or our problems."

"Ah, boss? You may want to take a look out the right window," Tre' said. They looked down and saw three police cars waiting for them on the runway.

Doc fastened his seatbelt and extinguished the cigar. "Marcus, you seem to draw a crowd wherever you go." Tre' banked the Gulfstream to the right and began the approach to the Bodo Airfield.

* * *

The black and silver jet with the lightening bolt across the tail wing, rolled down the end of the runway and stopped in front of the waiting policemen and boarding ramp. Marcus unlocked the cabin door and a short policeman entered. He approached Marcus.

"Are you Dr. Julian Sebasst?"

"Doc, someone wants to see you," Marcus said.

Doc grabbed his bag from the overhead compartment. "I'm Sebasst."

"Come with me."

"Whoa, hold up there, man. You can't come up in here demanding anything. What is it you want?" Marcus asked.

"An acquaintance is waiting to see Dr. Sebasst in the airport. You and the lady may come also, if you wish."

"I don't know anybody in Norway," Doc said with a puzzled look on his face.

"Please, follow me." The officer escorted them to a machine shop and told them to wait. He closed the door behind him.

Marcus sat on a stool with his legs crossed. "Don't cops in Europe have regular offices? I'm tired of being dragged to some back-alley room every time they have something to say."

The door opened and a barrel-chested black man with a cherubim face, and a watermelon-shaped head entered the room. "Long time no see, Doc. How's it hangin'?" Mallon Jefferson asked.

"What are you doing here, Jefferson?" Doc asked.

"Cleaning up some other country's mess, as usual. How about you?"

"You wouldn't be here if you didn't know that already."

The big man laughed. "Actually, I don't. I just got the word yesterday that you were coming in this morning. My people wanted me to meet you here."

"Who exactly are your people?" Marcus asked.

"The State Department."

"I can't believe you're still telling that lie. You need to come up with a better cover than that. What is it you want from me?" Doc asked.

Jefferson smirked. "You haven't changed a bit after all these years."

"Jefferson, what do you want?"

"Like I said, we're trying to clean up a little mess. What do you know of Admiral Terrance Bloodstone?"

"He's the British Royal Navy fleet commander—and jerk, from what I've read."

"That may be, but he's also one of the most powerful men in the British government. How well do you know his wife, Jordan Bloodstone?"

"Don't beat around the bush, Jefferson—get to the point."

Jefferson plopped his wide butt in the chair. "She disappeared right after her brothers' funerals, along with some classified documents she stole

117

from the British Defense Ministry. She used that information to find Leon-Francis and smoke Jason Worrick. She…"

"Hold up, man. Are you talking about Jordan Toussaint?" Marcus asked.

Jefferson was annoyed by the interruption. "Yeah, the same woman. Colonel Bloodstone has created a sticky problem for our two countries. She's an American citizen serving in the British military, with top military clearance, but that's another story. She steals top secret information, not to mention some sensitive electronic equipment, and then proceeds to wipe out half the male population of Norway. The NSA reports she's taking out people faster than cancer on some mountaintop near the Swedish border. If you ask me, the *sister* is crazy, but the fleet commander wants her back and safe. And so do we. But it must be handled discreetly. This can't look like the military came to rescue a crazed murderer. It has to be a civilian operation all the way, which is where you come in. We want you to locate her for us. We'll provide you with whatever you need for the job. You find her, give us her exact location, and we'll extract her."

"I don't believe you people. You have known about Devin Leon-Francis for years and have done absolutely nothing to stop him. Now that a British commander is upset and afraid that his black wife will embarrass him, you're willing to move heaven and earth." Doc pointed his finger at him. "If you had dealt with Leon-Francis, you wouldn't be in this position. My heart goes out to Jordan, it really does, but I have my own problems to deal with right now. And I don't work for the government anymore—in case you forgot. This is your problem, you deal with it."

Jefferson jumped from his chair. "Let me tell you something. If the Colonel is alive, she's going to stand trial for espionage and for murdering Jason Worrick—and God only knows how many more people. If she's lucky, she'll get off with life. Is that the way you think Momma Toussaint wants to remember her baby girl? The woman has already lost two sons, and you'll be responsible if her daughter is lost, too."

"Listen to me, Jefferson, and listen well," Doc said. "Don't you ever mention the Toussaints as though you are familiar. The only thing you know about the family or Jordan is what you've read in some government dossier."

"Look, Doc, all I'm saying is, we can smooth this all out for her when she gets home, as long as our governments are officially not involved. You're the only one who can help her at this point *and* possibly save her career in the process."

"Answer my question. Why didn't you do something about Leon-Francis a long time ago?"

Jefferson rummaged through his pockets until he found a cigarette stub. "It's not our job to go after every crook in the world. Unless they're a national threat, we could care less." Doc shot him another cold stare. "Hey, brother, I'm just telling it like it is, that's all."

"Where is Jordan, now?" Marcus asked.

"Somewhere in Lapland, around Kiruna. The NSA tracked a signal from the homing chip sewn in the liner of her snowsuit. But the signal hasn't moved in a couple of days, which may mean she's already dead. In that case, you're in luck. If she's alive, Leon-Francis' men probably have her by now. They've been tracking her for days."

"I don't like you, Jefferson, or your methods. You're a liar, and I wouldn't trust you even if you were saddled and had a bridle bit in your mouth. You want my help, then you help me first," Doc said.

"What do you want?"

"The truth, starting with how much you know about the Micheauxs and Merovingians."

"I know you're searching for the *Vincien Micheaux*, but you won't find it. It's sitting at the bottom of the ocean—you want the coordinates?" he asked, sarcastically. "We don't care about the freighter, or Sasha Micheaux. We're only interested in the headman, Anthony Chiapetta. He is the Medusa head, and the power behind the Merovingian council. We get him—the rest will crumble."

"You're crazy, Jefferson."

Jefferson leaned back on the door. "You made our job easier by taking down the Micheaux family a couple of pegs. With those homo twins out of the way, Chiapetta has to deal with their bitchy sister, and she's a handful. Chiapetta is old school and Sasha is twenty-first century, ambitious, and smart. She's a threat to him, and he'll do whatever it takes to get rid of her. He's vulnerable and he's going to make a mistake. Then we go after him."

Doc kept staring at him. "You're crazy."

"Yeah, you told me," he said angrily as he stomped his cigarette out on the floor. "Are you going to do this—or what!"

"Man, don't raise your voice up in here," Marcus warned. Jefferson relaxed and fell back against the door.

"What's between the Micheauxs and Leon-Francis?" Doc asked.

Jefferson sighed. "The Micheauxs have been trying to wrestle control of the Merovingian Council from Chiapetta for years, but Chiapetta has powerful friends backing him like Devin Leon-Francis."

"Leon-Francis and Chiapetta know each other?"

"Yeah, they have some history together. They were friends long before Leon-Francis went over to the dark side. They have an agreement. Chiapetta keeps the council's nose out of Leon-Francis' business interests *and* out of North America in exchange for Leon-Francis' continued friendship and support. With the Micheauxs in charge of the council, you can bet they wouldn't be so amenable to Leon-Francis' terms. Sasha wants to expand the council's influence to Quebec City—Leon-Francis' backyard. That's something he won't allow to happen. Consequently, there is no love lost between the two. Sasha Micheaux is Leon-Francis' worst enemy about now."

"So I guess the Micheauxs were never high on your priority list, either."

Jefferson tugged his pants up over his belly. "Like I said, Sasha is a small fish swimming with sharks. We want Chiapetta. Don't worry about her, she'll tumble with the rest of them when Chiapetta goes down. By the way, why does she have her ring in your nose? What's so damn important about that freighter of hers?"

"That's my business. If I do this, I want assurances that Jordan won't be screwed over like I was," Doc said.

"You've got it. I give you my word," Jefferson said eagerly. He extended his hand, but Doc didn't move.

"Your word is as worthless as monopoly money at Saks. I want guarantees from the Brits, Norwegians, and the U.S. that she walks away from this. *And* I want it in writing. Cabinet level only."

He withdrew his hand. "That's impossible. You know I can't get you that kind of approval."

"Then we're through talking."

"You know, you have sealed your friend's death."

"That's probably a kinder fate than what awaits her back home from people like you. I'll be in Narvik for a few days if you change your mind." Doc turned his back and walked over to Marcus and Sydney.

Jefferson slammed the door as he left the room.

Marcus looked at Doc. "Damn, I thought I was hard. You didn't give the brother any slack. Don't you think we could have brokered a deal with him to help us if we helped him?"

"Remember that incident I told you about when I was in the Secret Service years ago—involving the American diplomat who raped that little Portuguese girl?"

"Yeah, the guy you had to bust a cap on?"

Doc sat down on the corner of the workbench. "Well, Jefferson was the spin-doctor the government sent in to cover it up. He pretended to be on my side, but when he was through, he had turned a perverted diplomat into a patron saint, and the little girl was made out to be a prostitute. I got the blame laid on me, and Jefferson finessed the cover-up all the way through the Treasury Department and the Oval Office. By the time he was through with me, *I* almost believed his side of the story. Now, is that the kind of man you want to trust?"

"I don't like him, but we can't leave Jordan out to dry either," Marcus said.

"He'll have to eat a little pride, but we'll see him again."

Chapter 15

The Narvik police chief didn't like being intimidated by anyone, especially people like Mallon Jefferson. The obnoxious fat man and the Norwegian Prime Minister's office warned him to stop his investigation of Jordan Bloodstone. He'd considered backing off, until he woke this morning to news that two black Americans were in town asking questions about her and Tow-2-Tow International. Everyone seemed to have an interest in what had happened in his town, and he was about to find out why. He stuffed his bottle of antacid in his jacket and kissed his wife goodbye.

The ride to the hotel took ten minutes. The hotel manager gave him the room numbers of the Americans. He took the elevator up to the second floor and knocked on Sydney Bellashota's door.

Doc and Marcus were downstairs sharing a carafe of orange juice while they waited for Sydney to join them for breakfast.

"Didn't you say Sydney was leaving her room ten minutes ago?" Doc asked.

"Yeah, but she probably decided to change her clothes or something. You know how she is," Marcus said. He pulled out the business section of the newspaper. "Although, the last thing I would be concerned about out here is my wardrobe. This place is depressing, I'll be glad to get out of here."

"How's the acquisition of Cornerstone going?"

Marcus stuck his head around the side of the newspaper. "How'd you know about Cornerstone?"

"You aren't the only one that reads newspapers. I thought you were getting out of this kind of life," Doc said, buttering a muffin.

"This is a good deal. You know how much money there is to be made in insurance recovery. It's a great acquisition and Cornerstone is a natural fit for a man of my talents. You want a piece of the action?"

"No, but thanks for the offer. Since you seem to be an expert on financial matters, I've got a question for you."

Marcus folded the newspaper and laid it on the chair beside him. He looked at Doc over the rims of his glasses. "What's the problem?"

"Why would a man worth $80 billion risk everything he owns, including his daughter's love, for $200 million?"

"If you're talking about Leon-Francis, he isn't exactly your run-of-the-mill criminal, and he sure as hell doesn't think like one. Who knows why he does what he does. Something on Sasha's freighter was pretty damn important to him."

"I'm surprised he hasn't contacted Sydney by now."

"His old ass is too damn embarrassed. How is he going to rationalize this crap to her?"

"He's had this planned for a long time, and he had to have help on the inside to pull it off."

"Chiapetta?"

"He runs the council and is probably the least likely to be suspected."

"I saw the freighter's manifest list and there wasn't anything on that boat worth all this trouble," Marcus said.

"I agree. Do you still have a copy of your file on Devin Leon-Francis?"

Marcus stole a muffin off Doc's plate and took a bite. "Of course, Benno has it in our San Francisco office. What do you want to know?"

"Everything you have."

"Okay."

"I also want the information we collected on the Micheaux twins."

"The stuff we sent to the Feds?"

"Yeah, we still have a copy don't we?"

"Sure, but it's got to be six or seven hundred pages."

"Well, I need it."

"Okay, Benno will have it to you by tonight."

A few minutes later, Sydney got off the elevator with a tall stranger wearing a plaid mackinaw jacket. He had a thick mane of brown hair down to his waist, high Slavic cheekbones, and Asiatic eyes. They entered the café and approached the table.

The man pulled up a chair and flashed his badge. "My name is Jukurro. I understand you are inquiring about Tow-2-Tow International and Jordan Bloodstone."

"What do you know about her?" Marcus asked.

"First, tell me who you are and what you're doing here."

"My name is St. John. This is my partner, Sebasst. Jordan is a friend of ours and we're looking for her. We were told she might be in Narvik."

Jukurro eyed him suspiciously.

Doc interrupted. "Look. A man named Mallon Jefferson, who works for the U.S. State Department, told us she might be in Kiruna."

"So why are you in Narvik and not Kiruna?"

"We have some business here to take care of first," Doc said.

"What's your interest in Tow-2-Tow International?"

Marcus didn't like the Chief's pointed questions. He rudely picked up his newspaper and resumed reading.

"We're looking for a lost cargo freighter that disappeared near here. Tow-2-Tow answered the distress call, but the ship is still missing. The owner hired us to find it," Doc said.

"Who is the owner?"

"Micheaux Freight and Cargo."

"Any relation to the Micheauxs that I've been reading about in the newspaper?"

"Yes."

Jukurro tapped his fingers on the table. "What was the cargo?" Marcus held his breath—hoping Doc would lie.

"Two-hundred million dollars worth of art," Doc said.

"Damn!" Marcus said, dropping the paper to his side.

Jukurro's right eye twitched.

"I'm just being honest with you. You were bound to hear about it sooner or later," Doc said.

"How is Andy Preston involved in this?"

"You know Preston?" Marcus asked.

"He's the office manager of Tow-2-Tow, and a prime suspect in a murder investigation."

"Of who?" Doc asked.

"An American named Tiberius Woodberry. Do you know him?"

"He works for my father," Sydney blurted, without thinking.

"D.L. Francis is your father?"

"Yes."

"Do you know where he is?"

"No, I'm trying to find him."

Jukurro's eye twitched again. He put his notepad in his pocket. "Just exactly how many people *are* you searching for?"

"It's a complicated story," Doc said. "I will be more than happy to discuss it with you, but right now I need to know about Jordan Bloodstone. Do you have any idea where she is?"

"No. I am surprised that your friend Mallon Jefferson doesn't know. He seemed to know everything else when he paid me a visit the other night."

"He's not my friend."

"That's refreshing to hear. Jordan Bloodstone spent a considerable amount of time with Andy Preston before she disappeared a few weeks ago. I want to know why."

"You have to ask her. I don't know," Doc said.

"I see." He burped. "Excuse me." He quickly wiped his mouth with a handkerchief. "Now the Micheaux family is under investigation for art thefts. I assume the mysterious ship you're searching for is carrying contraband?"

"Probably," Doc said.

"I see." Jukurro sighed. "I appreciate your candidness, but I can't offer you any help. My only concern is apprehending Andy Preston, and the Tow-2-Tow office is off limits until I have completed my investigation." Jukurro groaned, clutched his stomach, and bent over in the chair.

"You okay?" Doc asked.

"Yes…just a little gallbladder problem. What's your first name?" he whispered in pain.

"Julian, but people call me Doc. You sure you're alright?"

"Yes. I'm fine," he said, rubbing his stomach. He turned to Marcus. "And you Mr. St. John—your name?"

"Marcus."

"No nickname?"

Marcus was losing patience. "Qwik—is there a point to any of these questions?"

"I like that name—Qwik. It seems well suited to you. I prefer dealing with first names, if that is okay with you?"

"Fine, call me anything you'd like. How about answering Doc's question."

Jukurro groaned again. "Marcus, you strike me as being an honorable man, and you're direct. I like that, too."

"Damn, are you like the passive-aggressive cop they keep for special emergencies around here? I'm going outside for a smoke." He got up from the table. "Is Jukurro your first or last name?"

"Just Jukurro."

Sydney also rose from the table. "I'll be back. I need to get some breakfast."

Jukurro watched them as they left through the lobby doors. "You and Qwik have been friends for a long time?"

"Since we were kids," Doc said, pouring himself another glass of orange juice.

"That's good. Everyone should have at least one good friend they can always count on. Sydney said you two are partners in a security company in California—the St. John-Sebasst Security Force."

"I own a piece of the business, but it's Marcus's company."

"I see. And how do you know Jordan Bloodstone?"

"I told you. She's a friend of ours."

"Why are you looking for her?"

"Our government wants her home."

"You work for the government?"

Doc's patience was thinning. "Are you ever going to answer my questions?"

"Maybe."

Doc waited for him to say more, but he didn't. "No, not anymore. I'm a pastor."

Jukurro's eyes lit up. "A pastor. Why is a pastor working for the Micheaux family?"

"It's personal. Let's just say the lives of some people I love are dependent on me finding that ship."

"And if you find it, what then?"

"We all go home."

"What happens to the artifacts?"

"That's not my problem. Look, Jukurro, I don't want to step on your toes, but I need your help. This is a lot more complicated than some stolen artifacts. And if I don't find that shipment soon, a lot more people will probably die."

"Tell me more about D.L. Francis."

"I can't do that. It's not my call. If you want to know more about Sydney's father you have to ask her."

"Fair enough," Jukurro said.

* * *

A foul odor filled the morning air. The snow-covered streets were polluted with the black resin of the rail yard. A truck carrying a load of precious coal sped through the intersection, spraying the sidewalks with its black slush. Sydney jumped back on the curb to avoid being hit.

She had on a blue leather pantsuit with dark, blue tinted glasses. One of the men said something funny, and she smiled. She was even lovelier than Carlos remembered.

He was across the street in a parking garage talking with his brother on the telephone. Enric Bourbon had bad news. Anthony Chiapetta had used his position on the council to transfer control of the Knight Guardians to

Eisenstadt. Together, they seized the Merovingian treasury in Languedoc-Roussillon, and were planning to convene a secret meeting of the council within the next forty-eight hours. Sasha had been right. Chiapetta and the council were making their move against the Micheaux and Bourbon families. The fate and wealth of the Bourbon family depended on the survival of the Micheauxs, and the Micheauxs were dependent on the Knight Guardians. Without the Knights, Carlos knew Anthony Chiapetta would be hard to stop. Sydney and the men crossed the intersection and headed toward the harbor.

"Enric, I have to go. I want you to follow Chiapetta wherever he goes. Find out when and where the meeting will take place." He snapped the cell phone closed and followed them.

They ended up at Andy Preston's office, at Tow-2-Tow. His office reeked of Old English furniture polish and saltwater. Doc raised the blinds and opened the louvered windows for some fresh air, but it smelled even worse outside.

Marcus stood guard by the window while Jukurro talked with Sydney in the other room. "I can't believe Jukurro gave you ten minutes in here. How did you swing that?"

"His people have been through every inch of this place—and they've confiscated the computers. He doesn't think we'll find anything." Doc opened the bottom drawers of the desk. "But there may be a manual log of some kind around here." He closed the drawers and started shuffling through the mountain of maritime books stacked on the credenza.

"This place looks and smells worse than the gym back home. I'm surprised you could find the top of the desk." Marcus's hand rested on a U-shaped counter littered with junked VHF radio equipment and electronics. An oversized book protruded from the bottom shelf. "Columbo, is that what you're looking for?"

Doc stepped over some boxes to get to the logbook.

"What's your read on Jukurro?" Marcus asked.

"He's okay...just a cop trying to do his job." Doc flipped through the pages. "This lists the names of the tugs, departure and return dates, but nothing about their destination." He studied the large laminated map stuffed with pushpins hanging from the wall. The map legend identified the vessel name and location. He glanced at the book again. "There are over sixty ships in this book, and half of them seem to be in service off the Norwegian coast."

"Which one was dispatched to the Micheaux freighter?"

"Impossible to tell by just looking at the map. I need to cross-reference the pins with the log. Doc pushed a pile of papers off the table so he could work. He laid the book down, and began writing. Marcus kept watching Jukurro through the window. Ten minutes later, Sydney signaled that they were through.

"We don't have any more time, Doc, Jukurro will be back in a minute."

"Then go out there and stall him. I'm not finished here."

Marcus pulled a knife from his pocket and slit the binding on the book. "Like I said, we're out of time. Take the ones you need—here." He handed the pages to Doc and threw the book under the table.

"And I suppose you're going to take down the wall, too. These pages are meaningless without the map."

Marcus patted his pockets for the miniature camera Sydney had given him. He took five snapshots of the map, and handed the camera to Doc. "Anything else?"

* * *

Jukurro locked the office door behind them and walked them as far as the railway terminal. "I have to make a stop. I expect you to give me a call if you find out anything I might be interested in."

Marcus smirked as the Chief walked away. "What makes him think we'd tell him anything?"

"We owe him, and we're honorable men. Remember?" Doc said.

Sydney walked between them as they began climbing the steep hill back to the hotel.

"How did it go with Jukurro?" Doc asked.

"He asked a lot of questions about Tiberius Woodberry, most of which I couldn't answer. He's one of three bodyguards who work for my father. That's all I know."

"Maybe your father is in Narvik," Marcus said.

"This is the last place he would be. Jukurro seems more interested in finding Andy Preston right now than my father," she answered solemnly.

"Andy Preston is as good as dead if he whacked your daddy's man. Things are bad when the rats start biting off each other's heads. This time your daddy has bitten off more than he can chew. With two of his top people gone, his organization is falling apart faster than Enron," Marcus said.

"My father will never allow himself to be caught, so don't fool yourself into believing that we'll succeed where others have failed. I'm here for one reason only, and that's to see my father. Nothing else. And then I'm going home."

"You're planning on sweeping all this stuff under the rug?" Marcus asked.

"There are always two sides to every story."

"Yeah, and both your daddy's sides are bad," Marcus murmured.

Sydney stopped in mid-stride and faced him. "Let it rest, Marcus!" Doc gently coaxed Sydney away from Marcus and steered her across the street.

"Where are you two going?" Marcus asked.

"We'll meet you back at the hotel in a couple of hours," Doc said.

Marcus watched as they walked back down the hill and disappeared. *"I'll be damned if I'm going to apologize every time I tell the truth."* He stuck his hands in his pockets and went to the hotel.

* * *

Doc found a secluded table in the German bakery shop, located in the train station. Outside the window, the sky had turned black. He smoothed the napkin over his lap. "Are you okay?"

"Marcus is getting on my last nerve with his constant digs against my father. How am I supposed to react?"

"You don't have to explain yourself to me, Sydney. He's your father and you have a right to defend him. But in all fairness to Marcus, there is a lot of truth in what he says. He may not be the most subtle person in the world, but he's not telling you something you don't already know."

"I know, but it hurts worse coming from him. Everyone thinks they're an authority on my father—including jerks like Mallon Jefferson and Jukurro. My father is not the sum of snippets of information contained in some Washington file, or the composite collection of stories and myths about him. He has another side, and that's the part I'll always love and defend to the death, if I have to. So yes, I get a little testy when people want to paint him with a broad brush as being the evil Svengeli of the world. He has always been there for me since my mother died."

"What kind of woman was she?"

"My mother?"

"Yeah."

"I don't remember much about her. I was only six when she died. But my father worshiped her."

"How did they meet?"

"My father hired her as an interpreter when he visited Sardinia on a business trip. They married a few months later."

"Fast courtship. An Italian Catholic marrying an American Jew must have created a local stir."

"I'm sure it did," she smiled.

"How did she die?"

"Tippi Sampa had her killed."

Doc stopped eating. "The Sampa crime family from Louisiana?" She nodded her head. "I'm sorry. I never knew."

"It's okay. I didn't find out the truth until years later, when my father finally admitted to me why he was so overprotective of me. Sampa wanted a piece of my father's business empire, and my father fought him. When negotiation failed, he tried intimidation. And when that didn't work, he had my mother killed. My father was never the same after that. He killed Sampa and his family, and took over their drug and gambling operation in Louisiana. He hasn't looked back since." Sydney pushed her untouched sandwich aside and folded her napkin. "The years went by and he made more enemies and went underground more often. But he always took care of me and saw that I lived as normal a life as possible. He's sacrificed his life to ensure my happiness and safety, and I can't ignore that, especially knowing that his life would have been different if my mother hadn't died. People might not be so glib if they knew all the facts."

Doc picked up his croissant again and nibbled on the corner. "Sydney, everyone has a crossroad in their life where they have to choose their path. Some like your father's are clearly marked by tragic circumstances, while others aren't. I knew a man who was a loser all his life. He was a deadbeat dad, a misogynist, a drunk, *and* a crook. His oldest boy ended up being a wife-beating alcoholic thug like him, and is still in prison. The other son turned out to be a loving father and husband, and a responsible human being. If you ask the brothers why they chose the path they did, they would both say it was because of their father. Marcus's brother didn't expect to be anything other than what his father was, because that's what he saw modeled in the home. Marcus, on the other hand, didn't want to be anything like his old man. He decided to make something of his life, just as you decided not to follow your father's example. Your father chose the wrong path, and in doing so, he has hurt and killed many people. So you can't expect a whole lot of sympathy from people like Marcus. He's been there. He's entitled to blow off a few sarcastic remarks from time to time. That's how he deals with his frustration, and it's a small pain to endure."

"I still don't like it."

"I know you don't. I'm just asking you to be a little more tolerant of him. Try to ignore him as I do. It works every time." He saw a slight smile on her face. "I'll talk with him when we get back, okay?"

"Okay."

"Enough about your father. Tell me about you."

"Me? You know everything there is to know about me."

"I know you're Jewish, but are you a naturalized Israeli citizen, or were you born somewhere else?"

"Born in Jerusalem, 1970, if you must know." She pulled her sunglasses down over the bridge of her nose. "Are you trying to profile me, Julian?"

He laughed as he bit off another piece of croissant. "Just trying to fill in some gaps on the Leon-Francis family tree, that's all."

"I could tell you every place we lived and how long we were there. But it wouldn't help. My father is too smart to stay in any one place too long. By the time you think you know where he is, he's gone."

Chapter 16

Doc and Sydney took a walk along the harbor before returning to the hotel. Marcus was waiting for them in the lobby. Sydney's laptop computer sat open on the coffee table next to the television.

"What are you doing?" Sydney asked.

"I thought we were here on business, not a vacation," Marcus said. I've been waiting for you guys. You ready to work?" He turned the television off.

Doc connected Marcus's digital camera to the computer and uploaded the images of the map in Andy Preston's office. He cropped the five photos into one composite picture, and enhanced the size. "It's not Rand McNally quality, but it'll have to do." He unfolded the torn pages from the logbook and spread them on the table. The photo showed thirty-nine pushpins clustered in northern Europe. Doc sized the picture then cut and pasted it onto a blank template, along with the map legend. "Okay, let's see what we have."

Sydney and Marcus matched up the numbered pushpins to the vessel names, while Doc cross-referenced the names to the log sheets. When they finished, three vessels were unaccounted for.

"The *Cyrus*, *Norwegian Dawn*, and *Tempestroll*. Two oceanic tugs and a salvage rig. All three were dispatched to the Arctic Sea the same night the *Vincien Micheaux* disappeared, but it doesn't say why. According to the log, none of them have returned to Narvik. If Mallon Jefferson is right, and the *Vincien Micheaux* was sunk, then it's reasonable to assume that the shipment was transferred to one of the tugs," Doc said. He noticed a missed entry. "I found another one. A grain freighter—*Angela's Storm*, with Panamanian registry."

"*Angela's Storm*?" Sydney asked.

"Yes."

"My mother's first name was Angela."

Marcus searched the monitor screen trying to find the pin. "Here it is," he said, pointing to the placement of the pin on the map. "Looks like it's somewhere off the coast of Greenland."

Doc studied the log sheets. "That's odd. This is the only freighter in Tow-2-Tow's fleet, and there are no log entries telling us where it came from or where it went. I find it hard to believe it's out there circling the Arctic."

"Leon-Francis has a zillion-dollar yacht, but he names a freighter after his dead wife. What kind of sense does that make?" Marcus asked. Doc looked up at him. "What—I got a booger on my face? Why are you looking at me like that?"

"You may have a point. Why would he name the freighter after his wife? What's the name of your father's yacht, Sydney?" Doc asked.

"*White Nightingale.*"

"How often does he stay on the boat?"

"Rarely. He uses it mostly for vacations."

"So where do you two meet when you want to see each other?"

"Usually at my ranch in California."

"I didn't even know you owned a ranch," Marcus grumbled.

"You think he's on *Angela's Storm*, don't you?" Sydney asked.

"I think it's a good bet," Doc said.

"That's crazy," Marcus said.

"Actually, it's brilliant. Who would think to look for him on a grain freighter? With a couple of tons of grain on the deck for show and false papers, he could dock anywhere in the world. And he would have enough room in the hull to transport that helicopter of his," Doc said.

"I could see my father doing something like that," Sydney said.

"I'm betting that wherever the *Angela's Storm* is, those missing tugboats will be."

"Okay, if you're right, how do we find him?" Marcus asked.

"All countries keep shipping and commerce records of ships entering their waterways and ports. Finding the ships is the easy part."

* * *

Doc spent the rest of the day and evening sequestered in his hotel room, studying the 481-page report on Devin Leon-Francis. Some of the information was inconsistent with what Sydney had told him. The biggest discrepancy surrounded the eight years Devin Leon-Francis vanished without a trace. Six of those years were when he was married to Angela Lia Belleshota. He didn't resurface in public until 1978. *Where had he been hiding all that time?* Doc didn't find the answer in the mountain of papers he had scattered across the bed. It was 2:10 in the morning and he had a headache. He popped some aspirin in his mouth and found a spot on the bed to lie down, but his mind kept racing. Doc couldn't convince himself that Leon-Francis would roam the seas on a freighter for six years. He had to have a more secure hideout somewhere.

The telephone rang. Doc rolled across the bed and reached for the phone.

"I received your message. Don't you ever sleep, Dr. Sebasst?" Benno asked.

"Not when you fax me a report larger than the New York telephone book. I need you to do something for me. Contact the Seafarer Union and see if they can trace the ports of destination on a freighter named *Angela's Storm*. Then I want you to confirm the date Tippi Sampa was killed by Mr. Leon-Francis, and run a background check on Sydney."

"Ms. Belleshota?" he stammered.

"Yes."

"This will take some time. Your deadline with Sasha Micheaux is in two days."

"Don't worry about that. Just get it to me as fast as you can."

Doc hung up and called Marcus's room. He left the door cracked for him and went back to work.

Marcus showed up a few minutes later in pajamas and a sports coat. He closed the door behind him. "I swear, you must have vampire blood in your veins." He yawned as he sat on the edge of the bed. "It's three in the morning, Doc. This better be good."

"Do you know how ridiculous you look?"

"Save the flattery, what do you want to talk about?"

"Sydney."

"We've been over this before. I got the message loud and clear. I have no intention of mentioning her father to her."

"This isn't about Leon-Francis. It's about Sydney."

"Sydney?"

"Yeah. How long has she worked for you?"

"On and off, maybe ten years. Why?"

"Just curious. How did you two meet?"

"She was looking for work after she moved back to the states from the Middle East. She spent some time with the Israeli police and had great references, so I hired her. It's probably the best business decision I ever made." Marcus leaned back on the bed, resting on his elbows.

"How accurate is this information?"

"It's accurate. Why?"

"It says Sydney's mother died in 1974. Sydney says it was 1976."

"She's mistaken." Doc started to ask another question, but someone knocked on the door. Marcus jumped off the bed. "You expecting more guests?"

"Relax, it's only Sydney. I forgot we were going for a walk."

"A walk! This time of night?" Marcus peeked through the eyehole and saw a large black head. "It's your friend, Mellonhead." He opened the door. Mallon Jefferson gave him a contemptuous look as he entered. Jefferson was wearing the same rumpled suit he had on in Bodo and he looked like he hadn't slept since the last time they saw him.

Marcus rubbed his fingers on Jefferson's coat. "Brother, I can hook you up with a good tailor if you want."

Jefferson brushed past him and handed Doc a brown envelope. "You got what you wanted." Doc read the signed affidavits carefully before placing them back in the envelope. "Those signatures didn't come easily."

"Yeah, well, I really don't care, as long as you got them."

"We care. The rules have changed. You have to go in and get Bloodstone on your own. We'll evac her once she's safe, but your people do the grunt work. That's the deal. No negotiations. Take it or leave it."

"Where is she?" Doc asked.

* * *

A foul smelling fog descended over downtown Narvik, blackening out what little light pierced through the clouds. Sydney was outside the hotel waiting for Doc. Jefferson ignored her as he passed on the way to his waiting car.

Eleven minutes later, Doc came out. "I thought we were meeting in my room," he said, buttoning his coat.

They started walking. "I saw Mallon Jefferson in the hall and figured he had business with you. Any news on your friend, Jordan?"

"Your father is holding her in an iron mine outside Kiruna. We're going in to get her."

"Oh, that's a surprise," she said, smiling. "That's cutting things close. We only have a couple of days left to find the artifacts."

"Yeah, we're going to need some help." They crossed the street and walked down the hill toward the harbor.

Two men stood in the shadows watching them until they were gone. The men entered the hotel from the alley, slipped through the empty lobby, and sneaked up the back steps to the second floor. The smaller man stood watch over the elevators at the end of the hall. The Swede picked the door lock and quietly entered the room. He pulled a small piece of synthetic rope from his pocket, and approached the bed where Marcus was snoring. The big man slipped the rope over Marcus's neck and lifted him off the bed like a rag doll.

Marcus coughed and spit as he fought for air. He tried squeezing his fingers between the rope and his neck, but the man was too powerful. Marcus's eyes slowly closed and he stopped struggling. Thinking he was unconscious, the Swede lowered him to the floor. Marcus stomped his heel on the man's foot, and he loosened his grip long enough for Marcus to gasp air. He swung his elbow back into the man's ribs as they both fell backwards on the bed. Marcus turned around and head-butted him in the face.

The man at the elevator heard the Swede yelling for help. He ran down the hallway and burst into the room. Marcus grabbed one of his guns off the nightstand table and fired. The man stumbled back out the door. The stunned Swede struggled to his feet. He turned around just in time to see Marcus delivering a spinning back kick to his head. The Swede went headfirst through the glass window and landed on the sidewalk.

Marcus grabbed his other gun off the table and raced down the stairs to find Doc and Sydney.

* * *

Doc and Sydney walked along the water, passing the quays and railroad station before ending up at an industrial construction site, where they ran out of sidewalk and lights. They turned around and headed back.

"Since I'm risking my life for this woman, I should at least know something about her," Sydney said.

"I don't have much to tell. She's the youngest in the family and the only one to make the Marines a career. She was stationed in England, where she met and married Bloodstone. He's sixteen years her senior. Their marriage was in trouble from the beginning. Having a beautiful wife was one thing, but that she was black became a political liability he couldn't overcome. They separated a few weeks before her brothers died. The Toussaints are a close-knit family, but I would never have guessed Jordan would do something like this. Even if she makes it out of this alive, her career is over."

"I have mixed feelings about risking my life to save a woman who's trying to kill my father."

Doc stopped walking. "How do you think she'd feel being rescued by the daughter of the man she hates?"

"Yes, that's pretty bizarre, too. Let's keep moving, it's getting cold out here." She held his arm as they passed a construction trailer.

"Do you remember spending time on a boat or freighter while you were growing up?" Doc asked.

Sydney laughed. "I wouldn't forget something like living on a freighter, Julian. I told you I was too young to remember a lot about my childhood. But I do remember as a child having reoccurring dreams of being surrounded by walls and metal stairs, but it definitely wasn't on a boat or ship. I would see my father floating in the air, waving to me as he disappeared in the clouds. I always thought he was going to heaven and I would never see him again."

"And you don't think that could have been on a large freighter?"

"The dreams were too surreal for it to be an actual place."

Doc heard a noise behind them and turned around. Then came the voice.

"Sydney, step away from him—get out of the way." She pulled her gun from the holster, but still couldn't see the face of the silhouetted man. "Step away, Sydney, and you won't get hurt." The voice was familiar. Doc saw four men moving slowly toward them. He stepped behind Sydney as the figure emerged from the shadow of the building.

Sydney recognized him. "What are you doing here?"

"This isn't your fight, Sydney," he said.

Sydney pointed her gun at him. "Where's my father, Morgan?"

Doc inched his fingers in between the back vent of Sydney's coat and found the spare gun she carried on her waist. Morgan stood forty yards away in front of her. He signaled and the others came out of hiding.

Sydney and Doc stepped backwards as the men formed an arc in front of them.

A short man with a handlebar mustache suddenly appeared next to Morgan. It was Fisher—her father's personal bodyguard and a cold-blooded killer.

"What's this about, Fisher?" Sydney asked.

Fisher stood with his hands in the pocket of his trench coat. "Don't get in my way, Sydney. I only want Sebasst. It's your choice whether you want to join him or not. You have twenty seconds to make up your mind."

Sydney used her other hand to help steady her gun. "Don't be a fool. How are you going to explain shooting me to my father?"

"By telling him the truth. You chose your friends over your family. You have nine seconds left," Fisher said, as the men broadened the circle around them.

The situation was hopeless and Doc knew it. "Do what he says, Sydney." He reached over her shoulder and lowered her arm. "We're outnumbered—don't die because of me." Doc dropped his gun on the ground. "She gives up. Don't shoot." He stepped out in front of her.

"Julian!" she cried. Doc turned. She fired. Two bullets flew past his cheek and hit Morgan's forehead. She fired again, hitting Fisher. Doc and Sydney hit the ground as gunshots erupted. When the shooting stopped, Sydney rose to her feet. Doc stood up and shook the snow from his coat.

"Are you okay?" she asked.

He looked at the dead bodies lying on the ground. "Yeah, I think so. What happened?"

"I don't know for sure." She went over to Morgan's body. He was dead. Fisher lay beside him—his eyes open and a gunshot wound in the chest.

She pointed the gun at him. "Where's my father, Fisher?"

"Go to hell, Sydney." She fired twice.

"Sydney!" Doc shouted, grabbing the gun from her hand.

"I'm pissed right now, Julian. I never liked this guy and I wasn't going to lose sleep wondering if I'd see him again." She turned and walked away, shaking and confused by what had just happened. The only thing she knew for certain was that she saw the tail of Carlos Bourbon's white coat disappearing around the corner.

Chapter 17

Jukurro's head was in the toilet bowl when he received news of the shootings. Minutes later he arrived at the crime scene on the harbor, where he saw Marcus sitting on the steps of the construction trailer. He shook his bottle of antacid before getting out of the car. He ducked under the crime tape and went over to inspect the first body. When finished, he re-zipped the bag, and moved to the next one.

The trailer door opened, and Doc and Sydney appeared followed by one of Jukurro's men.

"How did it go?" Marcus asked.

"A whole lot of questions and not many answers," Doc said.

Marcus saw Jukurro watching them out of the corner of his eye as a police officer briefed him on what happened. "You know this dude, Jukurro, is a straight arrow who plays it by the book. He's not going to want to hear any self-defense excuses, and he certainly isn't going to let us roll up out of here unless we feed him a bone. We can't afford to be wasting our time in Narvik, Doc. Time is running out. We have to get Jordan." He flicked his lighter and touched it to his cigar. Jukurro broke off his conversation. "Looks like your boy is heading this way."

"You people have had a busy night. I understand these dead men also worked for your father?" Jukurro asked.

"Yes," Sydney said.

"And the two dead men at the hotel?"

"Yes," Marcus said.

"And they tried to kill you?"

"You think this is a tattoo stenciled around my neck?" Marcus asked, showing him his rope burn.

Jukurro lightly touched his finger on the raw skin. "I see," he said, scratching his chin. He twisted the bottle cap back on his medicine bottle and turned his attention to Sydney. "And just why does your father want all of you dead?" He took a seat on the steps next to Marcus, crossed his legs, and pulled out his notepad. He didn't give them a chance to answer. "Let's start from the beginning."

Sydney's eyes blazed with anger. "Look, Jukurro. I'll tell you everything you want to know, but we do it *now*, so we can get the hell out of here," she snapped. She flung the trailer door open and entered the office. "Are you coming or not?" Jukurro followed behind and closed the door.

Marcus chuckled as he picked up Jukurro's empty bottle off the step. "I think he's going to need some more of this stuff by the time Sydney is through with him."

Doc unraveled a stick of gum and shoved it in his mouth. "We need to talk," he mumbled, as he began walking away from the trailer. "Sydney only got off two rounds. Somebody else killed those four men."

"Who?"

"I don't know, but Sydney saw something."

"What do you want to do?"

Doc sat down on a pile of cinder blocks. "Nothing right now. Let's wait and see if she brings it up."

"Brings it up. Doc, we have enough crap on our plates already without having to worry if Sydney is having second thoughts about us. If she saw the shooter and isn't telling, I think we need to be a little damn concerned here. If she is protecting someone I wanted to know who and why, and I don't think that's too much to ask."

"You're right, but let's give it some time. I trust her judgment."

"I trust her too, but when you throw daddy in the mix, it makes me nervous," Marcus said.

"You can bet this is about more than keeping us from finding those artifacts. There's still some things about Leon-Francis' past that don't make any sense to me."

"Like what?"

"I'll tell you after Benno gets back to me with some more information. One thing for sure—we need more people working on this."

"For what?"

"I need to know more about Sydney's mother."

"Ask Sydney."

"She doesn't know anything. Besides, I'd rather not say anything until I'm sure of what I'm talking about."

"What does her mom have to do with any of this?"

"Maybe nothing, but I want to check her out."

"Okay, but searching through a bunch of records on a dead woman doesn't get us any closer to the pottery or Devin Leon-Francis."

"But it might explain what he's up to, and isn't that what you wanted to know in the first place?"

"Okay. We can use the Greek I was telling you about in Switzerland. In the meantime, what do we do about Sydney?"

"Nothing."

Sydney emerged from the trailer fifty minutes later, looking haggard and tired.

Jukurro looked worse. He felt like hell had made its home in his stomach. Sydney had answered all his questions about her father, but he still didn't have a motive for Woodberry's death or a suspect in custody. Andy Preston was probably gone for good and Jukurro knew he would never learn the truth—not that it mattered anymore. All he wanted now was to get his town back to some sense of normalcy, which would only happen once the Americans were gone. Jukurro handed them their passports. "I want you to leave Narvik within the next twenty-four hours, and please don't bother coming back."

* * *

"What did you tell Jukurro about your father?" Marcus asked as they walked back to the hotel.

"I don't want to talk right now," Sydney said as she brushed ahead of them. Her walk turned into a run and she disappeared over the hill.

"This crap is making me sick, Doc. I feel like I'm in a bad marriage all of a sudden. Sydney has been like another daughter to me, but I can't deal with this. I don't know what to say or do, and if I do anything, it's wrong. I've never seen her like this before and I'm starting to worry about her. We shouldn't even be here."

Doc looked at his friend and slung his arm around his shoulders. "Marcus, everything I say isn't gospel. In this case, you were right. Someone has to stop Leon-Francis, and apparently, we're the only ones who care enough to do anything about it. Sydney's tough and she'll get through this, but we have to give her some space. And we can't assume she's going to help us any more than she has."

"That vacation you were talking about is starting to sound pretty good to me right now. Sydney could use a break, too." When they got back to the hotel, they stopped at Sydney's room to make sure she was okay, but she didn't answer the door. Marcus went downstairs to the front desk, and returned five minutes later. "The manager hasn't seen her."

* * *

141

Sydney pounded her fist on the door of room eleven at the Nordst Jernen Hotel.

Carlos Bourbon answered the door in his pajama bottoms with sleep still on his face. "You." He rubbed his eyes and moved from the doorway so she could enter.

Sydney looked around at the yellow walls as he tried to find something to put on. "Mind if I use the head?"

"No, of course not. Make yourself at home. I mean..."

"I know what you mean." Sydney locked the bathroom door behind her and stared at her reflection in the small mirror. She was a wreck. Her leather suit was smeared in mud and snow, and her turtleneck sweater was more black than white. There wasn't much she could do about either. She ran water in the basin and washed her face. She hesitated before opening the door. Her focus had been more on finding him, and less on what she would say. Another look at herself in the mirror told her it didn't matter anyway.

Carlos sat in a chair with his white overcoat draped over his bare shoulders, asleep.

She kicked his chair leg and woke him up. "Wakeup asshole, what the hell are you doing here?"

He sat upright, blinking his eyes. "Please, no profanity. I don't like it, especially from a woman."

"What?"

Carlos sighed and closed his coat over his chest to keep warm. "It's a sign of a lazy mind and an inarticulate tongue, neither of which fit you."

"You don't know me."

"I know more about you than you think, and that's enough for me. Please, have a seat," he said, waving his hand toward the bed. "I don't have the energy to keep up with your pacing." Sydney stared at the handsome man, who seemed unperturbed by her abrupt arrival. He raked his fingers through his hair. "There's some hot coffee over there. It looks like you could use some." She stood watching him for a moment not sure of what to do. He stared back. "Please, Sydney, take the coffee."

She reluctantly went over to the sink and picked up the pot, while keeping an eye on him through the mirror. "You look like the one that could use the coffee."

"No, but thanks."

She slowly poured the brew into the Styrofoam cup. "Why are you here?" she repeated.

"Watching our investment and making sure you're doing your job. Frankly, I've got concerns about both." She walked over to the bed. "Please, sit. You make me nervous when you stand." She sat down hard on the mattress. "How did you find me?" he asked.

"It's not hard finding a man wearing this." She touched the sleeve of his coat. "I don't like being followed."

"You should be thankful that you were. And so should Dr. Sebasst." There was an unusual calmness and sparkle in his eyes.

"Yes, well thanks, but we didn't need your help. Julian and I were fine."

"I wasn't worried about Julian," he said, reaching for his pipe on the nightstand.

Sydney felt herself blush, and was mad because she couldn't do anything about it. "Look, I personally resent the fact that Sasha thinks it's okay to send her little lapdog after us. We're not about to hide from you if we don't find your precious cargo. So we don't need you riding our butts until then."

"I'm doing my job, Sydney, just like you." He struck a match to the pipe.

"Well, do it from some other place, and stop calling me Sydney."

"It's your name. Would you rather I addressed you as Ms. Belleshota, or Ms. Leon-Francis, or Sid—what?" he asked in frustration.

Sydney threw her cup of coffee at the wall, barely missing his head. "Don't call me anything, just leave!"

"I'm not going anywhere until I have my hands on what I came for. And the sooner you get that through that stubborn head of yours, the better off we'll be. You and your partners need to find our cargo, and soon."

"Sasha may have lapdogs like you jumping through her hoops, but I'm not one. Not you or anyone else is going to tell me what I should or should not do."

Carlos rested the pipe in his hand. "You know, that's the second time you referred to me using that word and I don't like it—even coming from your lips. You are a prideful woman and I respect that. I only ask you to show me the same respect."

"How can anyone respect you considering who you work for? Sasha Micheaux is as corrupt and as evil as they come, and you want my respect?"

"And what is your father, a saint? I admit my cousin is far from perfect, but so is your father. Nevertheless, you are willing to give your life for him if necessary. My cousin and I don't necessarily share the same views on life, and I am sure the same is true of you and your father."

"So why are you working for her?"

"The same reasons you support your father...loyalty and family. Mixed together, they are as irrepressible as the forces of nature, and just as hard to run away from. The Bourbons owe a great deal to the Micheaux family, especially Sasha's grandfather. Our family is the smallest and therefore the least respected. But he saw to it that we were treated as equals with the other families. So what my brothers and I do for my cousin is out of a sense of duty, appreciation, and love. I'm sure your reasons are no less compelling."

Sydney found herself staring again, and at a loss for words. "Do you always babble on like this?" she finally said.

He smiled. "Too often. Perhaps even a little melodramatically at times."

"Gee, you think? What exactly is it that you do, besides harass people?"

"I ensure the welfare of my cousin. The quicker you and your friends complete your work, the sooner I can go home and resume my life."

"You call this a life, playing nursemaid to Sasha?"

"Believe me, it's only temporary. Once I know she will be okay, I'm going back home to Quebec City and my farm."

"You're a farmer?"

"Among other things."

"Sounds like a great life," she said with sarcasm.

"I enjoy it. If you can pursue your passions and make a dollar doing it, you have a blessed life. How about you?"

"I'm not here to discuss my life. I want to know what you are planning."

Carlos chuckled. "That's like asking your opponent in a poker game to show you his hand. If you and your friends do your job, you won't have to worry about me."

Sydney smirked. "Valentino, you are the last person I'm going to lose sleep worrying about. And I'm not playing this little extortion game that you and your crazy cousin cooked up for us anymore. If you have a problem with me, then deal with me, and do it right now. I'm not about to leave here wondering when I'll see that coat of yours flapping in the wind again."

"Then we have a problem," he said, puffing on his pipe.

"No, you have a problem. You want your artifacts, then go get them yourself. I've got other business to take care of right now that's more important than finding some silly trinkets that don't even belong to you."

"You're making a mistake."

"I want you and Sasha to get out of our lives—that's it."

Carlos rose to his feet, and found himself staring down the barrel of Sydney's gun.

"That was quick," he said, both amused and annoyed. She had a wild look in her eyes. "Do you mind, I think I will have some of that coffee?"

"You don't want coffee, remember?"

"I don't, but neither do I like people pointing guns in my face. Perhaps if I occupy my mouth with a cup, you'll have a chance to calm down and we can talk."

"I don't want to calm down, and we're through talking. I've made it as plain as possible to you that this ends here. I'm not putting up with you following me all over the world. So make a decision."

Carlos slowly raised his fingers, placed them on the barrel of the gun, and lightly pushed it away from his face. "You don't need this, Sydney. At least not with me." He sat back down and lifted the pipe to his mouth. "I am not your enemy."

"Sure you're not," she smirked. "But given the chance to kill my father, you'd take it. Wouldn't you?"

"Yes, I would. He's out to destroy my family."

"Why?"

"I don't know and it doesn't matter at this point. He's on a vendetta and if he's not stopped, there won't be anything left for me to return home to—and that's not acceptable. If you want to shoot me, go ahead. Just realize your father is the bad person here. He makes a habit of interfering in other people's lives and then expects them to accept it. Well, I don't—and neither would anyone else with any self-respect, including you." The conviction in his voice and piercing eyes told her he wasn't afraid to die.

This conversation was going nowhere and neither was he. She was wasting her time. "Fine. Do what the hell you want, I don't care anymore." She shoved the pistol in her holster and started for the door.

Carlos jumped up and grabbed her hand. "Wait, don't go."

She yanked free from his grip. "Don't touch me again."

"I apologize... I'm sorry. Tell me at least if you're making progress."

"We've got other problems to deal with right now."

"I see."

Sydney knew she should leave, but she couldn't and she didn't know why. "When you're not bothering people, what do you do for fun?" She couldn't believe she asked him such a lame question.

"Sydney, do people like you and I have time for fun or even friends?" She liked the way her name rolled off his tongue. "I must admit I find myself somewhat envious of the relationship you seem to share with Dr. Sebasst. It's clear that you have a genuine affection for each other—as you do with St. John, of course."

"Julian is a good man. Not *my* man, but..."

"I understand. I haven't quite figured out St. John, but you two seem more equally yoked."

Sydney chuckled. "We understand each other. He's straightforward and direct, and you never have to guess where you stand with him because he'll tell you. He's a simple man, but he hasn't gotten where he has by being stupid."

"He doesn't care for your father, does he?"

"He hates him. But you already know that, don't you?"

"Yes. That must pose a difficult dilemma for you?"

Anger returned to her eyes. "I'm not here to talk with you about my father."

"He'll try again, but next time he'll send more men." Sydney knew he was right. Fisher and Morgan were gone, but her father had more men willing to take their places. "St. John is no match against your father. He's too impetuous—like a quarter horse racing against a thoroughbred he can't beat."

"Marcus only knows one speed and that is flat out fast."

"Then he's foolish and dangerous, and a dangerous fool will only end up getting you killed too."

"Maybe, but I love him. I mean...you know what I mean."

"Just watch your back a little bit better, because I may not be there the next time."

There was another moment of awkward silence where neither one knew what to say.

"I have to go," she said quietly.

He walked her to the door. She turned to face him. Her fingers touched the hair on his chest as she buttoned his coat like a mother sending a child out to play. "Unless you're looking to catch pneumonia, you better learn how to dress in this weather or turn up the heat. By the way, we're leaving in a couple of hours for Kiruna. If you're planning on keeping up with us, you're doing a piss poor job." She started down the hall.

146

"Kiruna? What hotel will you be at?" he shouted as she turned the corner. She didn't answer.

Chapter 18

December 26 was the worst day of Sasha's life. It started with an overseas wake-up call at 4:00 from her bank in Quebec City. The Canadians had found the secret bank account she had created to launder her brothers' illegal money. The only way authorities could have discovered that account was if someone told them where to look and the only person who knew other than her dead brothers was Anthony Chiapetta. Two hours later, the United States froze all her accounts in U.S. banks, quickly followed by Greece, Israel, and Italy.

She received another call from her bank in Geneva when it opened for business. The Merovingians were transferring their money from the Banque de Micheaux to offshore accounts in the Caribbean. Sasha tried to contact the council members by telephone. Frelinghuyen, from Switzerland was the only one to return her call.

"Your money is safe with our family, you know this," she said. I have doubled, even tripled, your fortunes over the years, and this is how I am repaid? My father and I have spent our lives and our money to support the council. Now…"

"Sasha, this is business. You should not take it personally. Some of the members are a little nervous about the news we have heard this morning. This is simply a precaution to protect our investments. None of the families can afford to have their assets at risk, God forbid something like that would happen. It is only a temporary measure, nothing more than that."

"Johann, I have the utmost respect for you, but you are being deceived by Anthony. He is out to destroy my family at any cost."

"Anthony has always been an ally of yours, you know that. He personally called each member to urge us not to panic, and to keep our money in place. It was Eisenstadt that convinced us to take action, and for once, the German makes good sense."

"Meinhard Eisenstadt is a gerbil following the rat. Chiapetta is a lecherous traitor sucking the council's lifeblood, and good men like you and Leopold are blinded by his lies. I have a deep fondness for you and respect for our friendship, but now is the time I need you the most. The families own sixty-six percent of the assets of my bank. It cannot absorb this great of a loss. It will ruin my family. Please, I beg you to speak to the others…intercede on my behalf. I will personally guarantee the safety of your assets against our portion of the treasury in France. You must help me expose Anthony

Chiapetta for what he really is. He is desperate for money and will do…" The phone suddenly went dead. Frelinghuyen had hung up on her.

She lowered the receiver on the cradle. She had lost Frelinghuyen, and without his support, she was finished. Sasha had a financial interest in over four hundred banks around the world, and owned eighteen percent of all the assets—none of which she could touch now. She knew her family's portion of the Merovingian treasury would be the next thing stolen from her, and there wasn't a thing she could do about it.

Sasha sat at her desk fighting back tears of frustration. She could stop Chiapetta, but she couldn't fight the man behind him. Leon-Francis was a phantom she couldn't touch. He was too clever and too strong. But she had to do something if there was any chance of salvaging anything. She had only one hope left.

An hour later, her secretary delivered another devastating message from one of her men. Leon-Francis had captured Jordan Bloodstone. Sasha balled up the piece of paper and tossed it across the room. Then she cried.

* * *

Three hundred miles away, Anthony Chiapetta and his mistress were having lunch at Gustavo. The chic restaurant in the heart of downtown Florence was his office away from home. Today was no exception. He ordered another bottle of Bassio to keep his girlfriend entertained while he finished his conference call with the council members. When he finished, he wiped the spaghetti sauce from the phone, and then went back to his meal. Everything was set. The special meeting of the council would meet at Eisenstadt's spa in Germany as soon as he returned from his meeting with Leon-Francis. Chiapetta already had his script prepared. He would make a feeble attempt to support Sasha—but Eisenstadt, the Spaniard, and the Englishman would push for full expulsion of the Micheauxs and Bourbons from the council, which they would get. Sasha's incestuous melding of the Merovingians on her bank's governing board would ensure her demise. The board would demand that she step down as president of the bank, and Chiapetta, a vice president, had enough votes to assume control.

He wiped his stained fingers on his bib, kissed his mistress, and excused himself to go to the men's room. His buxom girlfriend watched him waddle off between the tables. She then turned her attention to the dashing

Frenchman sitting in the booth behind them, who had been eavesdropping on their conversation.

Chapter 19

That same morning in Lucerne, Iggy Vasilakis received an overseas telephone call from Benno Rood in San Francisco. By noon, Iggy was on the short flight to Geneva and then the train to northern Italy. He rented a truck and drove through the Italian Alps until he reached a small village filled with sixteenth century stone houses and tunnel archways.

Oira had a population of two hundred people. The town hall had no information on the Belleshota family, except that they moved away in 1959. Iggy spoke with shopkeepers and the local priest, but no one knew anything about Angela Lia Belleshota or her family. He tipped his hat to a pair of young women as he hobbled along the narrow street back to the town square.

Iggy bought two apples from a fruit vendor who told him of a woman that might be able to help him. He followed a cobblestone path around the rock quarry, until he came to a brown house where an elderly woman was repairing a window shutter. He introduced himself and she invited him in the house.

"Arturo and Pelia Belleshota...very quiet and unassuming family. I lost touch with them after they moved to Florence, but we heard that Arturo became a very successful businessman."

"Did you ever hear from them again?" Iggy asked.

"No. I did receive a letter once from their priest informing me of Arturo's death, but nothing more."

"When was that?"

"1981, I believe."

"What was the cause of death?"

"Oh, my goodness, I'm sure it was his age. He was well into his nineties."

"Do you remember the name of the priest who sent you the letter?"

"Oh, heaven's no. That was many years ago. Too many for me to remember now. I do remember the church, though. St. Ambrosio, like the great cathedral."

"And his wife, Pelia. What became of her?"

"I never heard. She was considerably younger than her husband and could still be alive, although it is doubtful. The loss of her daughter broke her heart."

"Did you know Angela Lia Belleshota?"

"Angela was a fine young girl—very well mannered and bright, as I remember. She was Arturo's only child and very young when they moved away. The day I received word that she had died was a very sad day for me. She was such a vibrant young woman...full of fun, and very handsome."

"How did she die?"

"I was told it was an accident of some kind, while she was vacationing with her husband."

"When was that?"

"The year? I don't remember." She put her work gloves back on as she watched Iggy taking copious notes. "Is there anything else? I must get back to my chores."

"Just a few more questions, please, and I will be through. Are you aware that Angela Lia had a daughter. A grown daughter living in America?"

"America? How wonderful. Her father must be proud, but he must surely miss her."

"Miss her?"

"Of course. She lives in America and not in Italy. In my day, families stayed together in the same village."

Iggy stopped writing. "Excuse me, her father lives in Italy?"

She seemed annoyed by the silly question. "Yes, of course. Where else would he live? His family is there."

"You know the family?"

"Yes, all of Tuscany knows the Chiapetta family. They once were one of Tuscany's wealthiest families. Ernesto is the oldest boy, but now he is old and retired. We seldom hear anything about him."

"Who is he?"

"Have you not been listening? Ernesto Chiapetta...Angela Lia's husband. Everyone knows that. Whom did you think I was speaking of?"

* * *

Iggy got in his truck and sat his derby on the seat next to him. He started the ignition and eased the truck backwards down the steep dirt road to the highway. He scratched his scalp as he tried to decide his next move. The old woman's information about Angela Belleshota was sketchy at best, but that's all he had to work with. Iggy turned the truck around and headed to Olbia, where he caught a jet for the short flight to Florence.

Two hours later, the airport taxi dropped him off in front of the museum, downtown. He walked south on Arno until he found someone who could direct him to *St. Ambrosio.*

Iggy found the small sanctuary sandwiched in between two mid-rise apartment complexes. He opened the door and went in. The church was quiet. He walked down the aisle toward the altar, but didn't see the priest knelt on the floor, dusting a pew.

"May I help you?" asked the priest as he stood to his feet.

Iggy removed his hat, and told him what he wanted.

"Ah, that was so many years ago. Way before my time. I believe Father Isumani was the priest at the time. But of course he has passed now."

"Do you have any church records?"

"We are not as sophisticated as our impressive building might indicate. I believe we once had a meager archive collection of some historical significance, but that was destroyed in a fire many years ago."

"Is there anyone in the church that might have knowledge of the Belleshota family?"

The priest rubbed his chin. "I don't think so."

"Who was the priest that followed Father Isumani?"

"That would have been the parochial vicar at the time. Let's see...yes, of course, that was Monsignor Giacobelli."

"Is he still alive?"

"Very much. He lives only a few blocks from the church. I can call and see if he is available, if you wish."

* * *

Iggy had no problem finding the burnt brick high-rise across the street from the police station. The building had been recently remodeled, but the elevators were temporarily out of service. Iggy walked up six flights of steps, wiped the sweat from his forehead, and knocked on the door.

A man greeted him in white slippers and velvet robe. The monsignor was a robust looking man with jet-black hair, and an inviting smile.

"It is very kind of you to receive me, Monsignor," Iggy said, nervously massaging the rim of his hat as he stood in the spacious apartment.

"It is a pleasure. Please, have a seat. Now, the good father told me you are searching for information on Arturo Belleshota's daughter. I never met her, so I don't know how much help I can be. Father Isumani knew her quite well, I believe."

Iggy pulled his tattered notepad from his pocket. "Anything you can remember will be helpful."

"Father Isumani told me that Arturo's daughter entrusted a statue to him for safe keeping, which he placed in the rectory. Unfortunately, it was stolen along with other church valuables many years ago, when thieves invaded the sanctuary."

"When was that?"

"Early 1970's, I believe. Later, her husband sought me out and wanted it back. I felt badly having to tell him we no longer had it in our possession. As I recall, he was very upset."

"What kind of statue was it?"

"I believe it was an obelisk of some sort."

"Do you remember what her husband said to you?"

"Words I would prefer not to repeat."

Iggy blushed. "Her husband…you remember his name?"

"It was a peculiar name, but no, I don't remember."

"Ernesto Chiapetta?"

The monsignor laughed. "No, I assure you, neither I nor anyone living here could forget that name." He continued chuckling.

"Devin Leon-Francis?"

"Yes. That name. He is the one."

"Do you know Ernesto Chiapetta?"

"No, but I know of his family. Why do you ask?"

"I was told Angela Lia Belleshota was married to him."

A grim look clouded the monsignor's face. "If true, that is unfortunate."

"Why do you say that?"

"His life is an open book, and I do not care to gossip about him. But if he is the one you are interested in, the authorities will tell you everything you want to know."

Chapter 20

Kiruna was a wilderness frontier, half the size of Switzerland—but not large enough for Andy Preston to hide from Leon-Francis.

Andy made it safely from Narvik to Kiruna on the train, but not without a cost. He lay coughing in bed, talking on the phone with a ticket agent for Maris Cruises. Maris had a freighter cruise ship in Lulea, bound for Alaska. The ship was leaving port tomorrow, which meant Andy had to leave now if he wanted to book a ride. Lulea was 400 miles away, and the only way he could get there was by train. He grabbed a handful of tissue and caught the phlegm from his mouth as he coughed again. His chest hurt and he had a sinus infection, thanks to his exposure in the open locomotive and the trek through wet snow to get to the motel. He wiped his nose and went to the bathroom.

He threw a towel on the floor, and kicked it in front of the crack of the door to keep the steam in while he took a long hot shower. The hot vapors relieved the stuffiness in his head, but he was still nauseous. He stepped out of the stall and wiped the steam off the mirror and got dressed. As he bent over to get the towel off the floor, the door crashed in on his head. Two men slipped a black hood over his head and carried his unconscious body outside.

They shackled him to the bed of a military cargo truck, and pulled the tarp down over the back. Andy woke up in total darkness—the hood still secured on his head. He seemed to ride for hours as the squeaky truck made its way over rough terrain. The truck stopped twice. Each time he was dragged from the back and allowed to stretch for a few minutes, before continuing on. His captives never spoke to him, and he had no idea how many there were.

The third time the truck stopped, Andy knew they were somewhere in the mountains. Breathing had become more difficult and it was much colder. He could hear men's voices outside, but couldn't tell what they were saying. The minutes passed as he thought about his predicament. In the back of his mind, he imagined escaping from the truck, and somehow getting to Lulea in time to catch the freighter.

He heard the sounds of footsteps moving in the frozen snow toward him—and then there was silence. *What are they waiting for…why don't they say something?* The anxiety was too much for him. His muffled screams caused him to hyperventilate.

A man slapped him hard against his head. "Shut up," he said. He unshackled Andy from the rail and tossed him off the truck.

Two men grabbed Andy's arms and dragged him through the snow. He heard the echo of rusty hinges as a door opened. Someone cut the ropes off his hands and pushed him. He went flying downward, landing hard on his stomach. He rolled over on his back and pulled the hood off his head, grasping at the stale air. It took a moment for his eyes to focus in the dimly lit subterranean cavern. Two utility lights were suspended overhead, illuminating a still body lying on an army cot.

"Jordan?"

* * *

The Norwegian sat in the storeroom, drinking coffee and talking on the satellite phone to Leon-Francis. "Preston just arrived."

"Find out if he's talked to anyone else," Leon-Francis said.

"What about the woman?"

"You'll have to bring her to me. I can't get away right now."

"She won't make it."

"She's that bad?"

"Yes. I doubt she'll make it through the night."

"Okay, get rid of her, too. Then pack your gear. I'll be sending my helicopter to pick you up and bring you here."

"I thought you wanted me in Narvik."

"There has been a change in plans. I need you to oversee the transfer of some goods for me."

"What goods?"

"You'll find out when you get here."

* * *

Andy knelt on the damp dirt next to Jordan's cot. Her hands and feet were wrapped in surgical bandages and her face looked like worn patent leather. He touched her body. She was cold as ice and comatose. "What have they done to you?"

The iron door creaked open, and a tall shadow appeared on the landing above him. The broad-shouldered man with snow-white hair and a fu-manchu mustache came into the light. Andy clutched Jordan's hand. "Who are you?"

"That's not important," the Norwegian said.

"I know you. You work for Tiberius Woodberry."

"Until you decided to kill him."

Andy released Jordan's hand. "He was trying to kill me! What was I supposed to do?" The Norwegian held a gun in his hand. "Please, don't do this. Just let me speak with Mr. Leon-Francis."

"That won't change anything. The damage has been done. You and your girlfriend saw to that."

Andy's eyes widened when the Norwegian's eyes turned to Jordan. "No, she hasn't done anything."

"She killed Jason Worrick and almost killed Mr. Leon-Francis, and you don't think that's anything?" He placed the gun barrel against Jordan's head.

"No!" Andy yelled, throwing his body over hers.

The Norwegian lowered his weapon. "You want her to live, tell me who else you've been talking to."

"I didn't say anything to anybody, I swear. I would never betray Mr. Leon-Francis, he knows that."

"If that's true, then you should have been a little more discerning in your choice of women. Your lady friend's maiden name is Toussaint."

"Toussaint…" The name resonated in his head until he remembered where he heard it before. He began sobbing. "I'm so sorry," he cried out.

"So am I, Andy." The Norwegian shot him in the temple and pushed his dead body off Jordan.

Chapter 21

Carlos Bourbon's jet landed in Kiruna at 2:30 in the afternoon and it was already dark. He flirted with the clerk at the car rental kiosk, and walked away with the name of the bed and breakfast hotel the three Americans were staying in. St. John's jet was still on the runway being refueled. Carlos saw the pilot in the cockpit going over his flight plan. Whatever they were up to, they weren't planning on being in Kiruna long. Carlos dropped his bag on the front seat of the rental car, and called his brother on the phone.

Enric Bourbon told him of Anthony Chiapetta's teleconference call with the council members. "The meeting is set for noon on Saturday at Meinhard Eisenstadt's spa in Germany," Enric said. "He and Chiapetta will orchestrate our cousin's expulsion from the council, and then Chiapetta will introduce a resolution to permanently remove our families from the council. Our cousin will be allowed to keep a quarter of the family's holdings in the treasury, provided she relinquishes all claims to the Banque, and we Bourbons quietly go away."

"Anthony has lost his mind. Where is Sasha?" Carlos asked.

"In seclusion in Burgenstock with some of our men. She is safe."

"She will never be safe as long as Chiapetta is alive. How many men do we have left?"

"Six. I didn't want to tell you this until you returned, but you need to know. We lost Dauphine." Carlos was quiet. "Are you still there, brother?"

"I heard you, Enric, what happened?"

"His body was discovered in a river near Regensburg, Germany."

"He was supposed to be in Norway with Micah. What happened?"

"I don't know. They must have separated. We think Dauphine must have trailed Leon-Francis to Germany."

Carlos groaned and then his voice grew soft. "They were brave men. But if we don't act fast, more of our family will die. Sasha is not safe in Switzerland or France. You get her on an airplane for Canada tonight. She will only be safe with our family in Quebec City."

"I'll fly her there personally. Don't worry."

"No, I need you here. Where is the Mangusta helicopter you bought from that Chechan general last year?"

"In our warehouse hangar in Zurich." Carlos explained what he wanted.

"That's risky, brother. What if the families find out what we've done?"

"Then we'll have to deal with them when the time comes. Right now we have no other choice. Either fight to keep what is ours or we lose everything, and I am not going to let that happen," Carlos said.

"Armaments won't be a problem, but it doesn't look like an Apache."

"Paint it white—that's the only thing people will remember. Make sure you have it ready before that meeting. Our cousin's life and our family's future depend on your success. I'm sorry I can't be there."

"Don't worry about me, little brother. You be careful. Those Americans have no honor. If they find our possessions, they won't give them up without a fight. Remember, they betrayed us once before. They will try again."

* * *

Based on the map and directions Mallon Jefferson provided, Doc estimated it would take another hour for them to reach the mountain where Jordan was. They were on the highway near Lake Luossavaara, heading toward the massive underground mines of Kiirunavaara. Marcus drove while Sydney slept on the back seat of the Yukon. Doc tried to sleep, but his mind was flooded with thoughts about Jordan, Sasha, and Leon-Francis. He felt like a soldier fighting a war on multiple fronts, and now Carlos Bourbon was breathing down their necks. The cell phone in his pocket began vibrating.

"Did I wake you?" Benno Rood asked.

Doc cleared his throat. "I wish. What's up, Benno?"

"I found two of the missing tugboats. They are in a Glasgow shipping yard being repaired. The salvage tug, *Cyrus,* is still missing, but it passed through the Port of Tulcea four days ago, followed by *Angela's Storm*, the next day. Both were bound for Belgrade, but neither arrived. The ships have to be somewhere on the Danube."

"How long will it take you to find them?"

"Phew...I don't know. The Danube River stretches over 1,700 miles long, across eight countries from the Black Forest to the Black Sea. Not to mention the thousands of tributaries feeding into it. Ships could hide forever in those waters."

"We don't have forever, Benno. Let's eliminate the Balkan countries and Russia. Leon-Francis is too urbane for them. That leaves us with Germany and Austria."

159

"Okay, I'll start checking the ports. By the way, I did some more checking on the *Angela's Storm.*" It was built in San Diego in 1982, but there is no history of it ever entering a foreign port. My guess is Mr. Leon-Francis keeps it anchored in international waters and uses his helicopter for transport."

"That figures. Were you able to confirm the date Tippi Sampa died?"

"Yes, he was killed in 1974, not 1976—in New Orleans."

"Thanks." Doc turned off the phone.

Marcus turned the sports utility truck off the highway onto the gravel road leading to the mines. "What's up?" he asked.

"Benno has a lead on Leon-Francis' freighter."

"That's the best news I've heard since I've been here." Doc seemed disinterested as he stared at the bleak landscape out the window. "What's wrong with you? You look like you've just swallowed a box of prunes."

"Leon-Francis lied to Sydney about her mother's death. Tippi Sampa couldn't have killed Angela Belleshota, because he died two years before Sydney's mother's death."

Marcus glanced in the rear view mirror to make sure Sydney was still asleep. "I wouldn't tell her that if I were you. She's having a problem dealing with the truth lately," he whispered. "I thought her head was messed up before, but this crap will send her over the edge. She's not firing on all cylinders. And, this secret meeting she had with this Bourbon guy behind our backs proves it. The old Sydney would have busted a cap in him before he had a chance to open his mouth."

"Give her a break. She's been through a lot these last twenty-four hours."

Marcus looked at Doc. "Well, Mr. Gandhi, if it's all right with you I'll still be watching our backs, because I don't trust Bourbon. He was in Narvik for a reason, and it's not because he's using up his frequent flyer miles. We have enough problems without having to worry about him sniffing up the cracks of our butts."

"Forget about Carlos Bourbon for now—he's behind us. Worry about what's in front of us and Devin Leon-Francis."

Chapter 22

There were more than 400 miles of underground roads dissecting Kiirunavaara Mountain like Swiss cheese. It took Doc and Marcus over an hour to find the right road leading to LKAB's abandoned mine, Satan's Tomb.

Doc carried the propane lantern as he led the way through the dark cavern.

"These directions Mellonhead gave us are lousy. I could swear we've been in this tunnel already," Marcus said.

"We're okay. The connecting cave should be a few hundred yards ahead."

They splashed through ankle-deep water and mud until they came to an opening, which led to four more tunnels that went off in separate directions.

"Which way, now?" Marcus asked.

Doc looked at the map. "Straight ahead," he said, pointing to the tunnel on the left. "Another ninety yards and we should reach the stairs to the upper shaft."

"I see how this place got its name. A brother could suffocate up in here before he has a chance to get lost. I can't believe they carve up the inside of this mountain just for some damn iron ore?"

"It's a valuable commodity. You can tell your grandkids you hiked through the largest underground mine in the world. That's assuming we get out of here in one piece."

Marcus stopped. "Hold up for a minute."

Doc stopped. "What's wrong?"

Marcus wiped the sweat from his face with his handkerchief. "Don't you think it's time to let me in on your plan? How are we going to deal with these creeps when we run into them?"

"I don't have a plan. Three or four guys shouldn't be a problem."

"What if Mellonhead's information is wrong and there's an army of guys waiting for us?"

"If you're worried about me, don't. I can take care of myself."

"How, with that cross you're wearing on your neck? We aren't dealing with vampires here, Doc. These boys will try to take your ugly black head off. Don't make it easy for them."

"Marcus, what's your point? We have to go."

"Here, take one of my guns."

"I don't want it, I've told you that before," he said, pushing the gun back in his hand.

Marcus swore as he put his gun away. "Sydney should be here instead of your old stubborn ass."

"Someone needed to stay with the truck and watch our backs. Do you really want her here if we happen to run into her father?"

"Hell, no."

"Then stop complaining and let's get on with this."

Marcus took the lead. "Just make sure you keep your big head in back of me." They followed the cave to a flight of wooden stairs that led up and disappeared through the cave roof. "You better let me check it out first," Marcus whispered. He climbed three steps, and then the fourth one snapped under his weight. The noise ricocheted through the mine. He held his breath waiting for someone to appear, but they didn't. "I don't like this. It's too quiet up there." He made his way to the top and stuck his head through the opening. He saw daylight. "We're just inside the main entrance to the mine. "It looks empty."

Doc climbed up and joined him outside.

"There's nobody here," Marcus said, looking around in all directions.

Doc knelt down and examined the tracks in the snow. He ran his fingers across the small tire imprint. "A military helicopter has been here. Come on, let's see what's inside the mine."

They wandered through the passageway for eighty yards, before stumbling upon the supply storeroom with an open door. Inside, they found a table sitting in the middle of the room with a deck of cards sprawled on top. A portable generator hummed in the corner.

"Someone was in a hurry to leave," Doc said, flipping off the generator switch.

Marcus saw a small alcove in the corner of the rock wall. "Hey, Doc, over here." He pulled on the heavy door and saw steps leading down to a cavern glowing with iridescent light coming from an underground grotto. They made their way along the sharp rocks to the bottom, where they saw two bodies laying in the dirt on the other side of the pool. They waded through waist-deep water to reach them.

Andy Preston lay sprawled in a pool of dried blood. Jordan lay beside him on her side. Doc rolled her over and felt her pulse.

"Is she alive?" Marcus asked.

"Barely."

* * *

Doc contacted Mallon Jefferson, and within minutes, a British evacuation team met them at the entrance to the mine. Marcus helped the soldiers carry Jordan to the waiting helicopter.

"Where are you taking her?" Doc asked.

"To the *USS Abraham Lincoln,* in the Baltic. They're expecting her. Don't worry, they will take good care of her, sir," the lieutenant said.

The medic came over to see Doc. "May I speak with you?"

"Of course. What is it?" Doc asked.

"The colonel is in serious condition, but stable. Somebody had the foresight and knowledge to properly address her wounds and administer the right antibiotics."

"Are you saying her captives saved her life?"

"Someone most certainly did. Anyway, I thought you would want to know," he said, smiling.

"Thanks, lieutenant."

"Our pleasure."

The helicopter lifted off the ground. Marcus pulled his toothpick from his pocket and stuck it in his mouth. They walked down to the lower road where Sydney picked them up.

"There better be a shortcut off this mountain," Marcus said, climbing in the truck.

"Everything go okay?" Sydney asked.

"She's alive and on her way to the hospital. How's everything here?" Marcus asked.

Sydney slammed the SUV in reverse, spinning the tires as she backed up to turn around. "I saw my father's helicopter leaving the mountain twenty minutes ago."

* * *

Carlos was snacking on a basket of nachos when the white SUV pulled up to the café, which was across the street from the bread and breakfast. Sydney climbed out, followed by Doc and Marcus. They entered the café and took a booth at the opposite end of the room from where Carlos was sitting.

The waiter poured them coffee and left the pot on the table.

"Thanks," Marcus said. He tore open a package of sweetener and dumped it in his cup. "I don't understand why they didn't kill Jordan," he said, stirring the coffee.

"Maybe they thought she was already dead," Sydney said.

"You sure that was your father's helicopter you saw leaving the mountain?" Marcus asked.

"Yes."

"You think your father was on it?" Marcus asked.

"I don't know or care any more." Sydney stared at the tabletop, ignoring her coffee.

It was time to change the subject. "What did Benno have to say about Satan's Tomb?" Doc asked.

"The LKAB closed it down in 1954. He's checking to see if they still own it. He'll call you later about the other matter," Marcus said. The minute the words left his mouth he knew he had screwed up.

Sydney raised her eyes. "What other matter—what's going on, Julian?"

Doc sighed. "The only way I'm going to find your father is by knowing how he thinks. And the only way I'm going to accomplish that is by finding out as much about him and your family as I can. Benno is working on some things for me, which I hope will lead me to your father."

"You said you were after the stolen artifacts."

"I am, but now it's only because I know your father will be there, too. He has tried three times to kill me, Sydney. Do you really think he's going to give up, even if Marcus and I walk away right now?"

"He'll try again, count on it," Carlos Bourbon said, suddenly appearing next to the table, with his basket of nachos in his hand. "May I join you?"

Marcus looked at the oddly dressed man wearing a tie and white wool overcoat. "Who the...is this Carlos?" Marcus asked.

"Marcus, meet Carlos Bourbon. Carlos, meet Julian," Sydney said with indifference.

Marcus ignored Carlos's outstretched hand.

"May I sit down?" Doc scooted over and made room for him. "Devin Leon-Francis' men will not be as careless next time, and they won't miss. I can help you find him."

"You must be nuts. I'd sooner swim the English Channel with a millstone around my neck than take my chances with you. You're no better than Leon-Francis."

164

"I only want what's ours, and I can help you get it," Carlos said.

"If it wasn't for your crazy cousin we wouldn't be in this situation in the first place. Tell Sasha we don't need her help," Marcus said.

"This is my decision, not hers," Carlos said.

"So what's the urgency now?" Doc asked.

"Nothing has changed. It only makes sense that we work together."

"You have to do better than that. Why does Sasha have us on such a short leash?" Doc asked.

"My cousin's future is dependent on those artifacts being found by tomorrow."

"And that's a bad thing?" Marcus asked.

"I've already lost a cousin and a brother to Devin Leon-Francis. I won't lose another. Especially my cousin."

"Sorry about your kinfolk, but why should we trust you?" Marcus asked, reaching for the coffeepot.

"Because I think I know where Devin Leon-Francis is."

"Where?" Sydney asked.

"Southern Germany—near Regensburg."

"Regensburg is about one hundred miles from the Danube River. He could be right," Doc said.

Chapter 23

On Friday, Devin Leon-Francis' helicopter landed on a roof of a downtown building in Florence. Anthony Chiapetta held onto his hat as he quickly made his way to the craft.

Devin Leon-Francis was sitting in the co-pilot seat. "Get in back, Tony."

"My old friend, I was not expecting you to come." Leon-Francis helped him squeeze in the tight space. He tried to catch his breath and find a place to sit. "This is a beastly craft, how do you endure such tight quarters?"

"I'm not used to having visitors. Take it up!" The pilot lifted off the roof and headed northeast.

"How long will our trip be?" Chiapetta asked.

"Relax."

"That is difficult. I have not been this excited in years. Tell me what the treasure looks like."

"You can see for yourself. Everything is waiting for you. When you are through, my people will ship it wherever you want."

"Excellent."

"What are you going to do with it?"

"It is already sold to the South Americans. They much prefer to pay my price for the return of their cultural treasures than to incur excessive costs of litigating their claims in court."

"And I'm sure you're selling it to them at wholesale prices."

Chiapetta laughed. "My friend, true art is rare *and* valuable. One must expect to pay for quality."

Leon-Francis smirked. He touched his pilot's arm, signaling him to change course. "Put this over your head." He handed Chiapetta a black hood.

"My friend, this is not necessary. After all these years and all that we have been through, you still do not trust me?"

"Put it on, Tony."

Chiapetta continued to chuckle as he slid the hood over his head. "Is this sufficient?"

Leon Francis pulled the drawstring, cinching it tight around his neck. "It'll do. Relax, we'll be there in twenty minutes."

* * *

Benno's telephone call woke Marcus up from a light sleep. He'd been trying to contact Doc, but he wasn't answering the phone. Marcus called his room, but there was still no answer. *He's probably downstairs feeding his face*, Marcus thought. He brushed his teeth and slipped on his robe and socks. "Damn!" he said as he stepped into the cold hall and saw his breath in the air. It was no wonder no one else was staying at this seventy-three dollar a night dump. He hated this self-accommodating bread-and-breakfast that had a name he couldn't pronounce. He hurried to the stairs that took him down to the kitchen. Doc wasn't there, but he saw Carlos and Sydney sitting in the living room alone. They were wearing the same clothes they had on yesterday. Marcus quietly closed the swinging door behind him as he left.

He ran back upstairs to Doc's room and tried the door. It was unlocked. He let himself in. The bathroom door was closed. Marcus banged on the door. "Doc, come out of there! Doc!"

Doc flung the door open. "What, you can't wait?"

Marcus snatched the stack of magazines from Doc's hands. "You haven't changed since we were kids. You're the only person I've met who has to take a library to the crapper every time you go. No wonder you never answer your phone. You spend your whole life in this place."

"Marcus, what do you want?"

"I thought you might want to know that Benno found *Angela's Storm* and the salvage tugboat, Cyrus. The ships are twenty-two miles off the coast of a city called Passau. You know where that is?"

"Yes, it's a little frontier town near the Austrian border. Anything else?"

"He hasn't found anything on Sydney yet, but he had some luck with the Satan's Tomb. The LKAB bought the mine in '56' from a company called Hammershield Mining, which just happened to be owned by the Prince of Darkness, himself—Leon-Francis."

"Give Benno a call back and have him check to see if Hammershield or LKAB have any other property holdings in Austria or Germany."

"Why can't you call him?"

"I'm going back to the restroom and finish what I started, if that's all right with you."

"Okay, but hurry up. We need to talk."

"About what?"

"Sydney—she's with Bourbon downstairs in the TV room."

"Okay…so?"

"You don't have a problem with that?"

"What—are they mud wrestling on the table—what?"

"This isn't funny, Doc. I'm serious about this. The man is no good for her and you know it. This is the beginning of problems to come if we don't nip this in the bud right now. I don't know what she sees in him anyway."

"Then you're blind. As far as his character is concerned, let Sydney make that decision. You aren't her father. Besides, a lot of people thought Caitlin was crazy for hooking up with you, remember?"

Marcus gave him a cold stare. "I know you're not telling me that—that curly-headed, nacho-eating, Zen-talking, Rico Suave is anything like me. Is that what you're saying?"

"I'm saying, I'm tired of you wasting my time talking." He grabbed his magazines out of Marcus's hands and slammed the door. "Make sure the door is locked when you leave—and call Benno back."

* * *

Doc showered, but he didn't bother getting dressed. There wasn't any place to go. The brutal storm that had raged across Norway and most of Northern Europe for a week was now pummeling Sweden with its forty-mile-per-hour winds. Outside the window, Doc saw seventeen inches of fresh snow. The café across the street was the only visible building for miles, but even it seemed to be disappearing before his eyes as the snow seemed to swallow it in whiteness. There was a discomforting calmness about this place that made Doc nervous. He hated waiting, but that's all he could do now. Benno and Iggy had to come up with something fast, or they'd be stuck here, and another day would be wasted. Doc stayed in his room the rest of the day waiting for their call, but it never came.

He skipped dinner and went to bed early, but was too restless to sleep. He called Marcus on the phone, got dressed, and went downstairs to the kitchen to make a sandwich. Light streamed from the living room. Sydney was stretched out on the couch with her back to the snow-filled television screen. Doc gently coaxed the TV remote from under her arm and turned off the television.

"I'm not asleep," she moaned.

Doc rested his hand on her waist. "We're leaving in a few hours. Go up and try to get some rest."

"Where are we going?"

"Germany."

She rolled over and looked up at Doc. "You found my father?"

"No, but if we don't get airborne now, we may never get out of this place once it starts snowing again."

"What are we going to do in Germany if we don't know where my father is?"

"Hope we get a break. I can't sit around here anymore doing nothing." Sydney rolled back to her stomach. "You okay?"

"I'm fine," she whispered.

Doc was never short on advice, but now he was lost for the right words to comfort her. They both knew they were on a collision course with her father. He gently massaged her back. "You want to talk?"

She rolled over. "I'm okay…I told you."

"Sure you are. You want a bite of my half-eaten meatballs?"

She laughed, pushing away the disgusting looking sandwich he held up to her mouth.

"Okay, if you're not going to eat, at least go to bed. We may have a long day ahead of us. Once Benno gives us a location, we've got to be ready to roll."

She looked at Doc. "I can't do this, Julian. My father may be a bastard, but I just can't do it." She turned her face from him and cried. Doc stroked her hair.

* * *

Marcus was already aboard the jet when Sydney and Doc arrived. He couldn't wait to leave. His only regret was that he wasn't going home. Maybe it was the foreboding weather that had worn him down. No matter where they went, the snow followed them like a shadow. Maybe it was the grind of chasing a phantom for almost four weeks. Whatever the reason, he was tired. He missed his family and wanted to go home, but he couldn't. There was no way he was going to let Carlos beat him to the shipment of artifacts. "You guys look like crap," he said, lifting Sydney's bag off her shoulder and storing it in the closet. "It's this crazy place. Night when it should be day, and vice versa. No wonder no one lives up here." He grabbed Doc's bag. "Is this all your gear?"

"Yeah," Doc said.

"Okay, let's roll up out of here."

"Hold on, Carlos is coming," Sydney said.

Marcus saw Carlos walking across the tarmac toward the jet. "Oh, no. Hell, no. I agreed to let him come, but I sure as hell didn't say he could ride with us. He's got his own plane, let him fly that."

"That's stupid," Sydney said.

"No, what's stupid is him thinking he's catching a ride with me."

Doc dragged Marcus away from the door and pushed him down in the seat next to the bar. "Relax—we've got other problems to deal with right now."

Carlos entered the plane and occupied the seat next to Sydney near the door.

Marcus reclined his seat. "I still don't like that dude, and nothing you say or do is going to change that—so don't try."

"I haven't said a word."

"Yeah, but I know how you think. You only want to see the good in people, and thinking like that will get you killed."

Doc cinched up his seatbelt and relaxed. "You actually think he's a danger to us?"

"Hell, yes, I know it. He may not be Sasha's clone, but he's her robot. And a robot will do whatever its master tells it to do."

"That's ridiculous."

"You think so, huh. Let Romeo over there get a glimpse of that pottery before we do, and you'll see his true colors. The boy is money hungry just like the rest of his lot. Why do you think he's making a play for Sydney? He knows she's loaded."

"I can't believe you said something that ignorant."

"Well, I did. I don't have to like him and I sure don't have to trust him." He adjusted his seat some more and relaxed. "Now, what's so damn important that you want to talk to me about?"

"We can't count on Sydney. She's sitting this one out."

"Good. I mean, we could really use her, but if I have to worry about whether she's the one trying to take my butt off, I'd rather she stay. This has been some heavy stuff for her to swallow. She doesn't need anything more screwing up her head." A light on Marcus's armrest blinked.

He picked up the telephone. "It's Benno—he has Iggy on the other line and they want a three-way with you." He passed Doc the phone and unbuckled his seat belt.

"Where are you going?" Doc asked.

"Up front. I wanna make sure Tre' doesn't fly *Thunder* into one of those mountains trying to get us out of here."

* * *

Carlos passed Marcus in the aisle as he returned from the restroom. Neither man spoke.

"I don't think St. John likes me," Carlos said as he reoccupied his seat next to Sydney.

"He's like that with everyone at first. People have to grow on him. Don't let it bother you. I'm not even sure if I like you." Sydney gave him a smile.

"What are you going to say to your father if you see him?"

"I don't want to talk about my father," she said, in a tone warning him not to pursue the question. "Tell me about the family you lost."

"My oldest brother, Micah, and my cousin, Dauphin, were two of five men sent to find your father. They've all disappeared. Dauphin's body is the only one we've found."

"So you think killing my father is going to even the score?"

The airplane's engines started. Carlos tightened his seat belt. "I honestly can't tell you what I'm doing anymore." He picked up her hand and cradled it with his. She looked into his gentle face, which showed signs of fatigue and the pain of loss. Fifteen minutes later, *Thunder* lifted off the frozen runway and headed southwest.

* * *

Chiapetta woke up in a room with concrete walls, a platform bed, air vents that substituted for windows, and the worst headache in his life. The last thing he remembered before losing consciousness was riding in Leon-Francis' helicopter and the odd scent that smelled of rancid figs. The electronic steel door slid open and Devin Leon-Francis entered the room. Chiapetta stood to his feet, and then his wobbly legs collapsed under him.

Leon-Francis caught him before he fell to the floor. "You'll be okay in a minute after the anesthetic wears off."

"Am I a prisoner?"

"No, this is just a security precaution."

171

Leon-Francis held Chiapetta's arm. "You feel well enough to walk?" he asked, guiding him from the room onto an underground paved street and fresh air. An electric-powered shuttle cart passed with men on board. Chiapetta watched in awe as the cart entered a concrete catacomb and disappeared. Towering above him were four floors of steel platforms connected by a steel **staircase** and glass elevator shaft.

Chiapetta couldn't believe what he was seeing. "What is this place?"

"Home."

"You," he said, waving his finger. "This is your sanctuary. The place where you hid from my brother all those years."

"And others. When you're feeling better I'll give you a tour, and of course, take you to see your merchandise."

"Excellent."

"We've encountered some logistical and weather problems. Shipping will be delayed for a day. Until then, you can relax here."

"I must be in Germany tomorrow for the council meeting," Chiapetta said.

"Suit yourself. You can leave tonight and I'll see that the artifacts are delivered to you." Chiapetta thought for a moment. Eisenstadt could handle the council for him. "Tomorrow will be fine, but first I must make a call."

"To whom?"

"The council members. They will have to proceed against Sasha without me. You may listen to the conversation if you wish."

"I may do that."

While Chiapetta was on the phone, Leon-Francis took the stairs down to the loading dock, where the Norwegian was waiting with a group of his men.

"Everything ready?" Leon-Francis asked.

"As soon as the trucks arrive and your guest inspects the shipment, we'll be ready to move the artifacts to the *Storm*."

"The weather is causing problems. The trucks won't be here until late tomorrow. I want you to handle the transfer personally."

* * *

Marcus returned from the cockpit to find Doc still on the telephone. Marcus pulled a gun cleaning kit from underneath the seat and sat it on the table beside him. Sydney was asleep—her head resting on Carlo's shoulder.

As much as the sight irritated him, Marcus took some comfort in knowing that at least she had someone to share her pain with. He disengaged the magazine from one of his Colts and started cleaning the barrel. Doc hung up the phone.

"What's Benno talking about?" Marcus asked.

"Hammershield Mining owns some property northwest of Passau in the mountains."

"Then, that's it—that's got to be where Leon-Francis is, right?"

"Probably."

"You could show a little enthusiasm. You were right."

"Yeah, and I was right about Sydney, too, but that doesn't make me feel any better. Iggy found out that Sydney's mother was already married when she hooked up with Leon-Francis."

"To who?"

"A friend of Leon-Francis'. A man named Ernesto Chiapetta."

"Tell me this isn't the same Chiapetta that Mellonhead was telling us about."

"It's his brother. According to police records, Chiapetta was suspected in killing Angela Belleshota, not Tippi Sampa."

"You have got to be lying."

"I wish."

"So this Ernesto dude, is he alive?"

"Yes."

"Well then, he didn't kill her. Devin Leon-Francis doesn't let anyone get away with anything, and he sure as hell would have killed this guy if he were responsible for his wife's death."

"He did something worse. Two months after Angela Belleshota was killed, a car bomb tore off the lower half of his body in the explosion. He's been living in a nursing home the last thirty years."

"Damn. If Chiapetta killed Sydney's mom, why would Leon-Francis lie and tell her that Tippi Sampa did it?"

"My guess is Devin Leon-Francis is not Sydney's real father. Chiapetta found out that Angela Belleshota was having an affair with Leon-Francis, and beat her half to death. She ended up in a hospital in Florence. Medical reports showed she was seven months pregnant at the time. Chiapetta kept her under guard around the clock to make sure she didn't leave the hospital, but eleven days later, Leon-Francis found a way to sneak her out. They vanished shortly after that, and it took six years of searching before Chiapetta's men tracked them down and killed her."

"So how do you know that Chiapetta is Sydney's father?"

"There are no public records of Sydney's birth. Not in Italy or Jerusalem, where Leon-Francis said she was born. And it makes sense. It explains why Devin Leon-Francis had been so protective of her. He never wanted Chiapetta to know she existed."

"You really believe that?"

"Yes, I do. The man has gone to extraordinary lengths to keep Sydney's identity secret. I used to think it was because he thought his enemies could get to him through her, and that might have been part of it. But the real reason may have been to protect her from Chiapetta. If his hatred drove him enough to kill Sydney's mother there was no guarantee he wouldn't try to kill his own daughter if given the chance. The tragedy is that Sydney's whole life has been built on a foundation of lies that Leon-Francis spent his entire life protecting."

"Even if this is true, how does this get us any closer to the pottery?"

"Sydney's mother gave an ebony obelisk to a priest for safe keeping. After her death, Leon-Francis tried to retrieve it, but it had been stolen. Probably by the Micheaux brothers."

"How do you know that?"

"Call it an educated guess. I checked the *Vincien Micheaux* manifest and found a listing for a black Egyptian obelisk, which was acquired in Italy before winding up at the Corinth Archaeology Museum in Greece, where it sat for thirty-six years. According to Italian police records, the obelisk and 300 other pieces of art were stolen from the Greek museum two years ago by the Micheauxs. Sasha told me that Jason Worrick tried to purchase a special piece from her brother's collection last year, but she nixed the deal when she found out Worrick was working for Leon-Francis. Less than a year later, we find Leon-Francis hijacking a Micheaux freighter filled with art. That's too much of a coincidence. I believe he tried to buy the obelisk. When that didn't work—he stole it. I think he's known all along where it was. As long as it was protected in a museum, it was safe. Once it fell in the possession of the Micheauxs, he couldn't take the risks that they or anyone else might discover whatever secrets it holds. The funny thing is—the Micheauxs never knew what they had."

"He went through all this work for a stinking statue?" Marcus asked.

"It holds some significance for him and he'd do anything to get it back, and take pleasure in eliminating the Micheaux family in the process."

"Now *that* I can understand. Are you going to tell Sydney any of this crap?"

"Don't you think she deserves to know?"

He returned to cleaning his gun. "You can't prove anything you've just said. And even if you could, what would you say to her? That her real father may have killed her mother and that she could be a member of the whacked out Merovingian kennel—*and*, that her uncle is the chief dog in the litter. What's that going to accomplish? Sydney may deserve to know, but she doesn't *need* to know. Let sleeping dogs lay, Doc."

Chapter 24

They landed in Germany just before noon, and they found themselves stranded on the Munich runway full of snow. Marcus viewed the long line of airplanes in front of them waiting for clearance to approach the terminals. "We're going to be here a while," he said, settling back in his chair. He looked at a photo picture of a black obelisk that Doc had printed off the computer. "It looks like the Washington Monument."

"Only it's twenty-six inches high, according to the description," Doc said.

"There's nothing unique looking about it. Why would my father go through all this trouble for that?" Sydney asked.

"I don't know," Doc said, as he got up to get the incoming fax.

Carlos looked at the picture over Sydney's shoulder. "May I?" Marcus passed him the photo. Carlos studied the picture and passed it back. "This isn't authentic. There's an inscription on the crown of the pyramidion. Inscriptions are commemorative notations telling us who carved them, not what they represent. It's a fake. A fine one, but nonetheless a fake."

"It's worthless?" Marcus asked.

"Not necessarily. See those small notches?" He pointed to the barely visible indentations at the sides of the base. There should be two more on the other side you can't see in the picture. All you have to do is press them in the right sequence."

"And?" Marcus asked.

"It opens. It works like a puzzle box."

Sydney saw Doc staring at the fax. "What is it?"

"It's a set of directions and a map from Benno." Doc frowned.

"What's wrong?" Marcus asked.

"The mine no longer exists. The Austrians leased the property for several years before giving it back to Leon-Francis. It's now an abandoned missile silo, covered by a twenty-seven-inch-thick door of concrete."

* * *

It took them two hours to get through German customs. They rented a jeep and drove thirty-nine miles to the outskirts of Passau, where they ran into heavy rain and wind. They continued southeast through a national forest until they reached Govinaha Falls, where they abandoned the vehicle and set out on foot. A small fire trail behind the waterfall led them six miles upstream through dense woods to the top of a plateau of overgrown grass.

"I don't see anything," Marcus said.

Carlos swept the binoculars across the flat meadow. "Neither do I."

Doc pulled out the wet map. "It should be north—to your right."

Carlos searched to the east. "There's nothing but grass and a few tree stumps out there." He lowered the binoculars.

Sydney wandered off into the trees, where she spotted tire tracks in the tall grass. "There's a road over here."

* * *

The dirt road led to a security fence lined with razor wire and surveillance cameras. They took cover behind the trees. Beyond the locked gate and chain-link fence was open meadow.

"This is just the other side of the same field we were in," Carlos said.

"They don't have a high-security fence and equipment up here for nothing. Something is out there," Marcus said.

Doc adjusted the binoculars. "There's a concrete slab of some sort." He moved closer to the fence. "It's a helicopter pad. The entrance to the silo must be out there, but it's hidden. There has to be another way in the place."

There was the loud cracking sound of thunder, followed by lightning and a downpour of rain. They ran for cover underneath the trees.

Doc stretched out the diagram of the missile silo on the back of a piece of bark. "The main shaft runs about 2,000 feet down from the top of the blast door to the launch control center at the bottom. Four fabricated tunnels of corrugated steel are connected at the bottom of the shaft like tentacles on an octopus. Each tunnel leads to an underground pod with its own independent ventilation and environment control system. The pods were designed to work independently and separate from the whole, in case the control center became inoperable during a nuclear attack."

"So farts smell downwind. I don't get it," Marcus said.

"It means there is probably an emergency exit at ground level," Carlos said.

"Right. And it has to be below us. We need to go back downstream," Doc said.

They backtracked down the hill and followed the trail for a quarter of a mile before they heard the noise of spinning tires in mud coming from deep in the woods. Getting closer, they saw the front end of a military transport truck stuck in the middle of a mud sinkhole. Three more trucks were lined up behind it, bumper to bumper, waiting for someone to figure out how to get them out of the mess.

"Let's go," Doc whispered. They snaked their way through the forest following the road, and came to a hillside and a concrete door framed between two retaining walls. The forty-seven-ton door sat on steel wheels, supported by railroad tracks mounted in concrete.

"How are we supposed to get past that?" Carlos asked.

"Hope those trucks don't take all day getting here," Doc said.

They regrouped under a cluster of trees trying to keep dry and warm, but the cold rain was relentless. They waited.

Sydney pulled a gun from her waist and checked the clip.

"I thought you weren't going in with us," Marcus said.

"I changed my mind." Marcus started to say something when they heard the trucks coming. The concrete door slowly rolled open.

"Those must be the trucks they're using to transport the artifacts," Carlos said, checking his gun. "There will be a lot of men in there."

"Oh, you can bet on it, brother," Marcus said, retrieving his twin automatics from under his coat.

Sydney handed Doc her spare gun. Take it." She forced it in his hand. "Forget your principals for once, Julian. If you want to live to see your child, you need to protect yourself. Take it." The last truck entered the missile silo and the doors began closing.

"We've got to go now before the door shuts!" Marcus shouted.

Doc tucked the gun in his belt as they ran for the door.

* * *

Eisenstadt welcomed each member of the council as they exited the bus in front of the Agippa Palace Conference Center. Knight Guardians escorted the group up the marble steps to the geodesic-domed conference room. Wine and refreshments awaited them as they relaxed and enjoyed themselves before the meeting started.

"This is a marvelous place you have here," the Dane said.

"Yes, opulence and excess seem to agree with you," the Austrian said. "Just ensure that our Knights do not become too distracted by the beautiful women I see bathing below in your pools," he chuckled.

The old men leaned over the brass rail, watching the young women playing in the atrium.

"Yes, quite beautiful. I should hope this meeting would not be too long." A chorus of laughter broke out in the room.

Eisenstadt sipped his wine. "Gentlemen, as you know our chairman was unavoidably delayed. However, he has instructed me to act as his proxy at this meeting. While we differ on the solution, we are resolved in doing what is best for the council. With that said, we shall proceed. Please, take your seats. I anticipate that this will be a brief, but fair and impartial meeting. We must move swiftly in deciding the fate of Sasha Micheaux. Afterwards we will retire downstairs with our waiting guests and see if our Austrian friend can still fit in a bathing suit."

* * *

The door to the silo closed behind them. They hid behind a parked shuttle until the trucks were out of sight.

Carlos marveled at the paved street he was standing on. "What kind of place is this?"

"A two-way highway to hell, if you ask me," Marcus said. He smashed the security camera anchored to the concrete wall. "We're in a world of hurt. We need to get moving."

They jumped in the cart and jetted through the tunnel. Marcus drove with Doc in the front and Carlos and Sydney sitting in the back.

"When the shooting starts, I want your butt right next to mine. You understand, Doc?" Marcus asked.

"I can take care of myself."

"No! You stay with me. Is that clear?"

"Okay, okay, I hear you. Just keep your eyes on your driving."

"Carlos and Sydney, you're on your own." Marcus slammed the brakes just before reaching the control center. They got out on foot. "Men are going to be crawling over us, so the best thing is to split up. We meet back here in fifteen minutes, or get out the best way you can."

The tunnel exited onto a circular plaza with a loading dock. Trucks lined up in front of the bay as workers loaded them with crates. Anthony Chiapetta stood on the loading dock supervising the operation. Suddenly, the wailing of the alarm flooded the silo, and the men stopped working.

Chiapetta looked around nervously. He saw a man run from behind a stack of crates with a gun in his hand. Chiapetta squinted to get a better look. "Carlos?"

A bullet from Carlos's gun shattered the glass figurine in Chiapetta's hands. Chiapetta yelled. The workers scattered. Chiapetta took cover inside the loading bay as a security team rushed out to the dock. The first guard through the door ran into bullets and went down. More men streamed out and Marcus and Sydney opened fire. Soon, the sounds of heavy gunfire filled the silo. They shot their way over to the loading dock where Carlos had taken refuge. He was reloading.

"Damn, you're crazier than me!" Marcus said, peeking around to see where everyone was.

Sydney jumped up and made a run for the control room door. "Cover me!" Doc tried to stop her, and a bullet bounced off the crate in front of him.

Marcus pulled him down. "Are you stupid? Let her go!"

Carlos shot two men as he chased after her. "Come on, we can get to the bay."

They raced down the hall to a steel door and more guards. She fired the first shots and they fell.

Carlos shot another one coming up from behind as Sydney stood riveted to the wall. "Sydney, what are you doing?"

She stood looking in the glass cubicle that led to the control room. "I have to get in here. I've been here before." She hit the button on the wall and the door slid back. The round room that was once a missile control center was now a plush carpeted suite decorated in modern Scandinavian furniture. Her mother's cello reclined in the corner next to her father's bed, with the cello bow locked in a curio cabinet. Sydney unlocked the door and removed a picture frame from the top shelf. The silver-framed photo was of a young woman with a long chestnut braid that fell to her bosom. She sat in a rocking chair, wearing a simple green and yellow floral dress that was too big, and a face that showed the stresses of a hard life. Neither could detract from her natural beauty or the sparkle of her eyes as she cradled her newborn daughter in her arms.

Carlos tapped her on the shoulder. "We need to go." Sydney didn't want to release her mother's picture. He pulled the frame from her hands as the guards broke through the door. She and Carlos began firing.

* * *

Marcus and Doc fought their way through the infirmary and out to a small hallway, where workers ran past them like they were invisible. Two guards stepping off the elevator ran into them. Doc knocked out the first one with a left-right combination. Marcus kicked the other one in the groin, followed up with a fist to the jaw. They jumped on the elevator and pushed the button to the next floor.

Devin Leon-Francis was in his office on the third level, watching the monitors. He called the Norwegian on his phone. "Where are you?"

"Top level, heading your way. Are you okay?"

"Who the hell is in here?"

"Your daughter and St. John. I'll be down there in a minute."

"Forget that. Meet me on top." He pressed the intercom button under his desk. "Bring my helicopter around, now!"

* * *

Sydney and Carlos made their way back out to the main corridor. Carlos saw Chiapetta at the opposite end, stumbling around, lost.

"Go after him, I'll be okay," Sydney said. She held his face and kissed him. "Be careful."

He raced after Chiapetta and disappeared around the steel steps at the end of the corridor. Sydney remembered those steep steps, the ones she played on when she was a child. The ones she would stand on and watch her father take the long ride up to the surface. She tucked her gun in her belt and raced for the stairs.

* * *

Marcus and Doc stepped into more gunfire when they reached the third level. They raced along the platform and more security came running from the cafeteria. Doc saw an open door, grabbed Marcus, and pushed him inside. He closed the door and locked it behind them.

Marcus was breathing hard. "Looks like we found the devil's den," he said, releasing the empty gun clips to the floor as he looked around.

181

The small room was a media haven, filled with computers and sophisticated electronic communications equipment. A large picture of Sydney hung on the wall behind Leon-Francis' desk, along with an open wall safe.

"It's empty. Leon-Francis is catching his ride, let's go!" Doc said.

* * *

Carlos searched for Chiapetta for ten minutes before he found himself lost. He wandered down a ramp that led to a pantry. The room was dark and empty. He turned to leave, but thought he heard a noise. He searched along the aisle of storage cabinets and found Chiapetta trying to hide his massive frame behind a wine rack.

"I had nothing to do with this, Carlos. You must believe me." Carlos raised his gun. "Wait, I can straighten this matter out. I only need to speak with Sasha and Eisenstadt. I will even resign my position on the council and see that Sasha is installed as..."

"It's already straight, Anthony."

He stepped into the open. "I am unarmed. See, no weapons." He had his hands raised high as sweat poured from his face. "You cannot shoot a helpless man."

"That doesn't make you any less dangerous." Carlos pulled the trigger.

* * *

A white Mangusta helicopter suddenly appeared over the northern horizon. It made a pass over the complex and then circled back—headed straight for the conference center. Several guests stared at the military craft hovering over the conference center. Eisenstadt and the other council members watched from the dome as the helicopter moved closer.

"Is he mad?" a member shouted. Eisenstadt stood riveted in fear as he watched the smoke tail of the first incoming missile. The massive explosion blew the conference center off the mountaintop.

Enric Bourbon turned the helicopter around and headed back to Zurich.

* * *

Sydney ran up the stairs as fast as she could, but there were too many steps and not enough time. She heard a familiar humming sound and looked over the rail. He was coming. The elevator ascended and she saw her father standing tall and erect as he always did, with a large man in a fu-manchu holding his bags. Leon-Francis' face turned solemn when he saw his daughter waiting for him. Their palms met briefly on the glass, as the elevator continued rising to the surface. Sydney ignored her tears and started up the steps again.

Marcus and Doc made their way up to the top level, where they ran into a hornet's nest. They took cover behind the generator, which was elevated on a seven-foot-high platform. Doc saw the emergency ladder that led to the blast door. He and Marcus worked their way toward the ladder when Marcus suddenly lost his balance and fell off the platform. He groaned as he tried to raise himself off the concrete, but two men sprayed their automatic weapons in his direction and he went down. Doc jumped off the platform, firing as he went. A bullet hit one man, but the others missed. The second guard was out of bullets, and so was Doc. The man charged him with a knife. Doc sidestepped his lunge, circled his arms around the man's wrist, and pulled the knife into his stomach. The guard collapsed on the floor next to Marcus.

"You okay?" Doc asked Marcus.

Marcus held his side as blood oozed through his fingers. "Yeah, give me a hand."

Doc lifted him to his feet. An explosion rocked the silo. They held onto the railing until the shaking stopped. "What was that?" Marcus asked.

Doc saw the black sky overhead. "They just blew the blast door open to the outside. Leon-Francis is leaving."

"Go after him, Doc, you can't let him get out of here…I can't make it."

* * *

Sydney found her father's abandoned elevator in the docking station. She crawled up the last nine rungs of the ladder to the outside in time to see her father and the Norwegian walking to the waiting helicopter. "Daddy!"

Devin Leon-Francis stopped and turned. His daughter was fifty yards from him, but he could still see the sadness on her face. The two stood silent for a moment—each knowing they would probably never see each other again.

"Why—where are you going?" she asked.

"You'll understand, one day, honey. Remember, I always loved you." He gave her a weak smile and a wave, and then stepped into the helicopter.

Doc reached the surface just as the helicopter lifted off the ground. He aimed his gun, but remembered he was out of bullets. It didn't matter anyway—he couldn't kill him. He stood with Sydney, watching.

Marcus dragged his tired body from the hole. When he saw the helicopter hovering, he fired until his gun was empty. The white helicopter flew over the trees and disappeared. Marcus dropped his gun in the grass, and clutched his side in pain. "I can't believe he got away!"

"He won't get far," Doc said.

"That bastard is like the energizer bunny. He'll be on our ass again."

"We'll never see him again," Sydney said, staring at the empty sky.

Doc placed his hand on Sydney's shoulder. "Come on—let's go find Carlos."

* * *

Marcus and Sydney found Carlos in Leon-Francis' office, sitting on the corner of his desk holding his shoulder.

Sydney poked her finger though the red hole in his jacket. "You okay?"

"I'll be fine. How about you?"

Marcus saw the satellite telephone sitting on the desk. "Who's on the phone?"

"My cousin. I called to tell her that I've recovered our artifacts."

"Yeah, but you're not taking them anywhere."

Carlos rose slowly to his feet.

Doc was on the telephone with the Austrian authorities when he heard Sydney calling his name. He raced along the platform to the office, where he saw Marcus and Carlos standing toe-to-toe, like tired boxers getting ready for the final round.

"Stand down." Doc said. The men didn't blink.

Doc moved in between them. "I said, stand down!"

Carlos blinked first. "My cousin would like to speak with you on the telephone."

Doc picked up the phone and walked over the corner. A minute later he tossed it back to Carlos. "It's settled. The artifacts go with Carlos."

"What, I can't believe you. You can't let them take this. It's like stealing twice!" Marcus shouted.

"Consider it their fee for services rendered."

"What services…what the hell are you talking about?"

Doc helped his friend back on his feet. "Come on, I'll explain it to you on our way home."

Epilogue

On New Years Eve, Devin Leon-Francis sat in his chaise lounge eagerly awaiting the fireworks show. He pulled the blanket up over his chest to keep warm. The obelisk rested on his lap. The Norwegian stood by his side as the lighted boat flotilla made its way through the canal. Leon-Francis tilted the obelisk on its side, turned the triangle blocks into the correct position, and then twisted the top. The bottom sprung open and a discolored envelope fell in his lap. He opened it and looked at the birth records for Silvianna Luisa Chiapetta. He hadn't seen them in thirty-four years. He handed them to the Norwegian, who burned them and then tossed the ashes in the bay.

Leon-Francis' telephone interrupted him. He picked up the phone and talked to the woman on the other end. "Are you sure?" Leon-Francis swore and slammed the phone down on the table.

The Norwegian stood behind him. "What's wrong?"

"I thought I told you to kill Jordan Bloodstone."

"Those weren't my orders."

"I told you to make sure she was dead before leaving the mountain!"

"What makes you think I take my orders from you?"

Leon-Francis tried to turn his head to look at him, but the Norwegian's twenty-two-inch biceps held his fragile neck in a headlock.

"Who are you? What's your...?" He gasped.

"My name is not important. What is important is the message from my cousin, Sasha Micheaux. She sends you her warmest regards and hopes your journey to hell is a long one." He flexed his muscles until he heard the sound of cracking bone. Leon-Francis' body slumped over in the chair. The Norwegian propped his lifeless body upright and smoothed the blanket back out over his lap.

He stood at the rail as fireworks exploded in the night sky over the water. When the New Year's celebration was over, Micah Bourbon finished his champagne, picked up the obelisk, and called a taxi to take him to the airport.

THE LAND OF PROFIT
(An Excerpt)
By Dwight M. Edwards

The cabbie dropped them off on Aurora next to a sleazy motel that looked more like a depression-era flophouse than a place someone would pay money to stay at. The Cameroon's weather-beaten exterior was as black as the aged-old dirt on the windows. Its guardrails bowed out as though being blown by the wind.

They found the entrance through a side door in the alley, and up a long staircase leading to the desk. The overweight proprietor in the caged office smelled as bad as his pee-stained walls. He told them that Constantine's room was on the third floor.

"I sure want to know why Dr. Constantine is staying in this rat hole," Marcus said as they made their way up the stairs. Three men sat in the lobby on a broken down sofa, staring at a television that didn't work. They eyed the fancy dressed men as they passed through to the corridor. The glare from Marcus's eyes told them they weren't easy prey. "We must be crazy to come up in here."

"Come on," Doc said, pulling him by the arm.

Marcus cupped his hand over his mouth as they searched the hallway for Constantine's room number. "This place stinks!" he muffled. The wail of babies crying was heard through the paper-thin walls. An old man opened the door, and quickly shut it again when he saw the two black men in the hall. Doc found Constantine's door and knocked. There was no answer. He knocked again, louder. A baby started crying again.

A young man across the hall opened the door. "I don't think he's there. He had visitors late last night and it sounded like there was a fight. I think he left with them, or…" He paused as if he just realized the alternative. "Or he could still be there." A teenage girl with a swollen belly joined him at the door and clutched his arm.

Doc tried the doorknob, but it was locked. "What did the visitors look like?"

"A short man in a black suit and stripped bowtie. He was with a tall thin woman, but we didn't see her face," the girl replied.

"Sounds like it was Kane," Marcus said as he pushed Doc aside. "We got to get in there." He kicked the door, and the door jam splintered into pieces. The sparsely lit room was empty, except for a single-sized bed, a table, and two chairs in the middle of the room. There were no clothes, papers, or anything else to suggest that someone was living there. But something was wrong. Doc could smell it in the air.

"You smell that odor?" Doc asked.

"Yeah—butt farts. This whole place smells like it," he said, as he knelt to look under the bed.

"No, I mean the sweet fragrance. Come over here."

Marcus went over and stood next to him. He sniffed the air like a puppy. "Yeah, I smell something. Citrus?"

"Tangerines," Doc said as he took one more whiff to confirm his conclusion.

Marcus stood with his hands on his hips. "So, where is the good professor?"

Doc looked around the room again, and then as if by default, walked over to the closed window. Droplets of dried blood were smeared across the window sash. He lifted the window open and looked down to the alley. "We can start by looking down there."

* * *

Doc found more blood on the lid of the dumpster. Marcus rousted a homeless drunk from his sleep while Doc searched the alley. Two wallets fell from the man's ragtag coat as he turned over and tried to go back to sleep.

Marcus picked them up off the ground. He opened the first one and tossed it back on the ground. The second one he kept. "Hey, Doc, over here—I found something." Marcus nudged the man with his foot. "Hey, where did you get this?"

The man stirred, and tried to focus his eyes on the wallet in front of him. "Hey, mister, that's mine," he said as he tried to grab it from Marcus's hand.

"I asked you where you got this?" Marcus repeated, brushing the man's hand away.

"Over there by the dumpster, after it was emptied this morning."

"Marcus pulled Constantine's driver's license from the billfold. "Have you seen this man?"

"Mister, I ain't seen no one," he said, without looking at the photo. "I only come back here to sleep. Can I have my wallet back now?"

"Does this photo look like you?"

The man squinted through one eye as he looked at the license again. "No, it don't."

"Then it's not yours." Marcus walked over to Doc. "Take a look at this," he said, handing Doc the small slip of paper that was folded in Constantine's wallet.

Doc held it up toward the streetlight. "This is a courier receipt from Sydney and its dated yesterday. "It looks like Constantine gave her a package to deliver. I thought you told me she was on vacation."

"She is. She left Seattle three days ago for California." Marcus opened his cell phone and called Sydney's ranch in the San Joaquin Valley. Ten seconds later he flipped it closed. "The house maid said she never arrived."

"Try her cell."

Marcus punched the number, waited, and then closed the phone. "Her cell phone is not in service. I don't get this Doc, what's going on here?"

"I don't know, but Constantine does. We need to find him."

"Well, judging by what we've found so far, I'd say a good place to start looking for him is in the obituaries."

Printed in the United States
45570LVS00006B/139-147

9 781591 138396